Cutting

A NOVEL

Konrad Karl Gatien & Sreescanda

Cutting

A NOVEL

Konrad Karl Gatien & Sreescanda

IRP NOVELS
u.s.a.

For information, contact: irpnovels@gmail.com

2011 PAPERBACK EDITION PUBLISHED BY IRP (USA)

ISBN 978-0-9838188-2-3   EAN 9780983818823
FICTION
1st Edition/1st Printing

http://www.irpnovels.com

Library of Congress Cataloging-in-Publication Data

Gatien, Konrad Karl.
Cutting: a novel / Konrad Karl Gatien & Sreescanda.
Summary: "In the alleys off Castro Street in San Francisco, young couples are getting off
blood as an aphrodisiac. It was only a matter of time before a killer broke loose.
(Provided by the publisher)
ISBN 978-0-9838188-2-3
1. Crime--Mystery--Fiction. 2. Crime--Police Procedural--Fiction.
3. Crime--Thriller--Fiction. Sreescanda. II. Title.

For my wife, Jennifer

-Konrad

One.

She was barely conscious.

Her knuckles were white, gripping the steering wheel with as much desperation as pain. She blinked furiously, frequently. Even found religion. *Lord, is this Your Vengeance? Am I paying for my sins and wickedness?*

She stubbornly staved off Death. Hope kept her going. Hope and maybe a last minute reprieve in this post-ultimate hour of purgatorial judgment. She reacted to the waves of pain by pressing and releasing the seven-inch gas pedal. The radial tires lurched. The champagne colored Lexus shifted erratically from lane to lane, erupting with speed and slowing down. Herky-jerky.

The woman faded.

The Lexus veered dangerously into oncoming traffic. Horns blared. A series of blinding neon reflections crookedly flashed off the windshield. She came alert just enough to swing the car back. Picked up landmarks. Her mind wandered. Few people fit an environment as perfectly as she did this city.

San Francisco.

Enchanting to even the most ardent cynic. The vertiginous declivity of her streets and the Moorish allure of her waters, she captured the passion of aspiring artists, the finest haute couture connoisseurs, and her most promising professionals.

San Francisco.

The symbol of elegance, audacity, and rebirth.

Much like the forty-three hills she was built on, the city underwent constant change. It began from her very inception, when she was hoisted up on the mighty shoulders of the North

American Plate. Thousands of years later, while the Nation was busy declaring its Independence, the Europeans slipped in and established the first permanent military outpost in the Presidio. Seven times, debilitating earthquakes and scourging fires had tried to crush her out of existence. All seven times, she'd risen from the ashes. In 1850, the city was re-christened from Yerba Buena, the name bestowed by Franciscan missionaries.

The dying woman did not have to dig deep for this knowledge. It was her sales pitch.

"Turn left now," the GPS purred, jarring the woman out of her death-drift into history. She realized she'd zoned so far out, she never heard the GPS's two prior warnings of the upcoming turn.

The intersection came upon her fast. She urgently swung the wheel. The momentum of the Lexus and sudden turn twisted her body. A fresh wave of agony scorched up her spine.

"Aaah!" she gasped.

The car headed straight for a young couple walking hand-in-hand. Engrossed in their romance, they never heard the danger hurtling toward them. *Screech!* The violent scrape of the low fender on the concrete pavement came loudly and suddenly as the car climbed onto the curb. They whirled around. The headlights placed them in full-blazed view for the woman to see the terror in their eyes. The car closed in a flash!

Its perforated grill bloomed in the man's glasses.

Panic synchronized their leap for safety.

The headlights fired past the young couple's tumbling feet. She glanced up into the rear-view mirror. They were dusting themselves back onto their feet. They could not have escaped with their lives more narrowly. She wanted to stop. Offer apologies. But their brush with mortality affirmed the tenuous thread by which her own life hung and fueled her to feed the Lexus with power. She couldn't hear them, but saw them screaming. San Fran natives, she knew at once, who probably thought she was another distracted tourist.

The mirror shook violently when the car jumped untidily off the curb. *Focus!* She admonished herself, trying to steady the headlights weaving in a dire, drunken gait. She reined in the Lexus. For the next several minutes, the car became one with the light, brisk traffic.

11:48 PM, glowed the digital clock, the exact time she felt consciousness desert her again. Waves of black stole her eyesight as she turned into a deserted alley. She did not—could not—die, at least not until she got to where she was going.

If I don't, how will anybody find out?

The alley was utterly empty. Flanked on either side by dense urban infill—jargon she used daily, referring to homes over stores so residents could live and work close to the heart of the city. SF had been an early pioneer of this lifestyle—her lifestyle, too—largely due to a lack of space. The black sky, with stars twinkling like uneven pinholes of light, roofed over the alley, which reverberated with the V6 beat of the Lexus's pistons.

"Right turn approaching," the GPS warned gently.

The woman sharpened. At the end of the alley, seducing her mind again, was the romance of this living, breathing, complex, brightly jeweled grid.

San Francisco.

A rare and radiant thing that bedazzled.

As she did every night, when darkness descended, she pulsed alive with lights that coursed through the city from end to end like lifeblood. The windows of the closely nestled houses and jostling skyscrapers sparkled, creating that familiar, fabulous skyline. The moisture thrown up by a brief evening downpour converted every twinkle into a brilliant starburst. The wet asphalt looked polished, glistening with prisms of illumination trapped somewhere in the depthless sheen. Street lamps, softened into iridescent halos, stood like benevolent sentinels along Geary.

Geary? She startled alert. *Fuck.* She could not remember emerging from the alley and turning onto this legendary four-lane. *Did I lose consciousness when I did?* Impossible. It was a hard right. She must have made it without even thinking. Like she used to make them daily—to, from, and during work. Such was her familiarity with the city. Directions came naturally, working in her subconscious.

The Lexus shimmied dangerously as she felt another wrack of pain. This time it did not stop. It came in white-hot, stabbing flashes. But she adamantly stayed alive. Not yet ready to become a Jane Doe in an overworked police department of a city that recorded one unnatural death an hour. She held the Lexus steady.

There was no room for error on this busy street. Cars passed each other with a couple of feet to spare. Pedestrians roamed the sidewalks littered with memories of the day just concluded. From the way they hugged their coats, she knew the brisk bay wind was icy. Yet no one seemed dissuaded. These were tourists unable to get enough. She could identify. She remained one even after living here all her life. She'd loved to walk—for the exercise, for the tangible vitality that the entire Bay area exuded. There was freedom in the air. Especially after the sun went down. To unshackle. To explore. To drop the pretense.

San Francisco.

The perfect city to live a double life.

Ever since she had turned sixteen, she lived an overt one in which she was liked and loved for her savvy, beauty, and intelligence. A corporate whore. She had to be. To finance and enjoy the life she lived entirely in the secrecy of shadows.

A bloody and sexually exuberant one that gave her both pain and pleasure.

Actually, it was pain *for* pleasure.

****

Detective Jeff Holland, better known as Dutch, barely noticed the nightly roster of usual suspects on slipshod wooden benches of the Golden Gate Police Station. Rustling and shifting and shouting, it was a deafening soup kitchen of patrons waiting impatiently for their meager portion of justice. The floors were filthy from this human traffic, which ebbed and flowed 24/7 through the revolving doors. Clogged roof gutters pasted the walls with a thick film of moisture, contributing to a frowzy upwelling of cheap perfume, sweat, and body odor. Then there was the language common to a muster desk. Profanity from the outer edge in every conceivable language by perps and police officers alike.

"Uncuff me from this bench, *maricon!*" Benny Benitez screamed above the numbing clamor at Dutch, who was busy running Benny's paperwork by Desk Sergeant Clyde Gantry. "I got fucking rights, you know!"

Dutch ignored Benny, a cut-rate punk from the Dominican Republic. His criminal ripples came from a prostitution pool, muling in underage girls from Miami in white vans. His AR—arrest record—listed him in for a Class 245—A&B with a deadly weapon. This assault and battery was Benny's second strike.

"You're kiddin' me, Dutch. This ain't Benny's MO," Gantry said and burst out laughing after he read the AR. "Holy Patron Saint of the Circus! Ten years, you'd think maybe I'd seen everything all right. But this takes the cake, the paper plate, and the plastic fork too!"

Dutch knew the MO that sent Gantry pealing was the A&B detail. Specifically, the half-eaten banana that Benny shoved down the throat of a john who refused to pay one of his fillies after a $10-throw in the front seat of the john's Lincoln Continental.

Gantry leaned over his desk. "Hey Benny! What's the matter? Your own banana wouldn't do? You got one of them little Ecuadorian bananas, is that it?"

"Fuck you in the ass with two dicks!" Benny spat back viciously. "*Soy màs grande que un burro, pinche Gringo!*"

"Ha!" Gantry shot back, holding up a pinkie. "My sister's got more hangin'." Gantry sat back chuckling.

Dutch belched, egesting a stench of the dinner he'd inhaled on the way back to the station—a hot dog with everything on it. He watched Gantry immerse himself in the paperwork with the inured disinterest that only thirty years in the force, the last ten behind this desk, could bring. Dutch knew Gantry's life story—the Desk Sergeant had shared it to break the ice when Dutch'd transferred here six months ago from Houston. When I first stepped off the bus from Owensboro, Gantry said, the worst thing I'd seen was a boy sew his arm back on after a tractor accident. He'd done a shit job, but the kid dialed 911 with his good arm. By the time the meds arrived, the kid had sewed half the damn thing up himself. Had his picture in the paper and everything. I thought *that* was fuckin' horrible, Gantry chortled, but within twenty-four hours I discovered I was in for worse.

Dutch had just listened and smiled politely. Gantry was telling the wrong guy. It had been a long time since something—anything—struck Dutch as oblique anymore. He was a foster child raised in an orphanage with jailhouse rules. Throw in where it was—Houston, a metropolitan redneck hellhole—he'd quickly discovered that each new horror became part of the daily routine until it seemed as natural as waking up in the morning and putting on his shoes. So, when he apprehended perps like Benny Benitez who had turned a fucking banana into a deadly weapon, Dutch wasn't shocked. He could care less. He'd booked hookers, muggers, murderers, wife beaters, husband bashers, child molesters, arsonists, petty thieves, carjackers, gangsters, hustlers, and every other kind of human refuse that oozed out of the swelling sewers of crime, so much so, that he'd become totally blind, deaf, and numb to the sights, sounds, and senses that paraded before him.

"Fruits and nuts," he monotoned to Gantry, "that's all you got in California. Fruits and nuts."

"You got that right," agreed Gantry and hollered across the room, "Lenny!"

They both looked up at the wall clock. It inched another click toward 12:00 A.M.

Their shifts ended at midnight.

Lenny, the zoo keeper, strolled up to take Benny to a holding cell. Dutch turned Benny around, who, he suspected, was on crystal meth. Dutch could tell. The addiction ran tellingly into their faces from the neck up. They sweated too much. Their eyes went rodent-red and slapped about like pinball flippers on full tilt. Parachute nostrils. Tongues constantly flicking over their lips—a reptilian habit Dutch found particularly revolting. Pill poppers, he thought, anything for a fuckin' fix.

"Be good, Benny," Dutch said, as Lenny shoved the pimp between the blades.

"Fuck you, Dutch," Benny scowled.

"You're welcome." Dutch waded past the sea of waiting perps and continuing pandemonium.

From inside, looking out, the glass panels of the double doors appeared opaque because of a brief lull in police traffic at the curb. The last radio patrol car had sped away to join a 502, 510 high-speed pursuit in the high-rent district of Russian Hill. Some stock broker's wife, ginned to the gills, was playing touch-and-go with her favorite boys in blue for another Sunday night soiree.

Something inside Dutch caused him to turn amidst the menagerie of faces and look to the front door. The noise inside the station was so loud, nobody else caught the thin swish of light that cut through the glass. In the brief instant, Dutch glimpsed the champagne-colored Lexus. The headlights shafted past and darkened the panels. Hard to discern smudges of light danced back on. He heard the tires squeal. The car was pulling up.

Then, silence.

Dutch started to look away, losing interest.

Suddenly! *Slam!* Two bloody palms struck the glass!

A blonde, twenty-six, if that, appeared between splayed fingers. She was pretty, even through the running mascara, tortured grimace, dilated eyes, and lips that trembled in fear-stricken panic. Closest to the door, Dutch momentarily felt her unbearable pain. Her chest heaved against the glass in fitful, explosive bursts.

The doors collapsed under her weight. Swung inward.

Little things immediately ticked off in Dutch's mind.

First, this caliber clientele didn't often do business with his precinct. She was a helluva woman. Dressed to the nines in a plain white Jackie-O style one-piece dress and three-inch Louboutin pumps. Make that one pump. Second, little of the whiteness of the dress remained. It was drenched in blood and it clung to her body. Finally, she had nothing on underneath the dress.

Then the booking area did something that Dutch knew to be unprecedented.

It went completely silent.

Every head of every cop and crook turned in synchronous beauty to watch the woman's dripping hands rise. Imploring. Her mouth dropped into a cavernous 'O,' but no sound emerged. She lost her legs from underneath and crumpled where she stood. Crack! Her kneecap struck the cold ceramic tiles. Then, in a final death throe, her back jerked straight as a razor and she toppled forward. Face down. A second *crack!* Her nose broke when she hit the floor. As painful as that sounded, Dutch knew it ended all the pain too.

Because she was dead.

Sprawled. Exposed. Dutch's skin crawled.

Not by the sight of the blood-wet body of a young woman stretched across the muster room floor. But by the back of her dress. It looked as if it had been dipped in a bucket of red paint.

Blood emptied in rivers from multiple wounds. Blood poured out of her gaping mouth. Blood flowed across the floor. Blood ran in rivulets. Blood filled the grout between the tiles and spread like a checkerboard. Blood formed a pool almost three feet beyond and on every side of her.

Blood, blood, blood, blood, blood.

"Jesus," Dutch heard Gantry exhale.

"Cinderella had a bad night," Dutch added, to conceal a couple of unprecedented sensations of his own—surprise and horror.

Dutch and Gantry looked at the clock simultaneously with the same thought.

12:02 A.M. Two minutes past the end of the shift.

At least this tragedy wasn't theirs.

Two.

A phone, atop the nightstand in the attic, rang. The coverlet on the wrought iron bed stirred. Stripes of sun and shade stretched all the way from the blinds, angled open to allow a one-way view to the outside. Dutch's hand appeared and groped toward the cordless instrument. Found it. Sleep tugged at his limbs like an anchor. Weighing him to the mattress. Clumsy and lethargic, his fingers knocked the phone off the bedside table.

His head nestled in the pillows, Dutch dipped his hand into the streaks of daylight and dragged it on the floor along the edge of the bed. By the fourth ring, he still hadn't located the handset and gave up. Dutch pulled the pillow over his head and resettled under the covers. The machine picked up.

"This is Dutch. Just your name and number after the beep." *Beep!*

"Dutch? Bishop." His partner on the force. Basso. "This is your early morning wake-up call. I left a message on your cell too. Don't forget, you're on the stand for testimony at nine. That's nine A.M. *Pacific* time. And Murdoch isn't known for his lenience, so don't be late."

Dutch squinted. Reluctantly awake. He swung his arm up. Twisted his wrist. The watch read 8:15 A.M.

"Shit," he growled and swung out of bed.

A tornado seemed have to cut a swath across the narrow but singularly long living room area. Clothes were scattered all over the floor. Mismatched shoes stood toe-to-toe. Rolls of newspapers, still wrapped by rubber bands, climbed in an unread pile behind the door. Empty beer bottles, six deep, rolled at the foot of a generously stuffed, three-cushion divan. A police scanner, atop a sofa table, chattered ceaselessly with the Dispatcher's monotone, directing officers from one crime scene to another.

He'd done little to decorate the compact attic apartment, though three large, black and white, utterly bleak landscapes did hang on the otherwise Spartan walls. A sea of burned stems at Yellowstone after the '92 fire. A sweeping shot of rust and decay in an abandoned junkyard. A dust storm blustering across a ghost town in Badlands, Wyoming. Elise, his wife—who told him to take them all when they separated—remarked how his taste in art spoke volumes about his psyche.

Dutch took a perfunctory shower. Dressed quickly. Headed for what had started out as an office nook. Now, it was just a mess of personal documents—bills, tax returns, crap. His driver's license peered out of the carelessly flung wallet on the empty chair below a shoulder harness, the only item carefully, consciously, and neatly draped over the backrest. The holster carried a Police-issue 9mm Browning automatic. Hooked into the holster was also a shiny San Francisco Police Department shield. These two items had not even a hint of dust or grime, not even in the ridges, because he cleaned and polished them both regularly. Cared for them like cherished trophies that—he had no qualms admitting—he arrogantly used to set himself apart and above the regular citizenry.

Dutch picked up his wallet, opened it to check how much cash he had, and noticed his driver's license through the transparent window of the front pouch. Aw, shit. He needed to get one issued by California. This still carried a picture of him when he first got it—at sixteen. He smirked at the picture. A striking, handsome kid with dark hair. A jock. Way, way before the ravages of experience and cynicism took their toll on his face. His green eyes, now jaded and melancholic, once glinted with an enthusiasm that carried over to an expressive mouth, the ends of which curled upward and stretched in that youthful eager smile of not knowing any better.

Dutch sprinted outside, struggling into a tan sport coat. His gun rattled against his ribs. He checked his watch. It had taken him twenty-five minutes to shave, shower, and dress.

Vertical lines dominated the quiet middle-class ghetto of closely packed Stick homes, the unflattering name for the most prevalent Victorian architecture in San Francisco. There were little or no setbacks separating these skinny wood frame structures with distinctive bay windows, false cornices, and square corners. Their narrowness made it look like a struggle to stay perpendicular on both sides of the steep, curving road.

Crowded bumper-to-bumper parallel parking reduced the street to a slender two-lane. The curbed wheels, turned outward uphill and inward downhill, protruded in varying degrees. The cars looked freshly cleaned, still showing off droplets from yesterday's short cloudburst. The lawns and shrubs were lush, their uniform green mottled with color wherever homeowners and renters had taken the time to plant flowers in their tiny patches of garden.

People, up and down the street, were leaving for work. Those with children looked a little more hurried. Cars pulled out of their slots randomly, the moisture in their exhausts discharging thick, white, reticulated trails. Forecasts predicted a day of clear skies.

A cable car rattled audibly in the distance.

"Eyeh, Dutch!" A young voice called out.

"Larry," Dutch waved back at the twenty-one-year old sophomore, who shared the house next door with two other students. The kid stood on a single-pulley scaffolding, hoisting himself up the facade filled with sunburst motifs. He was starting to paint the wide band of trim that formed a decorative truss with a brush of periwinkle blue.

Dutch rushed to the black, Hybrid SUV parked in the red reserved for the fire hydrant. That's one thing he hated about this city. Parking was a bitch. He had prominently displayed a police placard on the dashboard. Nevertheless, there was a ticket nestled beneath the driver-side windshield wiper.

"Oh, for crying out loud," Dutch groaned. Opening the door, he crumpled up the ticket and flung it into the back seat, where evidence gathered of at least a dozen prior infractions. That's when he noticed a yellow, rhino boot clamped to the rear tire. Dutch stepped back out and slammed the door. "I'm a cop, for God's sake! What is it with this town?"

"They got no respect for authority!" hollered Larry.

Dutch pivoted. "Can you see the Powell-Mason?"

"Let me check." Larry raised his finger, spun on his narrow, wobbly perch, and peered between the contiguous, multi-unit homes. "If you hustle, you can catch it at the coffee shop."

"Thanks!" Dutch shouted over his shoulder after he'd already started racing down the steady decline. He got there a minute too late. Breathing hard and heavy, he watched the cable car pass out of view. "Fuck me!"

He looked at his watch. 8:45 A.M. When he looked up, a black and white radio patrol car skirted around, heading his direction. Dutch leapt into the street and flagged it down.

A clean-cut cop peered over mirrored sunglasses. "What's the problem, sir?"

Dutch flashed his tin. "It's Detective. Let's go."

Dutch not only pulled rank on the wide-eyed uniform, but ordered him to flash and siren all the way. Still, it was stop and go through morning rush hour. He pulled out his cell and called Bishop, who didn't answer. Probably because he was inside the courtroom.

So, Dutch texted him, *'On my way. 10 min tops.'*

Bishop didn't answer. Pissed, probably.

Dutch ordered the rookie to pull a U-turn in front of the San Francisco Hall of Justice at Bryant and Sixth. He vaulted out of the RPC, darting indoors, when his cell rang. *Bishop.*

No point answering now. Dutch turned it off and kept running.

There were twenty-eight courtrooms in the Hall of Justice, eight dedicated to Superior Court rulings. He battled his way through lawyers, cops, plaintiffs, and defendants, reached the third floor, turned left, and entered Department 22.

The indomitable domain of Judge Marshal James Murdoch.

He was an austere looking man in his late fifties, with a bent nose and a long, hollow face so pale it could have been carved from a bar of soap. His gaze flickered briefly from Dutch to the court clock, which knocked the bottom of the hour—9:30.

"Sorry, I'm late, your honor," Dutch huffed, moving quickly down the center aisle to the front of the court room.

On the way, he passed his partner, Detective Brian Bishop, seated in the back row, who shook his head in disapproval. Bishop was a forty-two-year old, 6-2 linebacker-sized African-American. In the front row, the middle-aged Assistant District Attorney appeared flustered and putout. He looked like he'd received a barrage of abuse from the Court. Dutch shrugged apologetically.

"No rush, Detective Holland," said the judge, dripping acid, "the courts of the Great State of California are prepared to convene at your will and pleasure."

"I'm ready, your honor."

Dutch took a seat in the witness stand. He straightened his tie uncomfortably and glanced over to the racially diverse jury. He felt their acrimony. He didn't blame them. At ten bucks an hour, or whatever it was that they were getting paid, they didn't feel the delay was worth the soreness from sitting on the stiff wooden chairs—especially if it was caused by a city employee siphoning a salary out of an ever dwindling supply of taxpayer dollars. Even if the purpose was to serve justice on a young scumbag named Hector Alazando caught with his hand in the cookie jar.

A thirteen-year old cookie jar.

"Remember you're still under oath, detective," Murdoch told Dutch, who'd started his testimony the day before under friendlier circumstances.

Bishop and Dutch were the primary police witnesses for the prosecution in the case of the State of California vs. Hector Alazando, a twenty-year old Mexican gang-banger accused of sexual assault and sodomy of a minor. Hector had recanted his confession, claiming violation of Due Process.

Judge Murdoch nodded to the Defense table. "You may begin your cross-examination now, counselor."

Simon Winkfield, the stout, forty-year old, diminutive Public Defender rose smugly. "Thank you, your honor."

He bit the handles of his eyeglasses, then reseated them on the bridge of his nose. Dutch watched Winkfield peer through his polished spectacles. Son of a bitch was sizing up the jurors like a fox sized up a hen house. Maybe, he felt that it might just be possible if he could force that unguarded moment, when their desire for justice would be overcome by their indignation at the means of enforcement. Dutch had been on the winning side of that twinkling, when jury's deepest sense of privacy felt violated.

But he wasn't so sure about this group. Winkfield had picked a cosmopolitan blend of blue collar workers and lower echelon office employees—liberal and sympathetic, but not exceedingly zealous in their desire to reach a "successful disposition," which an attorney Dutch knew back in Texas had defined as one in which no side was happy with the outcome.

So, Dutch knew he had to be careful. Rein in his temper. It was no longer a pedophile on trial, but the very freedom guaranteed in the US Constitution. Winkfield had already set them up in his opening statement, "Liberty is such a fragile thing. And when handled indelicately, we all suffer. Because we all lose a little of our dignity. A little of our freedom."

Dutch looked over at Hector, who was no stranger to

courts and convictions. He never knew his father. He came out of a pregnancy by rape when his mother was barely fifteen. Despised by her, Hector grew up around hate and resentment. He was cruel even as a child, an attribute that earned him entry into street gangs when he was nine. He spent as many years in juvenile detention as out of it. Thoroughly familiar with the system, he had maintained a game face throughout this trial, appearing appropriately sorrowful.

When Winkfield stood up to cross-examine Dutch, Hector kept his solemn exterior intact, but Dutch observed that nothing in Hector's demeanor reflected the concern of someone who was facing the next twenty-five years marking time on the walls of a state penitentiary. In fact, the bastard's flat black eyes stared straight back. Mocking. Dutch set his jaw. He had no tolerance for bullshit and the blatant arrogance only kicked his anger into hyperdrive. *Did the asshole really think he was going to get off?*

"Detective Holland!" Winkfield startled Dutch with his tone. Dutch sensed the PD was setting his sights, circling the wagons, and taking long shots from the outside before moving in for the kill. "You've been with Robbery-Homicide how many years?"

"I'd call it an even...baker's dozen," Dutch replied, trying to ingratiate himself. *Mistake one.*

"And by that you mean thirteen years," Winkfield continued, with the corrective meter of a patient teacher.

"That's what I said." *Mistake two.* He sounded defensive. Dutch watched Winkfield. It was as if the umpire had yelled, "Play ball!" Nothing served his case for battery better than a hostile witness.

Then PD took another jab. "And isn't it also correct that you arrested my client based on a tip from a prostitute?"

Dutch nodded. "And the partials found at the scene. And a comparative match on the DNA. And—"

Winkfield quickly turned to the judge. "Objection, your

Honor! Nonresponsive."

"Sustained," Murdoch agreed. "Will the jury please disregard Detective Holland's last remarks and will the reporter please strike the witness's comments from the record."

"The girl was only thirteen," Dutch implored, trying to draw the jury's eyes to her parents, who could barely hold their emotions in check behind the Assistant DA. "Sodomized, then savagely beaten by this man—"

"Judge?!" pleaded Winkfield.

"I said, sustained, Detective Holland! The witness stand is not a forum for your diatribes. Maybe justices in Houston were more patient with your helpful disquisitions. But here in California, at least in my court, you will answer the question put to you. Is that understood?"

Dutch nodded, trying not to glare at the judge and failing.

"Speak up, Detective!" Murdoch went after him with a blade in his voice. "The clerk needs to record your response!"

Dutch glared. He didn't care that the tension in the courtroom had ratcheted up a notch. Nobody dared to move, rustle, scrape, speak, or cough. Even the defendant's *carnal* in the back sat perfectly still. Bishop offered a worried look and made a patting motion, palms down, signaling Dutch to get it under control and regain his composure.

Dutch backed off, "Yes, your honor. I understand."

"Then answer the question put to you."

Dutch swallowed an angry retort and spoke mechanically. "I arrested him based on a tip from a prostitute. It was a reliable tip. She worked for the defendant. He was her pimp."

Winkfield stepped forward with a photograph. A routine mug shot of the defendant with an ID number underneath the full face and two profiles. Unremarkable in every aspect. "I'm showing you what's been pre-marked for identification as Defense Exhibit 13A. Do you recognize this photograph, officer?"

"Detective," retorted Dutch, getting hot again. He knew

it and still refused to stop himself. "The title is detective."

"Of course it is," Winkfield deigned.

Dutch realized he'd been baited into another flare-up. The DA had warned him. Winkfield was good. He used to be a prosecutor who'd made boatloads of money. Now he was trying to shed the guilt of all those win-at-all-cost-wrongful convictions by switching sides. As if getting off guilty felons somehow restored the balance.

Dutch tightened his jaw to control himself from losing his temper and managed an even voice, "Looks like a booking photo."

"Very good, detective. That's exactly what it is. A booking photo from April 20th, the night of the arrest." Winkfield walked over to the court clerk. "Your honor, may the record reflect I'm presenting it to opposing counsel." Winkfield showed it to the Assistant DA and then raised it. "Your Honor, may the jury handle the photograph?"

Murdoch eyed the Assistant District Attorney. The young prosecutor helplessly shook his head. "We have no objection, your honor."

The judge nodded. "The jury may handle the photograph."

The photo went quickly from one jury member's hand to another. There was nothing much to see.

Winkfield produced a second photograph. "And this is a photo taken following your interrogation of my client three hours *after* his booking."

The photograph elicited gasps and expressions of disapproval as each jury member passed it to the next. Dutch knew why. The defendant's face resembled a broken picture frame. He had been beaten black and blue. His cheeks were lopsided and swollen. Contusions forced one eye shut. His nose was posted to one side. A dribble of blood dried in the hollow beneath his nostrils. His lips were distended and badly cut.

The last member of the jury, holding the photograph

was an elderly Latina woman with deeply etched features from years of toiling amidst ammonia and cleaner fumes as a hotel maid. A silent witness to many *gringo* excesses, Dutch suspected, and she looked at him with unconcealed contempt and hidden glee.

Dutch tried to appear contrite, but failed. This pig had raped, sodomized, and beaten a thirteen-year old girl. Something she was going to have to live with the rest of her life. *Who gives a damn if he got a little beat up?* The little girl was going to be seeing a community counselor for the next three months and that would be hardly enough therapy. This thing Hector so recklessly did was going to haunt her. She would live in fear of strangers. Harbor secrets she could never tell. After abuse, some kids never took a lover, or they took many, it could go either way. One thing was for sure. She would never trust anyone again. She would never place her faith in that great imaginary tranquility ordinary people took for granted. At thirteen, her life, her normal life, was over. Life as an addict or a drunk or an abuser herself might begin. *Fuck him.*

Dutch noticed Bishop lower his head in resignation. They'd not been partners for long but Dutch could hear what Bishop was thinking. *Damn stupid Dutch, always gotta be right even when he's wrong.* Bishop's congenial demeanor and propensity for ready advice made him a favorite around the station house. Dutch didn't even bother looking at the Assistant DA. He'd seen the photograph during Discovery and they'd discussed they were going to have to eat shit when it got passed around.

"Can you explain the difference in the two pictures, detective?" Winkfield inquired. A plain, on-the-face question. But it echoed in the courtroom like a gun whose hammer had just been drawn back.

"Holding cells can be rough on child molesters," Dutch shrugged.

"So, you didn't beat the defendant until he confessed?"

Dutch met Winkfield's accusing gaze dead-on. "No, sir, I did not."

So there it is, asshole. A standoff. Mexican punk says he did. White cop says he didn't. And then there's the girl, sitting in the front row, unable to look up. Unable to meet anyone's eyes. N*o matter what they think about me, anyone with blood running through their veins oughta feel for that little girl and put this bastard away.* At least, that's what Dutch was hoping. On any other day he might have been right. But not today. Dutch went still the moment Winkfield picked up a stack of papers. He recognized the seal on the top.

"I have here," Winkfield gestured grandly, "arrest reports and supervisory evaluations dating back thirteen years to your first year on the force in Houston, Texas."

Dutch groaned and cast an angry look toward the Assistant DA. He responded by rising from his chair but his body language telegraphed hopelessness even before he said, "Objection, your honor. Immaterial—"

"Overruled," Murdoch scolded.

Winkfield smiled. Dutch glowered. This was the vulnerable window the fucker had been waiting to open. Everything up to this point was a set up for this moment.

"According to inquiries conducted by the Internal Affairs Division," said Winkfield smugly, "you have been reprimanded not once, not twice, but *three* times during that period for violence against prisoners!"

Dutch could feel the mercury dropping, He was on his own for the remainder of his tenure on the witness stand. Half an hour before the noon recess, the Defense completed its cross-examination. The Assistant DA spared Dutch the redirect. Dutch stood wearily when Murdoch excused him. He left the courtroom filled with dejection, hatred, and self-loathing. As he passed Winkfield, Dutch kept both hands in his pockets for fear he might reach over and choke the shit out of him. The conniving son of a bitch had stuck to the letter of the law, rather than the intent.

Winkfield opted for a spectacularly overplayed closing statement in which he likened a dismissal of the case to yet another clear-cut victory against creeping fascism in local law enforcement. He readjusted the gleaming, gold-rimmed spectacles, forefinger to bridge and resumed his seat. Dutch hatefully observed the PD ooze the satisfaction of a successful disposition. Dutch had experienced what Winkfield was feeling—that rare unequivocal euphoria known as acquittal. *So this is how it felt to be on the other side.*

The jury deliberated for less than an hour.

Hector walked out, scot-free.

Bishop joined Dutch in the hallway. Dutch didn't say a word. He silently retrieved his gun from court security. As a cross-defendant in the case, he wasn't allowed to carry his weapon into the courtroom. If he were a witness or giving professional testimony for the prosecution, it would have been different. They started down the polished marble staircase.

"Pretty rough in there," Bishop said, unruffled, as always. In fact, every aspect of his demeanor, physical to psychological, spoke of a Zen-like acceptance of the world and his place in it. He had such a peaceful, organic fluidity about him, it was impossible to imagine him breaking up or falling apart under any circumstance. Keep quiet, maintain a low profile. It wasn't just a philosophy, it was a code Bishop lived by.

"That son of a bitch was guilty!" Dutch retorted. Just the opposite. Mercurial, whose pyroclastic outbursts lent any encounter an unpredictable edge. "You telling me if that girl was your kid, you wouldn't have done what I did?"

"Maybe so, but rules are rules," Bishop replied.

If you followed a case patiently and gave the suspects enough rope, he told Dutch when they first became partners, they'd hang themselves. Bishop was sure of that. Something about the criminal mind, perhaps a flaw in the sagittal plane, almost subliminal, always left trace evidence of their act. Either they couldn't live with the guilt, or they were compelled to accountability. Like a festering root pushing its way up through dirty soil, the exposure of the deed demanded the light of the visible world. And Bishop, the gardener, pulled up the weeds so the flowers could bloom.

"My father once told me if you don't stand for something, you'll go for anything. "

"Your father was a preacher," said Dutch. "It's easier for those guys."

"No it wasn't." Bishop shook his head. "He dropped a dime on an A&B before he got his shit straightened out. You want to go that way, too?" They descended into the lobby. "We don't invent the law, man, we enforce it. You gotta come to terms with that. You want to start making up the law, you got three choices. Become a politician, a judge, or God. All the rest is bullshit, and it's going to get your ass in trouble."

They went through the revolving doors one after the other and emerged outside. The sun stared down from a clear blue sky. Temperatures hovered around the pleasant seventies. Sporadic northeasterly gusts fanned in a generous, salty breeze off the Pacific Ocean. Dutch veered away, descending the sweep of steps two at a time.

"Hey! Where you goin'?" Bishop asked.

"I'll catch up with you back at the station." Dutch needed to be alone. Cool off. Ease the angry throb in his head. Bishop was just being too damn level-headed again. Once Bishop got that way, there was no reasoning with him. Dutch knew Bishop was right and it was pissing him off. After thirteen years on the force, he still could not keep an objective distance from his work.

He took the bus, dropped into a seat by the window, and stared out at the skyline.

San Francisco.

He'd been here less than six months, wasn't even familiar with all the streets yet, but he had quickly picked up on the attitude. An open mind. No barriers. If you couldn't accept, you wouldn't be accepted. What was it Bishop had said? Oh, yeah. *It's all about flow, Dutch. Feel it. It's all around you. The bay, the coast, the currents. Go with the flow, man.*

Dutch's eyes drifted along the flow of traffic, the flow of children in the Hayward Playground, the flow of pedestrians at the Buchanan Mall, the flow of tourists visiting the Alamo Square Historic District, before finally trailing up to the flow of cumulus clouds gathering in the cinder block skies.

The bus pushed its way through the stop-and-go traffic. Nothing in this town really fell into black and white, he thought, bemused. And since Dutch enjoyed existing in the gray, in those little zones in-between, he finally began to relax as a welcome thought went through him.

Maybe he did belong here after all.

***

Lieutenant Alan Schiff didn't mind being the Old Man. As such, he received all the love, animosity, and recrimination accorded the father of a dysfunctional American family. Fifty-five years in the making, he was a lean, peppery, twenty-three-year veteran of the SFPD who spoke his mind. Always.

So, he wasn't ashamed—in fact, he boastfully admitted—that he enjoyed being off the street and behind a desk. He got home at a decent hour. His wife liked that. They could finally plan their weekends together because he possessed the authority to delegate. Now, should some criminally-minded citizen unexpectedly try to disturb the peace at an inopportune moment, it was one call down to bunco, robbery, burglary, or homicide to ensure smooth sailing until Monday morning, 9 A.M. Granted, the pencil pushing got boring at times, but it came with a perk he had aspired to from his first day as a beat cop—being the boss.

Schiff looked up, ready to delegate, when Dutch and Bishop knocked and entered. First things first. He'd heard about Dutch's go 'round with Murdoch and figured it deserved a passing remark. "Turn around, Dutch."

"What for?"

"Just do it." Dutch did. "You're right, Bishop! He did get his ass chewed off!" Dutch grimaced. "Dutch, I'm gonna have to order you some new pants right away. With no ass, you must have dropped two sizes. Can't have you chasing skells with your slacks around your ankles."

Bishop sat down with a solid plop, chuckling. Dutch stared from Bishop to Schiff. Then he picked up the second chair, thumped it back a foot, and sat down.

"Hysterical," Dutch said. "Child molester goes free and you're telling butt jokes."

"Actually, it's not so fucking hysterical, Dutch," Schiff spat, turning serious just like that. *Snap!* Hot to cold. "It's your half-assed approach that puts them back on the street."

The disarming way he had of running his own good-cop-bad-cop routine, which required no partner and created a sense of unpredictability, had become legendary in the precinct. No one knew what to expect. He liked that. It discouraged direct confrontation. Little did they know he couldn't control his mood swings. One minute he could be laughing, the next, something happened in his brain and he'd sucker punch the opposition's self-confidence in a way that left them gasping. A complete transformation, instantly, right before their eyes. *Snap!* Just like that.

"So I was a little rough," Dutch retorted. "I got the confession, didn't I?"

"Yeah. But you got a history, Dutch."

"That was a long time ago. How long does one man have to pay for the same sin?"

"Ask a perp."

"Or Bob Dylan," Bishop joined in.

"Yeah." Schiff picked up the thread. "The answer is blowing in the wind."

Dutch stared. "What the hell is that supposed to mean?" Then he turned to Bishop. Schiff knew that look. He'd been part of a two-cop team. Being his partner, Bishop should've known better than to mix it up in this particular ass-chewing. "And who the fuck is still listening to Dylan when we've got Judy Henske and Bruce Springsteen?"

Snap! Mellow Schiff. He smiled crookedly. "Springsteen? Let me tell you something about Springsteen. You pour Bob Dylan into a glass, swirl it around, throw the whole thing out, and take a whiff. The whiff, that's Springsteen."

"That's not Springsteen," countered Dutch. "That's vermouth."

"In Bob Dylan's martini."

"Who's Judy Henske?" Bishop asked.

Before Dutch could respond, *snap!* Here came the fist to the stomach. Schiff barked, "You're running out of chances, Dutch. Your Lone Star ass is in a sling and I'm tired of taking the heat. You haven't solved a homicide in six months—"

"That's not true," Dutch shot back. "The goddamn court—"

"Discovered you lied on the search warrant on one, illegally seized in another, and hamfisted this morning's defendant."

"I did what I had to do to get them off the streets."

"But you *didn't*, Dutch. You *didn't* put them away!" Schiff raised his voice, aggravated by his detective's stubbornness. "If they don't do the time, you haven't solved the crime."

"That's beautiful," griped Dutch sarcastically. "You should find a frame for that. Hang it over your desk."

"Fuck you." Schiff slid his eyes sharply to Bishop, who had diplomatically stayed out of this final exchange. "And you! You're his partner. *And* you've got seniority. Next time his head is tucked up his ass, pull it out!"

Bishop nodded, his limpid eyes agreeable. "Next one is by the book."

Schiff and Bishop went a long way back. The lieutenant realized Bishop knew the concession had to come from the detectives. Schiff looked at Dutch for affirmation.

Dutch crossed his fingers in the signature Boy Scout pledge. "I promise."

"That sounded real sincere," Schiff glared. *Snap!* He was smiling again. Dutch and Bishop both blinked. Schiff was glad it was one of those things they never got used to no matter how many times they saw it happen. Dutch and Bishop rose in anticipation of being dismissed, when Schiff's voice cut in like an impatient dance card holder. "Your next one walked in last night. Some broad minced up like Chinese chicken salad, died right in the booking area. She's at the morgue."

Dutch stopped, confused. "I thought that DB came in after midnight?"

Snap! Instantly pissed, Schiff countered. "So?"

"Doesn't that make it Olsen and Jacobs?"

"Olsen and Jacobs got the B&E double homicide on Masonic."

"The college students?" Bishop asked gravely.

Schiff knew this one had struck too close to home because his own kid, like Bishop's, was applying to college in the fall. An overamped second strike popper on a bad trip was looking to score Blue Dot in Buena Vista Park, when he freaked out. Around midnight, he started climbing trees and leaping down at couples who were taking a late night stroll. Before the park police could catch up with him, he ran up Java to Masonic and spotted two UCSF med students changing out of their intern smocks. Mistaking them for doctors, he smashed through their window and insisted they hand over their drug supply. When they told him they didn't have any pharmaceuticals, he grabbed one of the broken shards of glass in his bare hands and stabbed them to death until he lost two fingers. Just a hideous fucking mess.

"So that's it?" Dutch asked.

"That's it," Schiff concluded.

Dutch and Bishop stood up and retreated.

Schiff caught them in the doorway. "Don't screw the pooch on this one, Dutch. I want every step to come right from the manual. Or I'll have your transfer put through with wings."

***

Bishop sensed his partner's anger and frustration as they stepped out of Schiff's office.

"Transfer?" Dutch hissed.

"I think that was his idea of a joke," Bishop assuaged.

"Some fucking joke," Dutch muttered.

Bishop changed the subject. "How 'bout a hot dog?"

An hour later, they arrived at the San Francisco General Hospital morgue. As they walked in, the odor of formaldehyde hit them with physical force. Body bags lay on gurneys that were gridlocked like an endless cortege of stainless steel traffic.

"How's it going with your wife?" Bishop asked, stepping around a sixty-five-year old Chinese man with multiple gunshot wounds to the chest, head, and throat.

Dutch shrugged.

Bishop had gone through some hard times when his own marriage failed and he remembered needing support. His son, Darryl, was an only child, who didn't understand why his parents were breaking up after eight years together. All Bishop could do was try to explain, in fatherly terms, what the courts meant by 'irreconcilable differences.' He recalled the conversation exactly as it had happened. Word for word. It was one of the hardest explanations he'd ever had to make as a father. "You see, son, your mother and I, well, she gets tired of staying up late waiting for me to come home, you know?"

Darryl's eyes started to get wet. He was a tough kid and

he wouldn't cry, but his hands were shaking.

Bishop took them and held them. "And, I love her, you know, but she's, well, she's just tired of waiting, that's all. So we're going to be spending some time apart for a while. You know...so she don't have to wait no more."

Darryl nodded, bravely. Bishop held him close. What Bishop didn't tell Darryl was that his wife, a teacher at Berkeley, had fallen in love with a stockbroker she had met at an alumni fund-raiser and had been sleeping with him for two months. He had suspected an affair. They had been fighting for a while, and the truth was, somewhere along the way, she had just let go. He consoled himself with a fifth of gin and a splash of tonic every night for three months before Schiff called him in, sat him down.

Snap! Straightened him out. "Listen to me, Bishop, I'm forty-five years old and I know what the fuck I'm talking about. Now this may sound cold, because you may not be able to see it clearly like I do, but you're young. And you're going to get over this. You hear me? And not too far down the road, you're going to have a woman that you love just as much, if not more, than Naomi, and you are still going to have your kid. And then, this whole divorce business, which appears so enormous to you right now, will be at the other end of the telescope. Like you are looking through it backwards. Got it? And it won't even seem like a major event. So forget about it. It's nothing."

That was ten years ago.

And son of a bitch, if Schiff wasn't right. It had been like he had reversed the eye-piece of the telescope. In the beginning of their divorce, every little detail had been magnified beyond reason. How many times a day had she called her lover from his house? The loss of warmth in her eyes. And the way she seemed so far way even when they were standing right next to one another in the same room.

It was so hard to accept that the woman, who had given

herself to him so freely, didn't care for him anymore. That he couldn't sweep her up in his arms and kiss her and hold her and laugh with her like he used to. Every shared moment that they had spent together was turned into a lie, somehow undermined by his new knowledge, to the point where he wasn't sure if any of it was genuine. If they had really shared the experiences and ideas and feelings he thought they had, and if she had ever truly loved him at all. Not if she could stop caring. It couldn't be. Not if she could love another. *God. It was unbearable.*

Bishop could see Dutch going through the same painful steps and he wanted to help his partner, if he could. But Dutch kept his distance. They talked openly about their work and things in general. When it came to his personal life, Dutch became tight-lipped. That bothered Bishop. He spent eight hours a day with the guy, five days a week, and he felt he should know him, but he had no real feeling for Dutch as anything other than a police officer.

Bishop waited for more details.

Dutch noticed and added dismissively, "She's not returning my calls."

"Divorce?" Bishop persisted.

"Maybe." Dutch didn't elaborate.

Bishop felt frustrated. He knew cops like Dutch—they believed performance on the job should be adequate to create a successful working relationship. Police work was different, Bishop had hinted to Dutch early on when he found the newly transferred detective from Texas taciturn to the point of non-communicative. Partners looked out for each other. And sometimes the familiarity, which allowed one to guess what the other was thinking, could be the difference between life and death in a lethal stand-off. Dutch did not bite.

Bishop wasn't giving up, though. He kept working Dutch. Building trust. Sometimes he wondered if he was wasting his time. Dutch seemed the type who compartmentalized. Even if they did become "friends," Dutch would divulge few, if any, details about his life away from the job. He seemed like that kind of a guy. With a dark side, perhaps even darker secrets. He'd seen how Dutch treated perps. Hector, for example. *Shit.* Bishop had been afraid for the pedophile. That kind of rage came from deep inside somewhere.

"Bishop! Dutch!" interrupted a high-pitched nasal voice.

Dr. Will Pease, the chubby Medical Examiner, a Georgia native, orbited around a gurney supporting the grisly, eyeless cadaver of a forty-five year old burn victim. Bishop loved Pease. The ME remained jolly even after eighteen years on the same job in a city where he'd seen fatal crimes escalate in number and brutality. Bishop had known him from the time the doctor had hair. His eyesight had deteriorated, but the one thing he had honed to a razor sharp edge was his inflammatory tongue. He never held it, arguing it was too late for the dead to take offense.

"Why'd they fire the nurse in the sperm bank?" asked Dr. Pease as he led the detectives toward the far end of the morgue.

"I don't know," Bishop said. "Why?"

"Drinking on the job!" said Dr. Pease, cracking up.

Bishop belted out a loud, healthy laugh.

"Funny, doc," Dutch said. He didn't crack a smile. He'd confessed to Bishop he wasn't fond of gallows humor. Especially down here. In a rare unguarded moment, he added that something about morgues always gave him the creeps. Everything was so cold. Endless lines of marble and steel. Refrigeration rooms maintained at a frigid 40°F. Dutch was all business. "What have you got?"

"What do you think? It's a morgue," Dr. Pease said, motioning to his crotch. "I got a stiff."

Bishop roared again. So did Dr. Pease.

"You know, doc, just because you laugh too doesn't make the joke any funnier," Dutch growled.

"Sure it does! Laughter is contagious!"

Bishop grinned. This only encouraged Dr. Pease. "Hey, did you hear the one about the woman who had an orgasm?" He paused, then blurted out, "Who cares!"

Bishop went off the scale on that one. Bellowing like a lonely walrus.

Dutch turned to him curiously. "What are you, banging his daughter, or something?"

"He's funny," dismissed Bishop. "He's got *panache*."

"*Panache?*"

"It's French. Means verve," explained Bishop. "My kid's in prep school. Now he's teaching me. Did you know nearly the entire English language was stolen from other cultures? French, Italian, German, Latin—"

"*Rem acu tetigesti!*" concurred Dr. Pease and tapped the tip of his nose with his forefinger. "You've touched the point with a needle. Latin, Dutch. High school honors was my forte."

"Forte!" Bishop latched on immediately. "French. You see, Dutch? All the best things in America come from somewhere else. Just like the black man. We're your original imports. And still the best deal you ever made."

"No," Dutch corrected. "Stealing Manhattan from the Indians was the best deal we ever made."

"Screw Manhattan," said Dr. Pease. "It's a lousy drink and a lousy town. And if you want to talk deals, let's talk the Louisiana Purchase. Doubled the size of the US for eleven million two-fifty, plus indemnities. Now that's a *ganga*."

Bishop and Dr. Pease looked at one another and blurted out simultaneously, "Spanish!" before breaking into a waterfall of laughter. Dr. Pease stopped in front of the refrigeration drawers. Ran his finger down the nameplates. Stopped at one on the third row from the floor marked: *Jane Doe*.

The unoiled rollers shrieked along the guides with an irritating scrawl as he pulled it out. Beneath the thin cotton sheet lay the dim outline of a human form. Dutch regarded the vague, anthropoid features with some reluctance.

"This is where it all begins," Bishop thought out loud.

Under the layer lay the mystery. And somewhere out there lay the answers to the big six questions: who, what, where, when, how, and most importantly, why. Time was of the essence. The twenty-four hours before and after the murder were crucial. Called 24/24 in cop jargon. That brief bracket of time contained the best leads to the killer's identity. Before and after that devolved into a period of exponentially diminishing returns.

Proof of the killer's identity was quickly contaminated, disturbed, lost, or destroyed by any number of factors. The list was endless. It started with the first person who arrived on the scene, who might attempt a rescue, save the dying victim, pick up the phone, walk through the scene, touch the body, touch anything, destroy trace evidence, latent prints, serology, impressions—basically do almost nothing right. And that was just for starters.

Then came the foot traffic.

If the first Jake to cordon off the area was lucky enough to keep away the curiosity seekers, friends, and family, the whole arsenal of the enforcement system was set up to work against maintaining a pristine crime scene. Beat cops, homicide detectives, the photo unit, assistant DA, crime scene artists, photographers, criminalists, medical examiners, print specialists, and videographers would all be trampling through the sensitive areas and rendering all but the perpetrator's most careless sanitization efforts effectively useless.

Then there were the wild cards.

If, by some miraculous twist of fate, the homicide division and its support teams were fortunate enough to be blessed with an undisturbed scene, free of ordinary human bungling, fate had a way of stepping in and tipping the scales in the perpetrator's favor. A slight breeze, sunlight, rain, or even moisture could become the subtle accomplices. Footprints could be erased, fingerprints smudged, vital fluids diluted or washed away, tire tracks altered, and blood spatter patterns modified or completely cleansed. All of the tenuous cairns pointing toward guilt and identity that lay about the scene of the crime could just as easily vanish without the benefit of human intervention.

Bishop took a deep breath. The odds were against them.

When Dr. Pease drew the sheet to the victim's knees, it was the point of departure for Dutch and Bishop. Where they began to sift through all the hidden factors and circumstances responsible for bringing this particular DB to the morgue at San Francisco General. They would commence with the body. With the help of the medical examiner, they would determine the cause of death. Find out if the killer had any kinky preferences. Was he a thug or an artist? Was the commission of the crime paramount, or, in a more sinister vein, were they dealing with a sociopath, who enjoyed the details of the act more than the act itself?

This, they would come to know all too well.

The woman's corpse was naked. Her blood had been cleaned away, revealing cuts which crisscrossed the front of her body from neck to navel.

A thousand tiny incisions. Slashed every which way.

Not randomly. But artfully. In a distinct, clover-leaf pattern.

"Je-sus," reacted Dutch, this his eyes swung to her crotch. "What the hell is *that?*"

"The ring?" Bishop asked. These were moments when Dutch's naïveté showed. "That's a chastity lock."

"Modern version," said Dr. Pease. Then to Dutch, "Though hardly adequate."

Dutch affected a pained expression. "Next thing you know, men will be piercing—"

"They already do," Dr. Pease confirmed.

Dutch winced uncomfortably. Bishop sagely tilted his

head.

"In this case," Dr. Pease resumed, "the ornament is decorative. There was penetration shortly before she was killed. There are some differences in the depression of bruises that could be evidence of a threesome." Bishop glanced at Dutch over the gurney. This little twist wasn't going to make the investigation any easier. "No semen though."

Bishop smirked, "Safe sex is the worst thing to happen to forensics. No semen, no DNA."

"Her back is cut as well." Dr. Pease motioned to a surgical tray where Dutch and Bishop could find gloves to help turn her over. "Same cloverleaf pattern. But not deep enough to kill."

"The fine lines between pleasure and pain," Bishop said.

"Huh?" Dutch looked up, puzzled.

"She's a scar lover."

"A *what?*"

"An underground blood sport lover. They get off on razors and knives—primal stuff."

"Self-mutilation is in," sang Dr. Pease in his best falsetto.

Dutch returned to his examination of the body, mesmerized by the multitude of artfully arranged cuts. "How did she die?"

Dr. Pease ran his finger along a line across the victim's throat. At first glance it looked like the vine from which the clover leaf scar pattern hung, but now that the ME pointed it out, the detectives noticed it was thicker than the other etchings.

"A quarter of an inch too deep here," he said. "Cut the carotid. And good night, Gracie."

"Weapon?" Dutch asked, finally.

"A barber's straight edge."

"Could it have been an accident?"

"No," replied Dr. Pease. He twisted the victim's head and pointed to uprooted follicles on the back of her scalp. "Someone yanked her hair from behind and slit her throat. Her documents—that's what they call this kind of body art—were executed within minutes prior and were probably healing until the attack. The trauma resumed the bleeding."

"How did she get to the station?" asked Bishop.

"Drove up to the door," said Dutch. "I was there when she came in and dropped dead."

Dr. Pease distracted past the two detectives. "Kimchi!"

Kim Lee, from Forensics, advanced across the room with a thick file in tow. They knew him well from their weekly poker game in the morgue. A native of Los Angeles, the third generation Korean-American took a lot of ribbing being a southerner in NoCal. Pease nicknamed him Kimchi—a Korean dish of pickled cabbage. They kidded him a lot, but when it came to lab work, nobody questioned Lee's credentials as a criminologist. Cops loved him because he was accessible and always on top of things in spite of the tremendous volume of evidence he handled. In court, defense attorneys had long ago given up getting experts to refute his testimony. His work was incontrovertible. Consequently, the DA often decided to prosecute or plea bargain based on Lee's conclusions.

"What's the capital of North Korea?" asked Dr. Pease, Kim's chief tormentor.

Dutch saw Bishop's jaw drop in anticipation.

"Five bucks!" Dr. Pease slapped his thigh. Bishop roared.

Dutch and Lee looked at each other. Neither cracked a smile. Lee's hectic schedule and self-imposed discipline afforded him little time for idle chit-chat. He saved that for the poker game. Lee motioned to the body. "The vic was probably attacked in the car and left for dead."

"Any sign of forced entry into the car?" Dutch asked.

"No."

"So she could've known her assailant," Bishop suggested.

Kim nodded. "Maybe."

"Do we have an ID?"

Lee read off the file. "Lauren Piolene. Real estate broker.

Part of the multi-million dollar club."

"Is that anything like the mile high club?" Yet another new voice.

Tony Magno, a twenty-something police tech with an eyebrow ring, strolled in with a T-shirt that could be deemed offensive because it read, 'If it swells, ride it.' There was no double-entendre here. Magno was a die-hard surfer who religiously took weekend sabbaticals to Half Moon Bay to catch the big wave. The youngest of their poker group, Magno typified the public perception of a California native, which he was, having been born and raised in Santa Cruz, just down the road from San Francisco.

"Hey, guys, wassup?" He spoke with that slow, laid back seaside affectation that sounded like the hardest thing he was going to have to do all day was get an even tan. "Lieutenant said I'd find you here. Got something." He eyed the corpse casually, raised his brows in admiration, and smirked. "Killer body art."

The irony of his last statement brought a smile.

"Know the cutter?" Dutch asked, because if anyone did, Magno would.

He nodded. "Heavy rep. Check it out."

Magno handed Dutch a plastic evidence bag with a crumpled, cloth napkin inside.

Dutch unfolded it and read the diagonal, across-corner embossing: *Scars.*

Three.

"You feeling happy yet?" Bishop asked, rolling his Toyota Camry to a stop at the intersection of Castro and 18th. The sidewalks bustled under the garish lights, slipper moon, and velvet sky full of sparkling pinholes. Ideal climate for a night on the town.

"No. Why?" Dutch replied quizzically.

"Cause you've just arrived at the 'Gayest Four Corners of the World.'"

As they looked for parking, Dutch got an unsolicited education from Bishop. In the 1970s, gays and lesbians had moved into this area located between the windswept hills of Twin Peaks and the Latino Mission District. They restored the Victorian houses, installed large windows and boldly brought their lifestyle, until then hidden by shame and persecution, into the public eye for the first time. Today, Castro Street was more than a homosexual nexus. It had emerged as the springboard for alternative lifestyles.

After circling the block a couple of times, Dutch said impatiently, "Let's park."

Bishop pulled into a red zone and flipped up his police placard. They climbed out of the Camry and stood out at once in their square sports jackets, ironed pants, nine-to-five office shirts, and ties. Suspicious glances followed their movements.

Tattoos, clothes, and hairdos were neither outrageous nor random fashion statements, rather they were a necessity dictated by the codes of counterculture. Like gang colors, their permutations identified the individual as butch, switch, gay, straight, lesbian, top, bottom, femme fatale, master, slave, kinky and all that it entailed.

Dutch and Bishop may have been embarrassed by the stares, but as it was, they were used to the 'us v. them' attitude that came with being cops. The two men turned down a narrow side street with no name and ran into a headwall of sound. The whiplash voices of barking street hawkers and music pouring from storefront doorways reverberated even louder in the slender space between walls that rose three stories high. Pop bulbs flashed in successive rows, falling around the signs like neon dominoes. The sudden assault of noise, chintz, and glitter caught the detectives off guard.

"Hard to imagine a classy chick like that coming down here," Dutch wondered aloud.

"Everybody's got a private world, Dutch," said Bishop solemnly. "A side they only show to certain people in certain places. A side their families, co-workers and friends will never fully know. And if it weren't for shit like this, we wouldn't know either."

Dutch looked away uncomfortably from Bishop's penetrating eyes, recalling that night at a bar with his now-estranged wife, Elise. They were still dating, but over those drinks they had started exchanging all the venial confessions that lovers share when they are on the verge of making a serious commitment. After a couple of stories about previous lovers and their initial sexual escapades, she'd come out and said point blank, "I'll never know everything that you're thinking and that bothers me."

At the time, he didn't get the full impact of what she meant and wrote if off to her relative inexperience and insecurity. She was still a virgin. She'd told him she had been waiting for the right guy, and until then, she had only given a few hand jobs to overeager high school boys in the front seat of their daddies' cars. Dutch couldn't believe that was as far as she had gone. She was twenty years old. A beautiful brunette with a diminutive, but perfectly shaped body and long, hard legs.

After a few more drinks, she admitted there had been one other guy. He noticed her eyes went dark and her body slightly rigid at the thought of him. When Dutch pressed her further, she refused to say anything else. What actually happened, there was no way of knowing. But only a few simple questions, which, under ordinary circumstances would have seemed harmless, set Elise trembling. And then suddenly, she broke down and cried. Dutch never asked Elise about him again. He held her close and let her keep her secrets, telling her everything was going to be all right. They'd had enough confessions for one night.

"What's on your mind, Dutch?" Bishop asked.

"Nothing," Dutch answered, coming back. "How much further?"

"If Magno's right, just around the corner."

Past Café Purr, which, according to Magno again, served the best latté, they steered into another unnamed narrow alley. The tech had told them they'd find no sign. Just a frontage set in a flourish of erotic color and shadowy, suggestive forms.

They almost missed the door. Magno had predicted they might.

The place catered exclusively to those specifically looking for it.

"Scars" was etched in an unsteady hand with a nail on the nondescript door, maybe out of a need to be unobtrusive and pass as graffiti, Dutch figured, or, considering this was San Francisco, where it was hard to discern between pretentious and artistic, the crudeness could be deliberate.

Dutch looked at Bishop and paused. He had to admit he was a little nervous. Especially after discovering a whole new world when they went online. A search for SIV—self inflicted violence—another of Magno's terms to describe cutting, produced several hundred sites that ran the gamut:

Body Modification: Deprive, Contort, Distend; The Gauntlet: A Fetish Haven; Skinworks: Best Temporary Scarring; Cutting Arts; Body Décor; the list went on. There were links to unique personal services: *Cupping, Waxing, Caning, Piercing, Skewering, Crucifixion, Flesh Hooks, Rape & Terror Fantasies, Torture for Thrills,* you name it. The merchandise list was equally esoteric: *Vampire Teeth, Executioner Hoods, Wurtenburg Wheels, Tit Clamps, Cock Screws,* and practically anything designed to titillate the fetish demon lurking within. Then there was the veritable buffet of employment opportunities: *Now Hiring G-Spot Lesbians, Eunuchs, Adult Babies, Boy Toys.* Combo packages offered services, toys and professionals: *Bottom Cocksuckers, Top Femme Whores, Androgynous G-Spot Fantasies.*

Dutch had been shocked, once again exposing his less-than-urban Texas background. Bishop had heard of these types of clubs before and smirked, "America's underside. Where it's all about what gives you the biggest woody."

They continued to stand outside the door. Who knew what they were going to encounter on the inside. Finally, Dutch motioned toward the door. "We gonna do this or what?"

Bishop nodded, pushed the heavy door open, and stopped.

"Damn, it's dark," Bishop exclaimed, his hand reaching reflexively for the butt of the .357 Smith & Wesson 686 he kept tucked in his shoulder holster.

Dutch remembered doing a double-take when Bishop had pulled his piece out in a foot chase through Chinatown. A father had skewered his daughter in an honor crime after he found her knocked up by a foreign student from Korea. Younger cops doing plainclothes work on the force had been required to switch over to the .45 and 9mm caliber handguns. They held more bullets and brought police up to par with the arsenal being used against them on the streets. Bishop, however, being a veteran, was allowed the right to choose.

He caught Dutch staring and told him he still felt comfortable with, and preferred, his .357 wheel gun. It didn't jam up like an automatic, so he could shoot right through his jacket, if he had to. A reserve of speed-load cartridges, clipped to his belt, enabled him to keep up with the extra ammunition, if and when the situation occurred.

"What's that?" Dutch asked, wary.

Ahead, in the distance, lights materialized. Faint, sulfurous worms. Writhing to and fro. Twisting and surging to a reverberant rhythm beckoning from the far end of the hall.

"Looks like snakes," Bishop answered.

"Or something."

As they moved further down the hallway, the lucent, sinewy forms garnered distinction. At first, it appeared as if the snakes were buffeted on roving hills of black. Then the hills knotted up like fists and fanned out into limbs. The limbs stretched forth from trunks and the trunks emerged as bodies. Naked bodies. A nontransparent, oleaginous paint coated the private parts, while blacklight fluorescent markings accented erogenous zones.

"Welcome."

Dutch and Bishop jumped. A face emerged from an underlit alcove they had failed to notice in their fascination with the nude dancers.

"The cover is fifty dollars."

That killed Dutch's enthusiasm. The detectives searched through their wallets, careful not to flash their tins. They didn't want to blow their cover, although their square clothes may have already given them away. Dutch came up twenty short and Bishop covered it, prompting the tony, handsome and somewhat androgynous doorman to ask, "Are you two together?"

Bishop looked at Dutch, who looked back at Bishop.

"Couples get a discount. Then it's only ninety dollars," the doorman said with a knowing smile.

Without a second thought, Bishop stuffed a ten back in his wallet. "Yeah. We're a couple."

Dutch was floored. He would rather have spent the ten bucks than have a bunch of sexual deviants think he was swinging from the other side of the plate. Dutch caught the doorman staring.

"Shy? That's all right. We get a lot of first timers. You know, just coming out." Then, confidentially nodding to Bishop," Your boyfriend is quite a catch."

Dutch was just about to bust him in the mouth to correct the misunderstanding, when Bishop said, "Thank you," turned around, and placed his hand on Dutch's shoulder. "Let's go, sugar."

Dutch heard the doorman remark with a faint-hearted sigh, "New love."

Dutch looked over his shoulder sharply. A lanky queen in a leather codpiece appeared and perched his chin over the doorman's shoulder. They stared straight back with smiles.

"I'd like to put some cream in his coffee," the queen winked when Bishop looked over. He laughed like a good sport.

"You silly slut," The doorman giggled. "Don't you have any regard for true love? Can't you see how those two care for one another? It's so...*romantic*."

Dutch self-consciously shrugged Bishop's hand off and noticed out of his peripheral vision the queen make a gagging motion with two fingers. "Grow up, puh-lease, little Ms. Disney. I swear, sometimes you are très, Snow White."

"Your secret is safe with me, Twinkie." Bishop reacted to Dutch's shaking head.

Dutch whispered, "For ten bucks? Are you crazy?!"

"I don't see the big deal."

"Well, I do! Jesus. Now you got everybody thinking I'm queer."

"Hey, if you're not comfortable with your masculinity—"

"Oh, I'm comfortable with it all right. I just don't want anyone else getting comfortable with it. That's all."

Dutch and Bishop entered the main staging area and were immediately struck by the feral atmosphere. Young couples, gay and straight, danced with uninhibited intimacy. Stylishly attired, though in various states of undress, this group was a cut above the glow-in-the-dark attractions in the central foyer. Off to the right and to the rear of center stage, a live four-piece band played on a raised dais. The lead singer looked like Marilyn Manson in an Armani suit with a MAC makeover. He moved gracefully. Etiquette tips, courtesy of Bryan Ferry. Voice, low and controlled.

Dutch recognized the tune as a not-so-bad rendition of a Velvet Underground song, 'Heroin,' popularized by footman Lou Reed in 1967. "*I don't know. Just where I'm goin'. But I'm gonna try for the Kingdom if I can, cause it makes me feel like I'm a man. When I put a spike into my vein. And I tell you things aren't quite the same. When I'm rushing on my run. And I feel just like Jesus's son. And I guess, but I just don't know. And I guess that I just don't know...*" The song was sexual in nature and built to a pounding climax, before slowing and resuming the insistent, steady refrain.

A pair of women brushed by the two detectives. They looked alike at first glance, except that the woman on the left carried herself with a slight hunch and eyes that avoided more than they made contact. Dutch and Bishop looked around the room and noticed others like her. From his research on the web, he knew they were called Tops, butch women whose name was derived from the dominant sexual position they preferred. They were distinguishable from Bottoms, who were friendlier as a rule. The one who brushed by frankly appraised Dutch and Bishop with a gelding glare.

The hypnotic, voluptuous strain continued. "*I wish that I'd sailed the darkened seas on a great big clipper ship. Goin' from this land here to that. In a sailor's suit and cap. Away from the big city. Where a man cannot be free. From all the evils of this town. And from himself and from everyone else around. Heroin. Will be the death of me...* " The melody suited the club. Suited Dutch. It picked up an unconscious rhythm in his head. "*And I guess, but I just don't know. And I guess that I just don't know...*"

It was all gray. Non-committal. Indistinct. Permissive undertones of hedonism and raw sexuality. Building to crescendo. He noticed that Bishop did not care for the beat or the lyrics. Clearly, he didn't get the blatant nihilism of the lyrics. Bishop was still stuck on '70s groove music and '80s feel good, when the lyrics were clean and filled with positivity. The Doobie Brothers, Donna Summer, Wild Cherry, Hot Chocolate, hell, Bishop had probably even given the Eagles Greatest Hits a spin or two when they still pressed vinyl.

Suddenly, the music stopped. Some dancers continued to sway, heedless of the abrupt silence, still moving to their own rhythm.

"Someone had the sense to turn off that shit," remarked Bishop.

Dutch shook his head. Bishop was such a prude. He couldn't wrap his head around today's angst and death and fucking around. Just couldn't tune in to that station. Dutch knew Bishop had a kid, Darryl, and heard him complain that kids had it easier now more than ever before. "Maybe that was the problem," he'd gone on in his diatribe. "You make something too readily available and nobody appreciates it. I knew a lot of brats like that in school. The ones who complained that the Beemer their dad gave them for their 16th birthday wasn't the right color. To hell with that, man. Fucking self-indulgent kids. Too much leisure time and not knowing what to do is what gets 'em all depressed. What they really need is a job and a swift kick in the ass. Then, when it comes time to relax, maybe they'll remember what it was like to have a little fun. And then they'll start appreciating songs like 'Peaceful, Easy Feeling,' and 'Love to Love You Baby' again."

Dutch nodded Bishop toward the bar.

"Oh, good. I need a drink," Bishop said, checking out the close-cropped platinum blonde in combat boots, camouflage shorts, and a ribbed, M*A*S*H halter top, who mixed and served well drinks.

"That so?" Dutch observed Bishop's eyes. "Then at least look up. She's not pouring from her tits." Her breasts looked like two wildcats trapped under a white blanket.

Bishop smiled, busted.

Half way to the bar, a hush descended over the entire audience.

A raven-haired woman in black latex pants and crimson tennis shoes emerged from a dark archway. Following her was a slender girl, young, maybe twenty-three, if that, her face striking without being overly pretty and attractive. She had a ring pierced through each nostril. A lentiginous dusting of freckles splashed over Mid-Western cheeks. A hat pressed down over straight, chestnut-colored hair which fell to her clavicle. She'd cut off the tattered jeans an inch below her crotch, accentuating long, coltish legs. Her champagne breasts bubbled over a Christmas-red push-up bra.

She received a smattering of applause from her friends and smiled back at them quickly, tensely, then extended a brief wave to her boyfriend, a young fresh-faced kid, who stood expectantly at the near edge of the proscenium mouthing silent encouragement. Christmas Girl followed the raven-haired woman to a hitching post. There, she spread her legs, her knee-high Tony Llama boots taking a stance just wider that her shoulders. Below, her feet straddled either side of a painted logo underneath the post, which read: The Spotlight.

On cue, the house globes dimmed. A single, white spot limned her frame and pinned her under its unrelenting stare. Center stage. Dutch recognized the look on Christmas Girl's face. This was her big moment.

"What do you suppose—" Bishop began.

Dutch raised a silencing finger. Intrigued by the show.

The raven-haired assistant secured Christmas Girl's wrists to the hitching post with lengths of corded leather. Thin, but strong. The boyfriend clapped and threw her a kiss. She arched her back seductively and pulled her shoulders together to allow the assistant easier access to unclasp her bra. Her breasts bobbed and rested, allowing Dutch and Bishop a pristine view of her blush-colored nipples that were hard as nails.

"That chick is totally turned on," Dutch murmured to Bishop.

Bishop nodded, inexorably drawn into the mysterious anticipation in the air. "High beams all the way."

Christmas Girl bent forward to strike a Figure 5, her arms at full extension beyond her head, which she bowed to the floor. She clutched the hitching post so tightly, the pressure of her grip squeezed the blood from her hands, leaving her long spatulate fingers as toneless as the stack of white linen napkins resting next to her. Dutch and Bishop noticed at once that the top napkin displayed the diagonal, across-corner embossing like the one found with the victim's body: *Scars*.

The silence in the room deepened.

The few who swayed without music moved off the floor. All eyes riveted upon the girl in the cowboy hat. She was nervous. Droplets of sweat beaded up and rolled down the gentle slope of her breasts before briefly hanging and then falling from her half-inch long nipples. The detectives walked with uneven strides. Now and then catching a glimpse of the girl through the throng which had constricted around the stage like a python awaiting dinner.

The air grew pregnant with anticipation.

Her boyfriend kept nodding and chuffing inconsequential words of encouragement, "This is it, baby, you're a star, you're going to be a fucking *star!*"

From the shadows of the pit, a sleek feminine form retrieved the stage mike. She spoke in a husky, contralto modulation that seemed to come from everywhere all at once. Yet, when Dutch and Bishop looked around, it was impossible to discern the source of the sound. It was as if it emanated from the very walls themselves. It gave the room a disturbing, animated, womb-like quality.

"Ladies and gentlemen, tonight, in the Spotlight, the virtuoso—Gillette."

The audience erupted!

A handsome, self-possessed man in his thirties stepped out of the dark archway. His attire matched the composure he seemed to exude naturally—spotless white blouson, full sleeves held tight around his wrists, studded securely with simple gold cuff links. Black leather pants that fit like a second skin over full sprinter's legs. And alligator skin boots with shining brass toes nesting his large, oversized feet.

The man crossed the stage to the Christmas girl. She saw him and caught her breath expectantly. Gillette's ultra-white teeth flashed a winning smile. But he said nothing. Gillette was a man of few words. He preferred instead, to play the game. Making a quick half turn, something bright flashed in his hand.

Bishop and Dutch stopped dead in their tracks. Neither could discount the coincidence. With an audible snap, Gillette swung open a spring-loaded barber's straight edge.

**

"You see that?" Dutch whispered as the room went silent.

"Uh, huh," breathed Bishop.

They could very well be staring at the murder weapon.

On stage, Christmas Girl tensed to the outer extremities. Goose bumps raced along her arms and legs. She squirmed anxiously. Excitement agitated her alabaster skin. The muscles on her back stiffened. Her nipples, hard before, now glistened like twelve-carat diamonds as they shrunk to an even more dense, bituminous state.

"Are you daddy's little girl?" Gillette asked with a satin inflection. He was wearing a microphone because his voice resonated over the speakers.

Dutch got the feeling this guy could read the newspaper and make it should like Shakespeare. On the other hand, Gillette could be an arch villain straight from the pages of the Marquis de Sade. Smooth, dark, and seductive. The kind that could make a person dance on the edge of a knife, or watch them bleed, with equal indifference.

"Yes. Oh, yes!" she exclaimed. A droplet of perspiration fell from her nipple. *Slap!* It struck the floor. Picked up by the stage mike, the impact broke the pindrop silence.

Gillette nodded to the band. They struck up an unintrusive instrumental of a Nina Simone song. Then he placed a hand on her nape and turned the barber's razor down. As he did, light glinted off the edge with a starburst. Sharp enough to split an atom. Gillette firmly ran the blade across her back. The skin broke.

Christmas Girl emitted a short, high-pitched shriek!

Blood folded out on either side of the cut in a slow, spreading wave.

"Jesus Christ," Dutch groaned. "We should arrest him just on principle."

Bishop shook his head. "Con*sensual* adults."

"Eyah, but don't you think maybe there's some room for interpretation between the letter of the law and...whatever *he's* doing?"

The girl writhed. Cheeks flush as a rose in full bloom. Her teeth, slightly crooked, clenched behind drawn lips.

"Don't stop," she hissed quivering with pain and desire.

The raven-haired assistant stepped in and patted her forehead, preventing a sudden tide of perspiration from raining down her face. There was something about this girl, Dutch thought, something in the way she received her pleasure that turned her otherwise ordinary features into extraordinary beauty. Her legs rocked and her hips bucked. Her wrists pulled at the tightly cinched leather laces that bound her firmly to the post. Her whole body quivered with transformational energy.

Gillette got in the groove, executing short, authoritative slashes. Quicker. Deeper. With each cut, the girl's screams intensified.

The detectives noted a shift in tone.

From pain to primal passion.

Her boyfriend beamed. The damn kid actually had a hard-on.

"Oh! Please! Oh-oh-oh!" Her moans became openly sexual. Closer together. Approaching orgasm.

Onlookers began to make out with their partners. Kissing, open mouth, tongues coiling. Turned on by Christmas Girl's outbursts. A flurried frottage of groping and running hands. Here. There. Everywhere. They stroked and squeezed and pressed against the hot zones.

"Look at 'em," remarked Bishop. "Men and women, women and women, men and men, hetero, homo, nobody gives a fuck in this place."

"It's all about the biggest woody," Dutch said absently. Engrossed by the cutting.

"You're a quick study, Dutch. You'll go far out here."

"I'm not sure I want to go that far."

Now Gillette began to moan with each cut. Swinging the blade flamboyantly. Christmas Girl's screams peaked in a final, keening wail just as Gillette finished with a flourish. The audience roared. A magnificent round of applause. Her boyfriend, pushed to the edge of his own orgasm by simply watching, licked his lips as if he were tasting her. Later, she'd be on top and he'd be on the bottom howling like a coyote. That was how it worked, Dutch knew.

Christmas Girl's real name was Betty Page, Dutch would discover when they questioned her in the ensuing days as the murder investigation probed deeper into the patrons of *Scars*. Just like the famous Hollywood pin-up from the '50s. She was regular to the club. Her step-father sexually neglected her mother. Then, when her mother went to the local GNC, where she worked as a nutrition specialist, he'd come in Betty's room and feel her up. Only, when he did it, he would hold a pairing knife under her jugular and tell her that if she made a sound, he'd cut her throat. So she did as she was told and whimpered while he ran his hands under her blouse and felt her soft, budding nipples. Some days, the pig rammed his rough, worker's hands between her legs and tried to squeeze them inside. She was ten. And she'd been frigid ever since.

That is, until her boyfriend introduced her to the loving walls of *Scars*. Here, in full view of the world, she could scream and writhe and cry and shout out her demons. They seemed to be released over the audience and cast out into the darkness as Gillette nicked her skin. He was her exorcist. Only now, she was in control. She embraced the knife willingly. And she took back all the power and all the self-respect she had lost. It was the best fucking therapy she'd ever had. So that's the way it was. And that's what brought her back to *Scars*. Like clockwork. Once a month.

Dutch and Bishop arrived at the bar.

They couldn't take their eyes off Christmas Girl. There was something so sexually free and liberated about her that she commanded their attention well after the peak of the show. Dutch took a seat on red leather barstool and looked away.

Immediately, he locked eyes with a hunter.

***

Dutch realized by the way the woman was staring from the end of the bar that she had been watching him before he noticed her. A cool, measured stare. Simmering light-gray eyes. Rimmed in gold, like the brushed back fur of something wild. Late twenties, he guessed. Exuding a confidence that was at once both intimidating and alluring.

The woman didn't look away when Dutch noticed her.

Continuing her analysis. Patient. Unblinking.

Until another sultry olive-skinned woman joined her.

"Hi, Nicole," the exotic woman greeted. Lips aflutter. Like butterfly wings.

"India," Nicole replied and kissed India so naturally, it didn't seem sexual, though watching two stunning women together affected both Dutch and Bishop.

"What is it with this place?" Dutch shook his head.

"Dunno," Bishop said. "But I wouldn't mind a membership."

Nicole casually tucked India's hair behind one ear so she could get a clear line of sight to the two men. It appeared so uncontrived and classy, Dutch wondered if he was being made by a pro. Nicole sized them up with aggressive, almost predatory, delight. Her eyes roved over their bodies with a restless precision, as if searching for a weak spot. When they finally stopped, Dutch noticed she was staring at their crotch. The two men self-consciously crossed their legs like synchronized dancers and averted their eyes.

"Man-eater," Bishop surmised in a low whisper

"You said it," Dutch agreed. True to the mark. "Good looking, though."

"You're on the rebound. Uncle Milty in a dress is gonna look good to you," Bishop shot back, referring to the burlesque comedian, Milton Berle.

On center stage, Gillette backed away and appraised his work with the same loving devotion an artist would bestow on a completed canvas. He gently straightened Christmas Girl, whose cries had died into gasping, fitful breaths identical to the aftermath of raw sex. She smiled through the pain. "God, I am so wet."

The band stopped playing and a low, tenor saxophone jazz ballad, à la Stanley Turrentine, crept in from speakers in the invisible spaces between the walls. It was a mixed track, Dutch was sure of that, because somewhere beneath the main score was embedded the sonorous rocking and moaning of a man and woman engaged in mutual pleasure. Once again, that mysterious quality of the music, that sourceless sound, which appeared to be coming from everywhere and yet nowhere, enhanced the sexual atmosphere, allowing the audience to feel as if they were in the same room with the couple making love.

"They ought to rename this place the Twenty-Four Hour Orgasm," remarked Bishop.

Gillette handed Christmas Girl back to the raven-haired assistant who led her behind the dark archway, dabbing her back with woven napkins as they walked. Gillette's white shirt was splattered. Rivulets of dark red blood dripped down his leather pants and onto his alligator-skin boots. For his grand finale, he took a graceful, sweeping bow, which elicited a quick acknowledgment of renewed applause, then followed the two women through the archway.

The Spotlight dimmed to an incandescent glow as the club crew took to the stage. Clearing it for the next act. They wore what looked like stylish, black overalls made of a synthetic, waterproof fabric resembling Gortex. Across the back was embroidered the club's moniker in gold brick letters. Quick, possessed of an economy of movement, within minutes, they mopped the floor with odorless antiseptic, removed the hitching post, and placed fresh napkins adjacent to the centerpiece for the next show.

A brazier.

It was made of lava rock and ornamented with bare bodies engaged in a bacchanalian orgy of forbidden delights.

Dancing couples stayed away from the stage. Reverentially. Like the aftermath of a sacrament. The remaining onlookers returned to their tables. Discussing the cutting in private conversations.

"Coke," Dutch ordered.

"Straight up," Bishop added.

Dutch's eyes drifted back toward Nicole.

"Forget about it," said Bishop.

"Why?"

"Because you're not walking on the same side of the street, that's why."

"I'll give her ninety seconds."

"Then what?"

"Then I buy your drink. Otherwise you buy mine."

"You're on," Bishop challenged confidently.

The next time they looked, Nicole was coming their way.

Dutch tapped his watch. "Fifteen seconds."

"Hell," Bishop grumbled, fishing the drink money out of his wallet.

"Virgins?" asked Nicole, arriving in a cloak of enticing perfume.

She possessed a voice that matched her looks. Throaty, polished enunciation that came from sophisticated breeding. Dutch and Bishop were intrigued by the question.

"That's what you are," explained Nicole. "If you've never been cut."

"And all these years I thought fucking had something to do with it," Dutch said.

Nicole laughed. A husky, sexy laugh. Teeth even and white.

God, she's gorgeous. Dutch caught Bishop's analytic stare. When Dutch looked at Nicole, he saw what she wanted him to see. The suggestion, full of possibility. The poetry in every connecting line. The entirety. Bishop, on the other hand, was going the other way. Examining, logging and separating the details with cynicism. Perfect teeth, the result of expensive dental work, not an inviting Cheshire Cat smile. Nice cheekbones, arrogance, not nobility. Expensive pageboy haircut, a well-coiffed ruse to cover an imperfectly-high forehead, not the perfect frame for a perfect face. Hell, Bishop should have hard-on, not a mental cock-block.

Dutch exhaled. He knew he had no chance of winning Bishop over. Bishop had chip on his shoulder about beautiful women generally, and affluent beautiful women in particular. Dutch surmised it was Bishop's baggage from his divorce.

Nicole held out her hand. "Nicole Gray."

Does she have any rough edges? Dutch took her hand into his own. "Jeff Holland." Then, almost as an afterthought. "Dutch."

"Obviously."

He noticed her immaculate squared-off nails tipped in white. His ex-wife had done her nails that way. His eyes lingered a little too long and Nicole caught it.

"You like them?" she asked, extending her hand into the light. They were painstakingly polished in an off-white pastel with an iridescent, glittery undercoat. "It's called Pimp."

"Of course," Bishop responded. "Brian Bishop. But nobody calls me Reverend."

Nothing. Not even a smile.

Nicole went on, giving Dutch her complete attention. "They're a new line of paper nails created by this wonderful protégée from Los Angeles. She was a chem major at USC and she dropped out to become a millionaire. Now that's what I call getting an education."

India walked up behind Nicole and encircled her waist. "Yeah. She comes up with the greatest names," India said. "Pimp, Porno, Jail Bait, Trash—and they're selling, like, unbelievably." India leaned over Nicole's shoulder, hand outstretched. "India."

"As in the country?" asked Dutch.

"No, the ink. My mother loved calligraphy."

They distracted momentarily. The band retook the stage and started up again. India wandered off to join the gathering fringe of onlookers.

"Who's next?" Bishop asked.

"Myke the Dyke," Nicole said.

"For real?" Dutch asked.

"You can check under the hood if you'd like," Nicole cooed. "I took his word for it."

Silhouettes of a new couple appeared underneath the dark archway, paused, then stepped forward, revealing themselves gradually.

"More theater," Bishop said.

"It's a show," Nicole nodded. "Catharsis."

The one on the left had hair the color of spoiled milk. Coifed into a crown of tawny thorns around his pate. He had broad shoulders. Hard, unsympathetic features. And the thin fissure of a scar running horizontally under his right cheek. In the light, Dutch noted the man sported a tiny blond mustache over what looked like pink lipstick. He wore a red bandanna, vest, baggy, brown, calf-skin pants, and boots, and he ambled with the low, cocksure gait of a Top.

"Say hello to Myke the Dyke," Nicole declared.

"You gotta be kidding me," Dutch said.

Beside Myke stood a redhead. Sateen tube bra securing taut breasts. Bright-patterned sarong floating over the floor as she walked. The band kicked up with a K.D. Lang instrumental. The redhead drifted to center stage. Unwrapped her sarong. And left an unmistakable impression on the detectives.

She was buck naked.

The redhead did a quick twirl, exposing herself to the audience. Unashamed. Her wild triangle of flaming pubic hair burning into their memories.

"Does this place have memberships?" Dutch asked, picking up the lingering thought Bishop had put down earlier.

The redhead bent over and Myke secured her to a stone bench reminiscent of a Japanese garden. She betrayed the same symptoms of nervous, sexually charged anticipation that

Christmas Girl had shown earlier.

"Need anything to drink first?" Myke asked, donning heavy leather gloves. Oiled to a shiny finish.

"No, thanks." She rolled her neck to catch a glimpse of his muscular physique.

Dutch noticed that her eyes were glassy, probably from inhaling premium hash or something like that before she came out. To dull the pain.

Myke the Dyke opened the brazier. Smoke plumed toward the ceiling. He reached in and grabbed the curved, filigreed handle of a finely wrought branding iron from the burning coals.

"Now wait a minute," Dutch drawled, rising slightly in his chair. "Is he really going to touch her with that?"

"Um, hmmm." Nicole smiled, amused by Dutch's naiveté.

The tip of the brand glowed with heat. Myke raised it in the air for the entire audience to see, then dropped it. Lower. Lower. Lower still. The redhead sucked in her breath as she felt the searing heat of the iron approach her bare skin. Then. For only a moment. Myke brought the iron into contact with her waiting flesh. She cried out! Her entire rear end shook in response to the white hot sizzle of the brand. Exhilarated screams from the audience echoed back. Their cheers drove her on.

Dutch saw India watching him. He realized he shared Bishop's sickened expression.

She smiled, "Obviously, this is not your cup of tea."

"Myke's good for a mark, but if you're looking to be cut, Gillette is the best," Nicole said, capturing their attention.

"That can't be his real name" Dutch asked.

"A sobriquet, yes," Nicole nodded.

Dutch shot Bishop a blank look. "French?"

"*Exactamènt,*" Bishop confirmed. "Means alias." Then, to Nicole, "I was telling Dutch how most of the English language was taken from other countries."

"Isn't that nice," Nicole said, more a statement than a question.

She shook a cigarette loose from a gold case and held it to her lips, which she pouted expectantly, and waited for Dutch to light. He did. A little courtesy went a long way and he had many questions to ask. He was trying to figure the right way to break the ice and begin the questioning.

"So, what can I do for you, officers?" asked Nicole

So much for the do-se-do, Dutch thought. Better off with the direct approach. He flashed his tin, "We'd like some information on a customer."

"Oh, you're *detectives?*" she said, then asked, "But isn't that kind of information confidential?"

"This is an *ex*-customer," Dutch answered tersely. And wondered again if he wasn't being fucked with. He watched her face for a reaction.

"Ex as in stopped coming here?" Nicole asked.

"Not exactly."

"What's her name?"

"How do you know we're looking for a woman?" Bishop pounced.

Nicole exhaled smoke in one long breath. "All my clients are female."

"Lauren Piolene," Dutch said.

Nicole wrinkled her forehead. "Blonde, twenties, good skin?"

"Not any more," Bishop said. He reached into his sports jacket and removed an autopsy photo. He and Dutch had carefully selected the one they were going to show. It had to be gruesome, but not sickening enough so the suspect could mask that all important first reaction behind a look of shock or disgust.

Nicole caught her breath, momentarily off balance for the first time that night. But then again, something about it was too perfect. The timing just right. As if delivered on cue. Still, Dutch couldn't be sure if it was just an act. She gave away nothing. Okay, that didn't work.

"We are the lead detectives on the case," said Bishop.

"Aren't you lucky." Once again, the question disguised as a statement.

Dutch looked at her eyes closely, really looked at them, but all he got was a featureless wall. Completely flat and unreadable. She wasn't letting anyone in she didn't want there.

Applause broke around the stage. Nicole looked away toward Myke the Dyke, who clutched an ice cold towel to the redhead's behind. When Myke removed it, a scarlet letter "A" swelled to the surface in sharp contrast with her milk-white skin. Myke helped her back into the dark archway.

"It's not what you think," Nicole offered without prompting. "It's not adultery the 'A' stands for. It's anarchy. Adultery went out with Nathaniel Hawthorn." Then she turned directly to Dutch, "You're not married, are you?"

Dutch's ring finger was unadorned. As a matter of pride, he had taken off his wedding band when Elise had asked for a separation.

"Some men, well, maybe not upstanding detectives like yourselves, but some men might say that an affair would add spice to their marriage. And those same people might even come to a club like this and take off their wedding bands looking for that extra...*ingredient*."

She held Dutch's gaze. He sensed Bishop's disapproval of his exchange. *Next time his head's up his ass, pull it out,* Schiff had said. Dutch realized his partner was about to use both hands to do just that, when India and Gillette, in clean clothes, appeared beside Nicole.

"Hi, baby," said Nicole and kissed Gillette, dipping her tongue into his mouth. He responded. They kissed long and hard. Deliberately. *For me.* Dutch smiled.

"Gillette," Nicole introduced after they pulled apart, lips

glistening. "Dutch and Bishop. They're homicide detectives."

Dutch noticed a shadow pass over Gillette's eyes. *Guilt?*

***

When Bishop was a kid, he had gone with his mother to pick up his father, Clevon T. Bishop, from the Sacramento State Prison. He'd been six at the time—conceived four years into his father's ten year stretch during a conjugal Valentine Day visit. Bishop Sr.'s first few years in the joint were rough. He turned to God and took Jesus Christ as his savior in order to get through. The day he got out, they all went to a malt shoppe to celebrate. There were pretty girls in summer dresses all over the place. Black and white polka dots, mini-skirts, and tan legs—it was a lovely afternoon. But something went wrong. Instead of his mother being happy, she was getting angry. Cold and quiet. His father started apologizing. Bishop couldn't figure what for, because his father hadn't done anything. After his mother left to pay the bill, his father pulled Bishop to his side and said, "Jealousy is a woman's game, son. It's best not to deal them any cards." That was the last pair of legs his father looked at other than his Mom's.

Bishop wondered if Dutch was even aware of the game Nicole was playing.

"Business or pleasure?" Gillette asked.

"One of our customers from last night was killed," said Nicole, with an undercurrent of what could pass for curiosity.

"You don't say?" Gillette responded, just as curious.

Applause rang out. Christmas Girl was back, a white shawl draped over her upper body. When she climbed on the dais, she searched the audience. Beckoning Gillette with a come-hither gesture.

"I need to show off my work." Gillette swaggered to center stage, accepted the continued applause and sashayed into a three hundred and sixty-degree spin before taking a deep, grandiose bow. Then, almost like a magician, he made an eloquent gesture and dramatically removed the white shawl from Betty's shoulders. As it fell to the floor, soft as doves' wings, Gillette took her for a runway stroll. The audience erupted.

The cuts weren't bleeding. They clotted in slender dark brown lines, which appeared as steady and precise as a fine pencil etching. The pattern, Renaissance in its intricacy, was simply breathtaking.

"They heal that fast?" Bishop asked Nicole, incredulously.

"Ever cut yourself shaving?" she asked. Bishop nodded. "Same thing. Only bigger."

"Much bigger."

Christmas Girl picked up the shawl, but didn't wrap it around herself. Several of the audience members wanted to take a closer look and scrambled onto the stage. Behind her, Gillette played the perfect star. Kissing, shaking hands, and smiling off the continuous shower of compliments.

"Ladies and gentlemen," the speakers moaned.

There it was again, that embryonic sound. Bishop and Dutch turned at the same time. It was the same emcee from the opening act when they first walked in. Both men noticed for the first time Nicole was gone.

She stepped into the splash of light center stag, a svelte silhouette under the hot lamps. "The Spotlight is closed for the evening. Please feel free to seek out entertainment and pleasure, however you like. We're open until 4 A.M. Thank you for coming." She took Gillette's arm and walked right by. "Good night, detectives."

"Wait a minute," Dutch stopped them. "Where are you going?"

"Wherever I want," Nicole replied.

"We'd like to ask you some more questions," Bishop said.

"Well then," Nicole sounded as if she were doing them an enormous favor, "let's go into my office upstairs."

Bishop had never seen anything like it. Glancing over, neither had Dutch.

About twenty feet square, Nicole's office stood on white marble. The tiles came from the same strain. So the grain ran continuously, rendering the joints nearly invisible and the floor almost seamless. Each wall, finished rough and painted white, displayed one-to-one dried-blood lithographs of cuttings sponged right off the body. The decor was completely without a table, filing cabinets, swivel chairs, visitors' seats and other accessories typically associated with business. Office supplies, Bishop guessed, must be stored behind the smoked glass shutters at the far end of the room.

Two extremely light gray couches faced each other. A portfolio lay between them on an alpenglow bath mat on the floor, arranged at a stylish, art house cant. Gillette slouched down onto the triple cushions and settled down straddling the crevice between two. Nicole took a seat beside Gillette.

The detectives sat across from them on an identical couch. Bishop picked up the portfolio, flipping through a showcase of Gillette's best work—Celtic knots, runes, tarot cards, and totems. He read the Artist's Statement: *Cutting is body art in the true sense of the word. Each person's cicatrix heals differently and creates scars that are his or her own, so you don't have the uniformity of tattoos, or their permanence. That's the appeal. Yet, if the client requests tattoo ink or wedge-cutting to make the break in the skin too wide to heal cleanly, we can create a lasting impression that takes the whole artistic expression to the next level. This is a showcase of my most sophisticated work, which I hope you, your family and loved ones will enjoy. Compassionately yours, Gillette.*

"Did you know Lauren?" Dutch began the questioning.

"Not really." Gillette heaved his shoulders in a noncommittal gesture. "I do half a dozen, sometimes more, every night."

Bishop's finger froze on a photograph in the portfolio.

The scars were identical to those on the victim. He closed the book, looked up, and saw Nicole's eyes locked on him.

"You that busy?" Bishop tried to play it cool, but it was too late. She'd watched him recognize the pattern.

"I'm booked three months in advance," answered Gillette with an undertone of arrogance.

"How much do you make?" Dutch asked.

"Five hundred a stretch."

"Three grand a night?"

"Give or take," shrugged Gillette.

Bishop shook his head. "All the money's in private practice."

"Cutting's not sleazy S&M," defended Nicole. "Our clients are stockbrokers, lawyers, doctors. My the cheapest cutters command one-fifty an hour."

"Myke the Dyke, too?" Dutch asked, surprised.

"Two hundred. But he's different."

"I'll say," Bishop added.

Nicole let the remark pass. "Myke specializes in branding. He's one of the best."

Dutch pointed to a framed trade school diploma on the wall. "Whose is that?"

"Mine," replied Gillette. "Computer graphics. Got swept into Silly-Con Valley for a while, but it didn't satisfy me artistically."

"So...you two are partners?" Bishop asked

Dutch and he would jump all over the spectrum, hoping to catch Nicole or Gillette in a contradiction.

"Think of it as a salon," said Gillette. "I used to own *Scars* one hundred percent. But I made some bad investments and Nicole stepped in."

Nicole laughed. "I was his best customer." She placed her hand intimately on his thigh. "Now I'm his working canvas." Nicole pulled the V of her blouse down, exposing an exquisite, three-dimensional flesh sculpture of a fish on her sternum, just where her cleavage started. Neither detective could escape the hint of the rose-colored areolae that were exposed. Nicole wasn't embarrassed.

"Nic lets me try out new techniques," Gillette said. "You know, before I perform them on my regular customers. I used sage ash in the cut. It acts like baking soda and makes the skin rise. Sculpture in flesh."

"Looks painful," said Bishop

Nicole released the blouse and looked directly at Dutch. "It's all the same, isn't it? Pleasure. Pain. Different sides of the same coin."

Dutch stared back. Shit. *There he goes again.* Bishop couldn't believe Dutch was buying this shit. *Pleasure and pain?* Bishop steered the Q & A back on track, "Did you see who Lauren came with? Who she left with?"

"I have no idea." Gillette sounded sincere.

"How often did she come? Was she a regular?"

Nicole held Dutch's eyes a moment longer, then slid them toward Bishop. "We worked on her about three months ago for a series of test cuts to see if she liked the way they healed—"

"You know, make sure we're on the same page," Gillette continued. "I remember it was especially important because she wanted both her front and back cut on the same night."

"Is that unusual?" Dutch asked.

Back in the game, Bishop hoped.

"Not exactly," replied Nicole. "But rare. You need a high threshold for pain to do both in one night."

"She had it," Gillette said. "I cut the front, let it heal. An hour later, I worked on her back. But it makes sleeping a bitch."

Bishop looked at Nicole. "Where were you around 1 A.M. last night?"

"On my way home."

"Anyone with you?"

Nicole rubbed Gillette's arm. "We car pool. It's the sensible alternative." Her eyes swung back to Dutch. "If you want to share the ride sometime, let me know."

"You have a rap sheet?" Bishop caught Gillette by surprise.

He didn't answer.

"We can find out," Dutch said. "But if you save us the trouble, you'll make one helluva first impression."

Gillette hesitated a moment, then confessed, "Second degree murder. Miami. I was acquitted."

"What happened?" asked Dutch.

"A cutting victim died."

"How?"

"Someone slit her throat after I worked on her."

Four.

Nicole broke the even stretch of the aluminum blinds ever so slightly and placed a single eye into the gap. The carefully manicured long lashes did not blink as she stared out. She watched the detectives climb into the Camry. They appeared to be having some sort of argument. The cops pulled out and away.

"What did you think?" Gillette asked, making a somewhat vulgar noise as he shifted on the luxurious cushions.

"About what?" Nicole asked, without turning. She waited until the tail lights of the car disappeared, then turned around. Gillette had his hand stuffed in the crevice between the cushions.

"The heat. You think they're going to be trouble?"

"I don't think so," Nicole sighed. "Dutch is cute and not too bright—I like that in a man."

"Yeah? But what about me?"

"I like that in you, too." Nicole advanced with a mischievous grin.

"Look, you were really coming on to what's-his-name." Gillette kept digging in the gap.

"Dutch."

"Whoever."

"Bingo." Gillette found what he was looking for. His hand reappeared with the shiny glass-and-metal object. "Come to papa." He lifted it to his lips and lit one end with a butane lighter, covering a small hole over the other end with one finger. "It's not gonna confuse the guy, you know. At the end of the day, he's still a cop."

Nicole went cold. "Who says I'm confusing him?"

Gillette watched smoke fill the tiny oval bubble. "Well excuse me, your highness. Who you fuck is your business. Unless, of course, it affects our business. Then that makes it my business."

"Gillette, dear, don't flatter yourself. I bailed out your leaky little one-man show and turned it into the hottest club in town. Try not to forget that."

Gillette dragged deep on the coke inhaler. His body shook several times as the stimulant hit his lungs and sent his muscles into involuntary spasms. "Magic, baby, just magic."

Nicole's eyes sparkled with lust. She straddled his lap and sucked on the inhaler. He zipped down and hiked her skirt up. She wasn't wearing any underwear. He thrust upward and she gasped loudly. They kissed, exchanging tongues of smoke. Arms and legs entwined in a fierce passion, they plunged through the Looking Glass together.

***

"I got a question for you, Dutch," Bishop bristled. "When does a murder suspect start coming on to the lead dick in a case?" Traffic was light. He pedaled down.

"When she finds him irresistible?" Dutch grinned. He couldn't get his mind off Nicole.

"Our Q&A went south as soon as you two started playing eye-footsies."

"She's different."

Bishop looked at him and burst out laughing. "Oh, man, you gotta be kidding me! Men have been telling themselves that since the Garden of Eden and you know what that led to?"

"Yeah," Dutch smiled. "Mankind." He got serious. "Kidding aside, she's well educated, she's got class, she's—"

"If the next thing out of your mouth is she couldn't have done it, I'm going to stop the fucking car right here."

"I didn't say that."

"You don't have to. Look at you. You're acting like you've got a schoolboy crush. That chick sponsors cutting and branding and all sorts of sex-freaka-doodle-doo shit for a living. You better get a hold of yourself before you start buying what your dick is trying to sell your brain, you got me? Why do you think she's hitting on you? To throw suspicion off her deviant little sexcapade business. So forget about this she's-different routine, because it's all bullshit. We're not reinventing the wheel for this case." Bishop pulled up at a signal, waited for the light to change, got impatient, looked both ways, and drove through.

"That was a red light."

"I know what it was, and don't get off the subject."

"Which is?"

"Nicole. Now, the next time you're with her, and you're looking into those cat-gray eyes, I want you to remember three things. One, upside down they're all the same. Two, all pussy's pink. And three, there's only one whore in the world with many faces."

"You're a real optimist you know that, Bishop?"

"Second time you put your hand in the fire, it still burns."

***

The squad room hopped with the usual bustle of cops and criminals, impact printers, and jangling telephones. The blues didn't mind the overlapping racket of voices and machines. It was a built-in security system. Just like a forest, any break or change in the ambience meant something was wrong. It could be anything from an IAD snoop on the premises, to a suspect on the loose in the station house, to a fellow officer getting his ass chewed by the brass. In the third instance, it went completely silent and everyone eavesdropped. It was that third kind of quiet Dutch heard, when Bishop and he passed the endless rows of standard issue desks on their way to the lieutenant's office a couple of days later.

"Anything?" Lt. Schiff asked before the door could even close.

The boot remained on Dutch's SUV, so Bishop had been picking him up. Nicole had been surprisingly cooperative, making the employees available for questioning. She'd even given them the contact info she had on *Scars*'s regulars. It became clear they weren't going to find a smoking gun.

"Zip." Dutch dropped the bomb.

"What about the cutter?" Schiff asked. "He has an identical prior."

"No good," Dutch said. "He shared the ride."

"Huh?"

"Car pool alibi," Bishop explained.

"We could bring him into the sweat shop for a chat," Dutch suggested.

Schiff glared at him. "Excellent suggestion, Dutch. Very by-the-book." Then, to Bishop, "What about the owner?"

"Nicole Gray. She's smooth as a silk snake. Got the city's top law firm on retainer. Says it's because of the kind of business she runs."

Dutch rocked back and forth in his chair. "So far, everyone Nicole fed us from the club has said that the victim came alone and left alone. But while she was there, they saw her with Gillette and Nicole before, during, and after her cutting."

Bishop spoke up. "I say one or both are guilty."

"Gillette?" Schiff asked. "What kind of pervert name is that?"

"A *nom de plume*," explained Bishop. The lieutenant looked at him vacantly. "An alias. An a-k-a."

"Then say so."

"I did," Bishop objected.

Dutch jerked a thumb. "His kid's in prep school. Thinks we stole the whole English language from other countries."

Schiff threw up his hands. "Don't look at me. I'm from Chicago."

"His real name's Lansing Genteel," said Bishop. "He was a sort of what ya call factotum before he found his *raison d'etre*."

"Cut to the chase, Frenchy, before *señor* becomes *señorita*," Schiff threatened.

"He was an everything man. No real direction." Bishop flipped through a hand-sized steno pad. "Started out collecting stubs in movie theaters and bussing tables. Then moved into haircutting, where he made enough money to get into a trade school. Came out at the top of his class in web design. But it didn't pan out. Then he hit rock bottom. His rent was two months overdue. They cut off his phone. Some loan sharks were going to cut off something much more important. Became the next American gigolo. Did that for a year. A friend told him he could make more money cutting chicks than fucking them. And that's when Lance went kinky and picked up a blade."

"Here's his priors." Dutch tossed a copy of Gillette's Miami acquittal on Schiff's desk.

Schiff scanned it. "What about motive?"

Dutch swung his head from side to side. "This S&M shit is perfect for a pervert picnic. I mean someone pulls a straight razor on you at home, you've got attempted murder. They do it in a bar with some groovy music and a ringmaster, you've got con*sensual* adults."

"Consenting adults," Schiff corrected.

"Not from where we were standing."

"I don't get it." Schiff was puzzled. "We're not dealing here with high school kids, or gangs, or dope addicts. This Lauren Piolene was a twenty-six-year old businesswoman. A beautiful broad like that could get any guy she wanted." Schiff opened her dossier and sifted through the Polaroids. "What drives them to do it?"

Bishop launched into a sustained peroration. "San

Francisco is a town where sex is complex. It's the hideout and hangout for leather doggies, G-spot hunters, and dildo specialists. Teenagers don't go to the prom around here. They get pierced and go to raves. And if they're not cutting school, they're cutting themselves." He shrugged. "We've got full page ads for bondage benefits for cryin' out loud, and we're probably the only city in the world where fist fucking is not a metaphor, it's another Kama Sutra position."

Dutch and Schiff stared at Bishop, mouths agape.

"Or so I've heard..." Bishop backpedaled.

"I guess you don't really know someone until you hear him talk about sex," Dutch smirked.

Schiff gave Bishop another long look. "After what happened the last few times with cases involving you two, the DA told me he's not putting his ass on the line in court unless there is enough evidence to rest it on. So I suggest you bring in a bicycle built for two."

The detectives emerged from Schiff's office to the usual buzz of activity and headed for their face-to-face partners desks.

"We'll start with the victim's car. Lee's going to be there," Bishop outlined their day's strategy. "Then Lauren's house tomorrow, when Magno will be going over it—"

Bishop trailed off and signaled with his eyes. Dutch discovered a man in a dark, but drab looking suit standing beside his desk. With no perceptible change in the din over the squad room, Dutch knew he couldn't be IAD.

"Detective Jeff Holland?" inquired the man with a lack of familiarity that immediately put Dutch on guard. "Who's asking?"

The man smiled. Dutch had a bad feeling instantly because that was the knowing smile of a man who knew his mark when he found it. Lips stretching briefly, like a rubberband, then snapping back into a spare, uncaring line.

"You have been served." He handed Dutch an envelope

with the address of a prominent law firm in the return corner.

Dutch tore it open, unfolding the single sheet. "I'll be damned." He snatched his jacket. "Let's go."

"What going on?" Bishop asked. Dutch tossed him the summons. Bishop skimmed it. "Oh, man. I'm sorry."

They didn't say a word the entire drive over. Dutch asked Bishop to pull over at Sacramento and Montgomery in front of the Transamerica Pyramid—San Francisco's tallest landmark at 853 feet. Bishop waited for the No. 41 bus to move away and parked curbside just beyond the stop. It was mid-afternoon. There were few people out, except clerks running errands, uniformed couriers making deliveries, and the rank and file going to and from that grand excuse used to avoid work—meetings. The sun lowered a column of light yellow brightness through a gap between threatening cloud banks, which had been gathering to fulfill the promise of rain predicted later that evening.

"That's her," Dutch pointed to a brunette, thirties, slender, conservatively attired in a brown pant suit. The two-inch heels on her dress pumps lifted her height to an attractive five feet six inches. She walked with the lowered eyes and quick-stride of someone who was rarely confrontational. A black handbag knocked against her hip, the strap strung over the opposite shoulder. She clutched an umbrella in her left hand in anticipation of the showers.

"Hold on, Dutch," Bishop said. "When you get bad news like this, the first thing you should do is wait. Calm down. Cool out. Get rational. Then deal with it."

"I am cool," Dutch returned, but his words were short and clipped. "It's going to be okay." Dutch got out of the car. He angled his approach to catch up with the brunette before she entered the Pyramid, where she worked as a secretary.

"Elise!"

***

Elise stopped in her tracks when she heard her husband's voice. She turned slowly. Her voice quavered, "Hello, Dutch."

He slowed to a jog, barely panting. She knew him to stay in great physical shape. He placed himself between her and the glass doors.

"You finally set the date," he held out the subpoena.

She tried not to look him in the eye and attempted to move around. "My lawyers don't want me talking to you."

Dutch wouldn't budge. "Fuck them."

"Okay, *I* don't want to talk to you." But her words rang hollow. Even to her. She looked at him, searching the features of this familiar stranger. But she couldn't find any feeling for him. She was filled with a sense of loss, not longing, for the time they spent together. He used to mean so much to her.

They had met on the University of Houston campus in the Spring of her Sophomore year. She had just turned nineteen and was working as an intern in the college President's office, when Dutch came to investigate a student homicide. They hit it off at once and he found every excuse to return to the University. They had lunch and coffee. They spoke of their families and upbringing—which sounded so similar, it created an immediate sense of belonging between them. As if they had known each other all their lives. He was as handsome and rugged as they came. She was attracted to his brash, outgoing demeanor, which helped bring her out of her shy, introverted world.

During the investigation, nothing physical occurred. A defense attorney would jump on that. So they flirted. When she finally got up the courage to give Dutch her phone number, he started calling after his shift and they spoke softly late into the night. When the case went to trial, Elise called in sick to watch Dutch in court. He was so confident. Dutch was testifying against a grad student accused of killing his adversary in the chemistry department. They were competing for an International Lead Zinc Research Program fellowship worth twenty thousand dollars. When traces of pharmaceutical grade bromate turned up after they pumped the victim's stomach, the student claimed Dutch had planted the evidence.

Dutch shook his head. "Dead men can't swallow."

The perp was Chinese. And one thing about Texas, it didn't care for the mix of races breaching its staunchly defended borders. It was proud of its reputation for the toughest law enforcement state in the nation. The deliberation was quick, and with a unanimous conviction out of the way, Dutch was finally free to ask Elise out on a real date. They'd gone out before, but under the guise of detective and witness.

They started with dinner, but didn't finish. Half way through the meal, Dutch stood up and said, "We've waited long enough."

They rushed back to his apartment. All their pent-up physical desire set off a night of unforgettable passion. Neither slept a wink. By morning, Dutch complained gratefully that his balls were killing him, and if she didn't stop, he'd have her arrested as an accessory. That was fine with Elise. She was so damn sore her legs were shaking. When she got up to take a shower, she sagged against the wall, exhausted, and there was Dutch, standing beside her with that raffish, lovable smile. He carried her into the shower, and she could hardly believe it, but they made love one more time under the raging water.

Thankfully, it was a Saturday. Elise had the weekend off. Dutch called in sick through Monday. Later that night, lying on top of him in the bathtub, under candlelight and warm bubbles, Dutch proposed. He didn't want to wait for a license or a church date. There was a flight to Las Vegas. They could be on it and return to work on Monday as husband and wife. It was the most spontaneous, most outrageous thing she could imagine. She laughed out loud and kissed him. Up until then, she had regimented everything with lists and schedules. Dutch's proposal opened a window to the stale, musty room of her life and the wind that poured in stirred her soul. He made her feel alive again for the first time in far too long.

The marriage turned out to be the exact opposite of their passionate weekend.

The charm and politeness he had exhibited during their courting gradually faded. They began to fight. He never did household chores. Rarely kept his promises to spend time with her. He started coming home late. Then frequently came home later. Then sometimes not at all. Every promise that he made was soon met with some excuse. The dinners she had worked so hard to prepare turned cold. Eventually, after innumerable disappointments, she gave up planning and preparing for their private moments. And sex—the roughness and command which she so enjoyed the first time—became the norm. He knew no other way to make love. And she needed tenderness.

Finally, Dutch started to bring his frustrations home from work, and she became privy to his dark side. He flew into fits of rage. Drank too much. Though he never hit her, sometimes she felt she might feel safer if he did. That way she could stop worrying about what he *might* do. Which she always imagined would be far, far worse.

Later, she discovered, his rage had found another outlet.

He was getting rough during interrogations. Two IAD probes revealed his brutality toward prisoners in his care. As rumors of a third circulated, their marriage went into a tailspin. Faced with dismissal and losing Elise, Dutch agreed to see a counselor, who, after a few sessions, concluded he was too dedicated to police work. Dutch needed to ease up. The therapist suggested a change to a low pressure environment.

Dutch put in a transfer for San Francisco.

"Jesus, Elise, moving out of Houston was supposed to give us a second chance," Dutch said.

Elise looked away, almost apologetically. "No. Moving out of Houston was about giving you a second chance. With the force. For me, it was all about closure."

"Well, serving me with divorce papers is one hell of a

way to prove it!"

Elise jumped at the sharpness of his tone. Suddenly, there it was again. Her old friend. Fear. Somehow he knew. He always did.

Dutch smoothed it over before she panicked, "I'm sorry, honey, it's just...I've been thinking a lot about how we were together. How good we were when we started. If we could just be together and talk, you know, like we used to, I could open up. Share more—"

Dutch stopped talking. Unable to find the words, he pleaded with his eyes. Sorrowful, romantic eyes. Exerting a force over her that could turn an out-and-out fight into a night of reckless passion. Making her laugh when she'd rather cry. Changing her entire mood in an instant. Usually they worked. Not this time.

"All you're after is control. I wouldn't let you control me and you couldn't handle it. This isn't about me, or our relationship. This is about you and your need to control. Well, I'm out, Dutch. Out from under you."

"I'll fight you."

"It's too late, Dutch." Elise's voice became staccato and shrill with emotion. "I don't want to fight anymore, and I don't...want...to see...you." Elise had a hard time getting out the words. But if she was ever going to get over him, she had to make the final cut. She stalked past him.

"Elise, wait—" Dutch started after her.

She stopped and turned around, using the few strides with her back turned to him to gather the courage to say in a firm voice, "If you don't leave me alone I'll tell them how you got away with murder."

Five.

The guard at the police impound allowed Bishop's Camry inside the rolling cyclone fence gate. Bishop did not have to hear what transpired between Dutch and Elise. Their body language had telegraphed it all. Then, the way Dutch had opened and slammed the car door shut confirmed the conversation hadn't gone well. Bishop kept quiet the entire ride over, allowing his partner his space.

Dutch should not have confronted Elise. All things should proceed outward from a serene place of knowing. Only then could the right path be chosen. Suffering injustice was the all important first step toward enlightenment. Prizing the essential over the trivial, accepting adversity with an open heart and without complaint of injustice, made sense, and enabled the harmony of reason.

During the drive, Bishop had looked over and could've sworn Dutch's eyes changed color. He wondered if it was just a trick of the light, the way the sea shifts during a storm. One second, a pure, clarion note of aquamarine as the surface was struck by a blinding shaft of light. The next, a jumbled gemstone of dire black and gray as the shadowy hand of a cloud plunged it into darkness. That a man's emotions might actually brighten or darken the hue of his iris had an appeal Bishop couldn't deny. The sea changes color, but the sea does not change, Bishop thought. The immutable soul, colored by emotion, endures.

He watched Dutch wrestle with his conscience. Struggling in silence. Trying to regain his composure and come to grips with the very real fact that his wife wasn't coming back. Bishop knew how hard the road could be. And he didn't envy the journey.

Bishop squeezed into a tight notch in the overcrowded lot. They got out and walked under a covered port, where Lauren's car was being examined.

The champagne colored Lexus was hardly recognizable. Fingerprint dust splotched the exterior, particularly messy around the door handles. Clear Mylar covered the plush leather seats. Inside, Kim Lee did a serology work-up. Taking swatches of blood with a gauze pad from the backrest of the driver's seat.

Bishop admired the deft efficiency that evolved from Lee's years of practice. "Mind if we take a look?"

The Korean criminalist glanced up and waved through streaks of blood running in arcs down the perfectly intact front windshield. "Hey, Dutch. Bishop. Just a sec." Lee placed the gauze pad in a paper envelope and marked it with a yellow evidence tag. "All right, go ahead and snoop."

Bishop and Dutch nodded, slipped on a pair of powder-free latex exam gloves and opened the right side door front and back. Both leaned inside. Blood evidence lay everywhere.

"All this one person?" Dutch asked.

Lee nodded. "Yup. We have a DNA confirm."

"How much is there?"

"Two, three quarts. All hers."

Bishop got curious. "How much blood in one body?

"A gallon. Give or take a quart." Lee flashed off a Polaroid, jotted down a note on the back "By the way, all indications point to a right-handed assailant." Then he began carefully triangulating the next patch of blood.

Bishop inspected the blood distribution patterns, angling up left to right as if thrown from the edge of a blade, across the front windshield. There was more everywhere he looked. Ceiling. Dashboard. Steering wheel. Gear shift. Hand brake.

Pedals. Lauren's bloody finger and palm prints smeared it all.

"Fucking blood bath," Dutch said, straightening back out.

After an hour of looking and asking questions, the two detectives headed back to Bishop's Camry. The clouds thickened and droplets came down infrequently.

"Can you take me by Parking?" Dutch asked, clicking his safety belt. "I gotta get that boot off my car."

"Just can't play by the rules, can you?" ribbed Bishop, turning the key and firing the engine.

"We bust our asses twenty-four seven. The least they can do is cut us a little slack."

Bishop didn't argue. By the time they arrived at Parking, a low-slung sunset beamed from a western horizon across snowy white clouds whose bellies were gilded with gold. A magnificent contrast of turquoise and copper reminiscent of the paintings made famous by Maxfield Parrish.

"You want me to wait?"

"No thanks, I'll be all right," Dutch replied. "You got somewhere to go? Maybe we can get a beer or something."

It was the first time Dutch had ever made a friendship gesture like that, and Bishop hated to refuse, but today he had to turn him down. "Can't. I've got to pickup Darryl."

"Sure," Dutch said.

"Some other time," Bishop offered, not wanting Dutch to think he was blowing him off.

"Cool," Dutch said. If he was disappointed, he didn't show it. "I'll see you later."

Half an hour later, Bishop pulled in front of a short parabolic driveway encircling a statuary fountain beset on all sides by fine, dense tufts of grass that reminded him of a putting green rather than the front lawn of a private high-school. At the base of the fountain, a plaque read: *St. Ignatius School for Boys.* A handsome, well-groomed kid, in a blue school blazer, bounded over to the car and hopped in. Wide, flat forehead. Thick, strong neck. Athletic build. Pressed nose, nostrils slightly flared. Heavy lips and large, kind eyes. He'd inherited almost every feature from his father.

"How are you, son?" Bishop asked.

"Yo, dad, what's up?" Darryl tossed his books in the back seat, co-opting California Sophocles, the local custom of answering a question with a question. On the Left Coast, no one ever answered how they were. They just repeated the question asked of them in a different form. It was as if they were afraid of figuring it all out, realizing everything might not actually be all that cool after all.

"How's school? All good?" Bishop asked, hoping to get a straight answer this time.

"*Comme ci, comme ça*," Darryl replied. "You know, same old, same old. How about you, dad? Working on anything?"

Bishop shook his head. "*Comme ci, comme ça*, same shit different day."

Darryl shook his head, smiling. "You're crazy, dad."

"How's physics?"

"Cool. You know, M.I.T. has this new laser imaging lab that is the shit. I wrote them for an ap."

"Go for it." They drove for a while, shooting the breeze. As Bishop descended a winding, two-lane drive down toward the Presidio, the houses began to take on the appearance of a country club. Bishop pulled up in front of a belvedere mansion. A tall, threatening expanse of masonry and bentwood that seemed to have its bluenose slightly upturned to the approach of Bishop's working class Camry. "How's your mother?"

"All right." Darryl's eyes shifted away. Evasive.

"She finish her Ph.D.?" Bishop was treading sensitive ground.

"Yup," Darryl replied. Staring out the window. Eyes fixed on the gleaming amber lights on either side of the front door.

"She gonna take that teaching job?"

Darryl shrugged. Bishop could really see himself and his wife, Naomi, in Darryl, who had lucked out on both scores. Luckiest kid in the world, Bishop figured. Blessed with his mother's intelligence and his father's bull-backed physical strength. Darryl was everything Bishop wished he had been at that age, and Bishop admired him for it. A black man with a mind could go anywhere these days. A world of opportunity lay before Darryl. Ripe for the picking. All he had to do was reach out and grab it.

Though there was one thing Bishop wished Darryl hadn't inherited. His mom's emotional distance. He couldn't put his finger on when it happened, but now that it was there, he couldn't seem to get around it. No matter how hard he tried. So, at the same time Darryl was coming into his own, really shining, showing the potential of the man he was going to be, he seemed to be drifting. The thought that he might never get to know his son on honest terms because of it hit Bishop like a bullet.

"Don't know," Darryl responded.

.   A silhouette passed by the front window of the house. Bishop recognized the proud cheekbones, hair swept back like two rolling waves into long, twisting braids that followed the curvature of her back to rising hips and firm, athletic legs. She moved gracefully. The anomalous quality of a statue in fluid motion. His heart leapt involuntarily. *Goddamn. Eight years since we divorced, and I still get jitters from the mere glimpse of her.*

They'd met at the San Francisco Opera at the War Memorial Opera House. Bishop used to go once a year. Being his annual big night out, he paid top dollar for front orchestra seats. *La Bohème* was playing. It was a lavish production, filled with spectacular set pieces and engaging performances by the lead tenor and soprano. Translations on the newly installed light board above the audience made it that much easier to follow.

Rudolfo, an impoverished poet, met his future wife Mimi, a seamstress, who embroidered flowers and a sparkling but ill-fated love developed. They were both young and idealistic and indigent, but so full of life. Bishop remembered clearly the moment when both the lovers' candles, the only source of light on the stage, went out. They searched for Mimi's missing key in the dark. Rudolfo found it, but hid the fact, so he might locate her by following the sound of her voice. When they touched hands, they fell deeply in love.

Something happened inside Bishop that made his head turn. The moment was pure magic. The most ravishing woman he had ever laid eyes on was looking right at him. Her skin was the color of rich, fertile earth and her eyes were lustrous and full of wonderful possibility. And damn him to hell if, right before she turned back to watch the performance, she didn't smile. He broke the ice during the entr'acte, bought her a drink and stole glances at her during the last two acts of the production. And there she was, staring right back at him. It was as if they shared some psychic connection. His palms began to sweat, his heart beat like a big bass drum, and his spine felt as if someone poured ice water down his back.

If this was love, Bishop thought, he was hooked. They went out to dinner a few times. Each place about as extravagant as he could afford on a patrolman's salary. But he was looking down the road. Like a horse with blinders on, straight ahead. Because when his wife looked back on how they met, he wanted her to have nice things to remember.

Strange, he thought, from the moment he'd seen her, he could never imagine her as anything other than his wife. He was constantly in awe of her brilliance and the infinite convolutions of her mercurial mind. She led him to places he'd hardly imagined and he loved her for it, every step of the way. Naomi had won a medal and a full-ride scholarship to Stanford for taking the 400-meter hurdles at the California state competition. As a freshman, she had been favored to win the NCAAs. Her qualifying mark had put her first in the nation, a sure bet for the Mexico City World Championships. Then, in her senior year, just before the Conference Championships, she tumbled over the last hurdle in the middle of a routine warm-up dash during the first hour of practice. In the blink of an eye, in a momentary twist of the ankle, in silence, with only the few attentive eyes of her teammates and coach, it was all behind her. She had ripped a tendon.

There would be no fame or glory on the playing field.

Her future quickly receded into what never was. A past that never acquired the benefit of a present. More a sound than a vision. An echo. A distant, fading echo. They had some hard times after that. When Naomi finally accepted the idea that her running career was over, she threw herself completely into her school work. She graduated summa cum laude with a major in African and Afro-American Studies and an honors emphasis in Children and Society. She won the coveted Robert M. Golden medal for excellence in the Humanities and got accepted to the Master's program at Berkeley.

Set to begin the Fall term, she discovered she was pregnant.

It was the hardest decision either of them ever had to face. They both wanted the baby, but neither wanted to give up their careers. In the end, Naomi postponed her entrance into the Master's program—indefinitely. Times got tougher. Raising a wife and kid in San Francisco on a patrolman's salary wasn't enough to butter anyone's bread. Bishop felt he was never good enough. That he would never be able to afford the kind of life he would like to give Naomi. When she assured him that didn't matter, it made it that much worse.

Darryl grew up around arguments and heartbreak, and Bishop was sorry for that. When Naomi finally went back to school, Bishop was plagued by constant doubt and fear. Doubt that she still loved him. Fear that she'd find somebody else. Somebody better. That he'd be exceeded by someone brighter, more handsome and wealthier. He'd heard of University professors making upwards of six figures and knew he'd never be able to compete with that. Even if he made detective in next year's exam.

He became jealous.

If she came home late, he'd question her repeatedly about where she'd been, who she'd been out with. Accuse her of everything from adultery to mental masturbation while basking in the glow of some erudite professor. The death knell sounded when Bishop got suspicious of her Cognitive Neuropsychology professor. Naomi figured she'd had all she could take.

"That's right!" she yelled back. "I sucked his cock! And you want to know how you can prove it? He's got the word Encyclopedia Britannica Volume Twelve tattooed to the bottom of it! That's twelve! As in inches!" And she stormed out of the room.

It was Puccini all over again. *La Bohème* with a ghetto libretto. Just like Mimi and Rudolfo, Bishop had chased her away with his jealousy. Ashamed of his lack of wealth. Feeling guilty for the delay her pregnancy had caused her career. Too insecure to show her love or accept her love in return. The police psychologist from Behavioral Science Services called it a defense mechanism. He was pushing her away, creating jealousy where none existed, so that she would leave him and he could stop feeling inadequate. But Bishop didn't give a damn about that. Not then, not now. Whatever the reason, it still hurt.

The days dragged and they drifted. Not so much living together, as co-existing. Bumping into one another in a house devoid of emotion. A dwelling shared by two people renting the same space. The same four walls. But everything had changed.

Bishop suspected an affair. Still, the day she confessed to it and asked for a divorce really took the wind out of him.

And now, as he stared up at the gables of her wealthy estate, he figured she'd gotten everything he thought she wanted. Nice income, fat home, handsome husband, intelligent friends, dinner parties. And Darryl five days a week. Darryl had become the common thread. But even that bond was weakening.

"Mr. Webber says that a man who can speak another language is two men," Darryl said, steering the conversation away from his mother. He could see that his dad still tore himself up over her.

"That so?" Bishop raised his eyebrows.

A remarkable, young looking black woman emerged at the top of the stone steps in the front door of the mansion. A tall man, whose rangy bespectacled frame spoke more of an introverted life, dedicated to numbers, as opposed to great physical activity, appeared behind her. That's him, Bishop thought, the stockbroker.

"He treatin' her all right?" Bishop asked, a jealous, protective undercurrent to his voice.

Silence. Then, Darryl surprised Bishop, "It wasn't about the money, dad. You know that. She just didn't love you anymore."

Bishop found that the hardest to accept. He still loved her. Her face, the grace of her movements, still colored his every mood. Why didn't she love him back? Bishop looked at the two figures on the steps. Misty-eyed. Moody. He looked down at the steering wheel for no apparent reason. "Yeah."

More silence. Darryl said finally, "Gotta go."

Bishop nodded. Darryl turned to leave. "Son?" Darryl stopped. "I'm proud of you."

"I know," Darryl smiled and raised two fingers.

As Bishop watched Darryl climb the steps to his second family, his second life, the husband that his wife now loved, and the father he could never be, he thought of Mimi's dying words from the final act of *La Bohème*. "I wanted to be alone with you, love. So many things there are that I would tell you. There is one, too, as spacious as the ocean, as the ocean, profound, without limit; you are my love, my all, and all my life."

***

Dutch caught a ride back with the city employee assigned to unshackle his car. It was dark when they arrived in front of his apartment. Every window shined brightly. The air was mild and inviting, carrying the sentimental aroma of wood-burning fires. A few residents walked their dogs. The street had the carefree quality of a Norman Rockwell painting.

These people are cut-outs, Dutch thought. Unsuspecting painted-in figures, who had little use for, and who paid little attention to, the realities of the urban environment. If they knew the kind of things that happened in Washington Park, right at the end of this very street, they'd board up their windows and wouldn't come out.

The boot came off with a mighty clang. Dutch thanked the driver, backed the SUV out of the red zone, and wearily climbed the stairs to his attic apartment. When he walked in, the dispatcher's non-stop chatter greeted him. His only companion in the cold, dark room. *Suspect is an Asian male. Consider him armed and dangerous. He just shot and killed another Asian male. Possibly gang related.* Dutch threw down his keys, kicked off his shoes and slumped into the couch. Undoing his collar, he pulled down his knotted tie. *We see him. Light blue shirt—He's shooting! Two women down! Jesus. Go! Go! Go! He's behind you! I see him, I see him. He's coming toward us!*

Dutch poured two fingers of Dewar's White label into a shot glass and tossed it back. *Now! Now! Now! StaticStaticStatic. Got him! He's down! He's down! StaticStaticStatic. He's not moving.* Dutch refilled the shot glass. *He's dead. Copy that. 10-54.*

Good, Dutch thought. *Serves him right.* Killed one,

wounded, possibly killed two others. Victims completely unrelated to the perp, the intended victim, or anything connected to the crime.

The innocent.

They did nothing, yet they suffered. They suffered physical pain, mental anguish, hospital bills…the list went on and on. And it didn't stop there. Their loved ones suffered, too. They would worry. Their lives would be disrupted. Their faith would be challenged. *Why her? Why this? Why now?*

The endless interrogatories.

The pain would ease, Dutch thought. The scars might heal. *But questions will endure. And the answers will never come.*

Dutch gulped down his second shot. Felt the familiar lightening of the senses.He had seen it too often. Time and time again. Too many times before. And he knew. The answers would not come.

Secure the scene for CSI.

As dispassionate and disinterested as the cop reporting the fatality, Dutch started to gulp down the scotch when he noticed the answering machine blinking. He never gave out his cell number. It was Department issued and subject to scrutiny. In Houston, his desk had been next to cyber crime and he'd learned that nothing could be erased off a cell or a computer. Unlike an old fashioned answering machine. That's why he still kept a land line.

Once. Twice. Three times. *Elise?* He leaned over and played it. The first two were hang-ups. The third was not.

"Hi, Dutch. This is India. Remember me?" The playful, sing-song quality of her voice started and stopped. Coquettish. Unlike Nicole. He didn't get the feeling he was being played. India's interest sounded authentic. "Nicole gave me your number." I didn't give it to Nicole. "I hope you don't mind. I was thinking about you. Remember what I asked for the other night? Would you like to do that? I'm here. At the club. And

I'm waaaaitiiiing." She giggled and hung up.

Dutch rolled the scotch in his mouth and considered the invitation. The variety and vigor of San Francisco's night life suited singles. But Dutch didn't like the dating scene and wanted nothing to do with it. He'd done his best over the years to separate himself from the certitude of ordinary life. He found he preferred his own company to sharing time with others. Yet, he found, as the saying goes, that no man is an island. So he chose his friends carefully and kept very few. Never letting anyone get too close until...

Elise.

He loved spending time with her, and opened up to her as much as he could, but it hadn't been enough. No matter how much he tried, it had never been enough. Now that Elise was gone, he felt more alone than ever. She had torn a giant hole inside of him and no matter how much of himself he stuffed into it, he couldn't become whole again.

Then came last night.

Something had happened at the club that resurrected him from his solitude. Now, just thinking about the sights and sounds from *Scars* and India's flawless olive complexion, started a wildfire racing through him. *What the hell?* Dutch jumped into the shower.

An hour later, Dutch entered *Scars.*

Scrubbed down, spotlessly clean, and casually dressed in a T-shirt and slacks, he looked more like a male model than a cop. Since this visit was orchestrated for pleasure, he felt remarkably more at ease. His casual look—hair tossed carelessly about his head—softened the hard lines of a tough cop deeply affected by the daily grind.

The same doorman greeted him. "Back so soon?"

"I'm not gay," Dutch said flatly.

"Uh-Hmm" the doorman murmured skeptically. When Dutch pulled out his wallet, the doorman shook his head. "No charge. India put you on the list."

"Great." Dutch continued inside. It was packed, but the Spotlight was empty. It looked as though they were between showcases. The band played a slow, sensual number that elicited intimacy. A Tori Amos song. Calliopean chords. Clear. Captivating. "...*and Southern men can grow gold. Can grow pertty. Blood can be pertty. Like a delicate man. Copper to steel to a hinge that is faltered. That lets you in, lets you in lets you in...*" A babble of gigglers surrounded a girl, barely twenty-one, showing off fresh scars from the session just ended—a devil with three phalluses.

Before he found India, Dutch found Nicole. It shouldn't have surprised him. She stood out in a crowd. She wore a scarf wrapped around her breasts and knotted in the back. Below, her bare midriff exposed a diamond studded hollow navel. His gaze lingered on her black netted leggings. She sensed his stare and turned. Their eyes met and she made no effort to conceal the fact that she enjoyed the way he was undressing her. She smiled invitingly, her perfect, white teeth glittering like sea shells beached on valentine lips ever so slightly parted.

Her scent was intoxicating. It lulled him into a false sense of well-being. Dutch was already losing ground. He felt himself slipping into those eyes. Water rising up to his neck. Drowning. He'd better do something. And soon. "I see you got my home phone number."

"I didn't think you'd want India calling you on your cell," replied Nicole. "It wasn't police business."

His eyes flare involuntarily. *Shit.*

She noticed. Smiled, "There are no secrets in this city."

"Look, you want to check up, that's, ah, one thing," he fumbled. "Invasion of privacy is ah-nother."

Nicole laughed. An easy, sexy laugh. "That's funny, coming from a cop."

They sized each other up. Squaring off. Nicole enjoyed it. He could see that. She knew he felt the nervous, sexual tension between them. She thought she would like to take him to the dark places he was haunted by. To see if there was anything she could do with it.

"I think you'll find I have a knack for getting what I want, Dutch," she said. "How's the cop thing going?"

"Leads didn't amount to much, if that's what you mean," Dutch said. Telling her what he presumed she already knew. "But I may need to ask you a few more questions—"

"Whatever," she replied huskily. It sounded like a dismissal, but it was far from it. The way she said it, Dutch had little trouble finishing the sentence for her. Whatever *you want.*

India joined them. Breaking the spell by placing a lingering kiss on Dutch's cheek. She whispered in his ear. "You came."

"Toodles." Nicole fluttered her fingers in goodbye and walked toward the Spotlight, where she picked up the microphone and made the usual introductions.

Gillette was up next. His canvas tonight was a platinum blonde. She lay on her back, straddling a cured leather pommel horse, in silver, opaque, wraparound sunglasses and little else. The dark chocolate color of Hershey's kisses, her nipples on small, firm breasts pushed into her silver stretch nylon T-shirt, standing out against the lustrous surface of the glittering nylon threads. She shuffled to the edge and parted her thighs. Calves pouring into blinding white boots capped with silver spurs.

Gillette knelt between Hershey Girl's legs. Caressed her taut, smooth skin. Touching the canvass, preparing the surface. She bit her lower lip. The throes of foreplay. The Universe was about to be created. And she was at the center. Waiting for the Big Bang. It came when he flicked open his barber's straight razor and whisked the skin of her inner thigh. The cut drew a sharp gasp.

Blood surfaced.

"The usual." India ordered a drink from the bar.

"MGD," Dutch echoed, forcing his eyes from the

Spotlight.

"Hmm, Miller, exotic," India teased.

"I'm a man of conventional tastes."

"*Qu'elle dommage,*" India offered apologetically.

"You aren't going to prep school, are you?"

"Actually, I'm getting my Masters at the SF Arts Institute."

Dutch gave her a second look, as if seeing her for the first time. "Doing what?"

"Woodcutting," she continued eagerly. "I make boxes. Little Japanese boxes. You cut figures or patterns in wood, dip them in ink, and apply it to poured paper."

"So this is what?" Dutch asked, gesturing to the club. "Night school?"

India shook her head. "It's more personal than that. There was this boy. Man. *Whatever.*"

There was that word again. She used it just like Nicole. Bestowing an off-handed sexual quality that was at once a dismissal and an invitation. He wondered if they were comparing notes, or if India was emulating Nicole out of habit. People often aped the affectations of the ones they admired.

"We went out three and a half years," India continued after taking a sip of her blood red Cosmopolitan. "Then it ended in a huge mess."

"Doesn't it always?" Dutch empathized.

"Usually, yeah." Dutch reached for his wallet to pay for the drinks. "Oh, don't worry about that," India said. "It's on the house." Dutch was about to ask why, when she continued, "I'm, you know, kind of like...Nic's girl Friday."

"You work for the club?"

"Not exactly. More of like, you know, personal services," she said with a faint blush singeing her cheeks.

"Oh. And she doesn't mind you seeing me?"

"Don't be silly. She's not the jealous type. I can do whatever I want just so long as I'm home by midnight and I make her come."

She giggled suggestively and flipped open her ring. It was silver-blue, Victorian in design, with a hollow cup under a false stone. A mid-nineteenth century device to conceal poison. Children of Goth used them as ornamental hideaways for their illicit drugs. The ring was the same, but the poison had changed. Now the glimmering gem could hide any number of methamphetamines, hallucinogens, or barbiturates. Kids today never had to worry about mood swings. They could simply pop open a cap and presto! A completely new vibe, courtesy of Dr. Feelgood.

India's, it just so happened, contained powder cocaine. "Candy?"

"That's not a solution."

"Works for me," India sniffed a capful. Her eyes suddenly braced him. "Hey, you aren't going to bust me, are you?"

Dutch thought about it. People were human after all. If he went around busting every Tom, Dick, and Jane with a snoutful of cocaine, half the lawyers in the city would be busy defending themselves. "I'm off duty."

"Good," India replied impishly, relaxing, and laughed, "because I got it from a cop. Anyway, after I broke up with Charles, him, you know, the boy I was seeing, I was so upset I got very, very drunk. When I was walking back to my dorm, I cut my wrists with my keys." She showed him three asymmetrical lines healed in ragged scars. Looking up, she caught a melancholy look in Dutch's eyes. "Bad day?"

Dutch took a deep breath and exhaled, "Close."

He didn't go any further. He had to keep the wall around his personal life high enough nobody could see in. I n d i a leaned forward. He could feel her breath against his neck when she whispered, "Let me inside."

***

"What?" Dutch pulled back. India had hit close to the

mark twice now. Was he that easy to read? Or, was she that good?

"Under your skin," India continued. "You know, like I said the other night. Let me *cut* you." She looked into his eyes with something more than indifference, less than love. "It's cathartic. Whatever worries you have will flow away. Come on. You can trust me."

Dutch swallowed. The line Bishop had predicted was being drawn. Not by Nicole, by India. The innocent one. It always came from the innocent ones. The least predictable. A warmth radiated to his extremities. Equatorial. Dizzying. Turned on by India, her proximity, and what she was saying.

"She's right," said Nicole, suddenly over his shoulder.

Dutch startled into a half turn. Hemmed in by both women. He could feel the heat of Nicole's bare skin on his back. The rough insistence of the diamond stud in the hollow of her navel rubbing against him. And India's scented breath on his lips.

"Think about what I said, will you? For me?" India slipped off the barstool, took two steps, and turned, "You two behave." She walked down the black stairs, alongside the stage.

Hershey Girl's first gradual moans reverberated over the audience. Nicole had placed the stage mike next to her lips, so the groans slipped from every corner of the room, like luscious incense pluming from the censer of her vibrating vocal cords. The audience, like marionettes, writhed to the command of her voice. Gillette carved convoluted lines down her inner thigh.

"The insignificant life of Dauna Dale," said Nicole.

"Who?" Dutch asked sharply.

Nicole nodded the Hershey Girl. "You're wondering about her."

Certain names, like power, were acquisitive. Gathering extraordinary dimensions. Bestowing brilliance, like a corona, around the dark edges of insignificance. Dutch could not associate any other name with the girl on the stage except Hershey Girl.

Like most San Franciscans, Nicole explained, Dauna came from somewhere else. The Great gesticulated Nowhere beyond California's borders. Tarrant City, Alabama, wasn't much to look at. It had less than ten thousand people when Dauna left. Her mother was forty-two, a check-out clerk at the local A&P, who'd married an abusive husband. Dauna got used to the beatings after a while. She'd hide in her closet or lock the door to her room and turn up the music so she wouldn't have to hear the unsettling slap of skin against bone.

Dutch wondered why Nicole was telling him this, but he didn't want her to stop. "How do you know so much about her?"

"I interview every girl who wants to be cut. To protect myself as much from liability as to make sure they knew what they were about to do." Seeing Dutch's eyes drift back to Dauna, Nicole went on.

Summers were the worst. Dauna's mother would wear long, uncomfortable dresses to hide the bruises, suffering blistering rashes from the sweltering heat, as she walked the mile and a half to the grocery. She stood straight and tall as she passed porch-bound neighbors, fanning themselves with whatever came to hand. She hoped they would remark how unusually cool, youthful and elegant she looked in her pretty dresses, under the hot, hot sun.

One day Dauna asked her mother why she put up with it. Dauna's mother suddenly looked old, tired and creased, like a balloon after the air had been let out. "I love your father," Dauna's mother replied, staring out at the chinaberry trees and weeping willows that lined the narrow two-lane county road that led to their saltbox house. "What would I have without him." She looked sad, not lost, just sad, Dauna told Nicole, and recalled her mother's words verbatim. "Besides, you don't see many men lining up to see me, do you, child? An old hen like me. Lucky to have what I got. And don't blame your father. He weren't always mean. He just grew that way is all. Tried hard, but never got what he wanted out of life—I couldn't give it to him—so he just gets mad sometimes is all. The world made him that way."

Dauna despised her mother for being so weak. She didn't understand her mother's unwillingness to change. To leave. Dauna took it out on her body—began to cut into it with bottle caps, pull-off tabs, whatever she could get a hold of. Scarring it over, hating it, trying to change what she could. Anything to take her mind off the possibility that she may one day live a similar future. She looked around. Her mother's story was every girl's story. Dauna turned sixteen and couldn't stop the cycle. She began working next to Mom at the A&P. Checkouts Four and Five. The Dale Girls.

So, Dauna continued the assault on her body. Cutting into it with safety pins, pairing knives, whatever she could get ahold of. Scarring it, hating it, using pain to forget the stomach turning sensation of seeing her life in twenty years. One day, she realized there was a point in life, in everyone's life, after a certain age, where won't became can't. She had just enough bus fare and used it all. Mile upon insignificant mile faded into the bismuth. When she wound through the Diablo Range on eighteen wheels, greased axles, and glaring headlights, she found three things waiting. California. San Francisco. And her alter ego: A woman of significance.

Nicole's telling of the story in a soft monotone played like an emotional undercurrent to the cutting, adding a layer of meaning Dutch had not felt the first night here. He was mesmerized.

"Gillette loves his work," added Nicole. "They love what he does for them. It makes them feel special. For a while. Then, in a couple of days, the scars heal and they're back to their ordinary lives."

"What's he doing now?" Dutch asked. "That design?"

"Gillette likes to borrow from the masters. German, Italian. The putto he's doing now is a Caravaggio. Charming, isn't it?"

Hershey Girl arched her back, shoulder's rippling, sweat sheeting down her lower abdomen, as Gillette carved the tiny, angelic figure.

"Eyah," Dutch agreed, watching the girl.

"Oh, God, don't stop!" Dauna cried, afraid that the muscular glutton between her legs might quit. Her hands gripped the edge of the bench above her head. Her feet pressed hard to the floor. Spurs digging tiny indentations into its polished surface. Her calves flexed, harder than stone. Gillette worked between her crotch and knee. The narrow strip of her silver sequined bikini dripped with wetness. The smell of her sex fueled Gillette's own lusty ambition.

Dutch stole a glance at Nicole. Her eyes stared in rapture at the cutting underway. Her tongue touched her lips, turned on by the thrill experienced by the platinum blonde. She felt Dutch's roving stare.

"You like watching?" She did not look at him when she spoke. She turned afterwards. The corner of her lips were coiled up in a smile.

"It's better than listening to your neighbors screw," Dutch said, then threw a curve. "Why did you give India my number when you wanted to see me?" It was a shot in the dark. A trick of the trade ingrained from years of police work. When you weren't sure what you were going to catch, you chummed the waters to see what surfaced.

"Is that what you think?" Nicole asked demurely. She was too good to fall for the easy setup.

So he played it straight. He motioned to Gillette on stage, "Yeah, I do. What about you and razor boy?"

"We're not involved exclusively."

"What about India?"

"We're not exclusive either." Nicole became coy.

"That's not what I meant."

"Oh. One's not enough?"

Dutch blinked. "That's not what I meant either."

"Maybe we could both do you. Would you like that?"

India walked up. "Like what?"

Nicole encircled India's waist with one hand and pulled her into her lap. "*Ménage-a-trois*."

India did not hesitate. She was up for it. "Sure."

Dutch looked from India's innocent face to Nicole's smile of complicity. "Pass."

India seemed hurt. Nicole shrugged, no loss.

She motioned to the bar for a drink, "Tom Collins."

India scribbled on a *Scars* napkin and handed it to Dutch. "Call me...or drop by. Won't you?"

She'd written her phone number and address. Dutch recalled the last time he had seen one of those napkins. And what had happened to the unlucky recipient. He stuffed it into his pocket and observed the applause for Gillette, who handed Hershey Girl over to his raven-haired assistant. Dauna shook her platinum blonde hair, walking awkwardly, like a fawn getting her legs, gently caring for the one Gillette had worked on. His white shirt showed the red, almost-black, color of blood. Tell-tale signs from the cutting. He disappeared through the archway after his bows. Just like a magician, Dutch thought. Only Dutch knew Gillette for what he was. An ex-hairstylist with an unusual night job.

Better check more closely on that prior, he reminded himself.

"Are you going to let India inside?" Nicole baited. "She's very good. Don't be afraid."

"I'm not afraid," Dutch's voice rose defensively.

"Blood is sexy," Nicole admonished with a wink.

Gillette swaggered up in a crisp, royal blue Armani silk shirt. "Sure is. And it flows green, baby."

He jumped on the barstool beside Dutch and ordered

a Jack and coke. Nicole retreated between Gillette's legs, deliberately grinding her ass into his crotch.

"Find anything?" Gillette asked.

Nicole smiled mockingly.

"I will," Dutch said.

Six.

Dutch drove Bishop in the SUV around the hairpin turns of Russian Hill, home to that tourist-infested stretch of Lombard Street called 'the crookedest street on earth.' Posh homes dropped in stepped plateaus on either side of the steep gradient. Mornings continued to be brilliant and cool, making San Francisco the envy of the country, which came under siege from heat in the southeast and southwest, rains in the northwest and Midwest, and a first cold front in the northeast.

"What a beautiful day, man," Bishop looked out the window and inhaled deeply. "Clean air, clear skies, water in every direction. *Bellisima!*"

"Will you knock it off with the vocabulary?" Dutch griped. "Your kid's homework is making me crazy."

"What's the matter? You don't want to expand yourself?"

"If I wanted to go back to school, I'd take an extension course."

"Fine. Live in the Dark Ages," Bishop said. "But remember, those who don't learn from history are doomed to repeat it."

"I'll keep that in mind," Dutch drawled.

They approached Telegraph Hill, named after the semaphore installed on the crest in 1850. Once home to immigrants and artists, who appreciated the spectacular view, today, the pastel clapboard residences were prime realty, accessible only to the Bay area's most affluent.

Dutch pointed ahead. "That's it, up there."

Police black-and-whites blocked the driveway of a single-family home in the middle of the block. Two adjacent lots had been unified, the structures joined together and renovated with multiple gables riddled with skylights. Yellow crime scene tape and uniformed officers kept the yard off-limits to the neighbors, who, despite their wealth, couldn't escape ordinary, morbid, human curiosity.

Dutch and Bishop parked behind the tech van, ducked under the tape and walked onto a professionally landscaped yard. The lawn didn't have a brown patch or errant weed to discolor the uniform green all the way to the house. An organic fountain of river rock and fluorescent lichen hid the entrance.

Dutch was greeted by Lauren Piolene. The dead girl. She was laughing, radiant, full of life, between her smiling parents from within a framed picture. It stood beside vases filled with dried lilacs atop an antique, redwood end table. Beyond the entryway lay a stylishly decorated home. Dutch found out just this morning that it had appeared in Architectural Digest. They'd already talked to the professional service that Lauren had hired to come in once a week to keep it up to standard. Even now, the interior looked immaculate—in spite of the half dozen techs sifting through the nooks and crannies, leaving nothing unexamined, unsearched, or undusted.

"Where's Magno?" Dutch asked nobody in particular.

The uniform guarding the door pointed through a doorway. "In the den."

Dutch veered in the direction of the tech's finger. "Is that the same as a study?"

Bishop drew level with him. "No. Study's for needlepoint. A den is a man cave used for apartment listings. You ever hear of one that reads bedroom plus study?"

Dutch had to think about that.

Lauren's den was designed to be a bright room. A massive floor-to-ceiling, plate-glass wall dominated the spacious chamber. Immediately outside, a live oak tree, transplanted at great cost, soared slightly off center. Within, modular shelves dotted the floor plan. They contained books, statuettes, several realty awards, and home-office accessories. A subtle touch of feminine prevailed everywhere. In the pink chintz of the curtains. The framed lithograph of Renoir's *Ballet Dancer*. The selection of authors and titles.

"You ever hear of Celine?" Dutch asked, picking one up.

"Don't touch that," a tech said impatiently.

Dutch slid it back in. "Yeah. The vic gets sliced in the car and then the cutter comes back here to read French novels."

"Dutch—" Bishop warned.

But Dutch was already on the move. Examining the lithograph of the *Ballet Dancer*. Just like a cat, Bishop thought. Always curious. Always getting into something. Dutch had become captivated by the peculiar picture. As he approached, he discovered why.

Except for droplets of red on the young girl's lips and shoes, the painting was awash in an atonal blending of grays. And, except for a slash of black across her throat, there weren't any distinct lines. Floors and walls were apparitions. The subject floated in a realm of suggestion. Free from boundaries. The delicate touch of the painter suggested liberation, completeness, and longing.

Inspecting it closely, Dutch couldn't shake the feeling that he was not only looking at the dead girl, Lauren, but at his own life was well. Rapid, liquid movement, safe within a soft gray landscape. As Bishop approached, Dutch wondered if he too could see the resemblance to Lauren.

"Legs are too thick," Bishop concluded, as if reading his mind. To Bishop, the girl looked nothing like Lauren, save for the fact she wore a thick black velvet choker around her neck that reminded him of the laceration that had brought her life to an abrupt end.

Dutch was entranced. Focused on the eyes. They were at once as sympathetic and endearing as they were haunting and plaintive. Importunate. Beseeching forgiveness. And demanded, with a certain subtle insistence, retribution. He saw Lauren in the fluid brush strokes more clearly than in the family photograph in the entryway. This was the real Lauren. The indistinct Lauren, who'd maintained a secret life well out of the oppressive illumination of public opinion. Lauren. The Shadow Dweller; the sweet little girl; the siren; the showpiece; and the sufferer. It was all there.

Dutch could see it as clearly as if it had been written on the incident report that noted her death. He wondered if people could see themselves in the art they chose. And if Lauren ever saw herself like this, the girl within the frame, when she meditated on it in her private moments. Or if she just saw a ballet dancer.

"Hey, guys!" Magno announced from across the room. "Over here. Got a client list off the hard drive."

Magno was seated at a sheet of reinforced frosted glass on four free-standing cylinders that served as Lauren's office desk. From a burgundy leather chair, he held up a sheet from the laser printer seated atop filing cabinets whose drawers were open and the contents rifled. Evidence of the techs' thoroughness.

"It's a Who's Who of low lives," grinned Magno, looking proud of his break-in.

Bishop perused it. "Oceanfront mafia."

"Explains how a realtor can own a house like this," said Dutch. "Check out the names."

Bishop scanned the list. Found Nicole Gray. "She helped Nicole buy her home."

"In Pacific Heights." Magno nodded, impressed. The Pacific Heights had become San Francisco's neighborhood of choice for the super-rich and famous. "Big Kahunas in the Heights."

"Seven million and change, Nicole paid," Bishop continued.

Dutch leaned over Bishop's shoulder and whistled. "No

way you can make that kind of money breaking skin."

"Only one name on the list is local," said Magno. "The rest are out-of-state wire transfers."

Bishop quickly singled out the name.

Manuel Briganza. No home address, but a working phone number was listed.

"Run a trace," Bishop ordered. "Let's see where it takes us."

It took them pier side.

***

Fisherman's Wharf was overcrowded even during the off-season. This afternoon, a traffic nightmare of overwhelming proportions backed up seemingly unconnected roads more than a mile away. Except for pedestrians, nothing moved in the radius of congestion. Even the cable cars ground to a halt, blocked in. The cause of it all?

A full-dress, cop carnival.

Every approach along the Embarcadero, from Hyde to Taylor, had been systematically blocked off. Black-and-whites were parked at reckless angles. A sea of uniforms moved urgently. Voices blasted out of radios. A crowd of onlookers and media strained against the police barriers. Two San Francisco Police Department choppers circled overhead, preventing newscopters from entering the restricted no-fly perimeter for the duration of this flush out operation. Snipers scaled onto rooftops.

Dutch's SUV entered the hot zone just as an ambulance and two fire engines pealed in behind the barriers, lights, and sirens at full-tilt boogie. Dutch, Bishop, the medics, and fire fighters cruised through the sea of law enforcement up to the main point of interest--the SWAT van. They climbed out and were met at once by a grizzled veteran who'd weathered worse stand-offs than this one, even if he did have to go back to the first Iraq war of '92 to prove it.

"Crayton. SWAT Team Leader." He didn't offer a handshake and it wasn't unexpected. His sandpaper voice matched his rough, no-nonsense appearance. Hair shorn to the scalp. Craggy cheeks protruding from brachycephalic features. Eyes recessed, hard as anthracite. Leaving the overall appearance of an impassive, cliff wall. Without wasting time, he pointed toward the focus of this massive deployment and started forward.

Dutch and Bishop ran the first few strides just to keep up.

"Son of a bitch fuckin' freaked," Crayton spat. "Cops caught him literally with his pants down, hosing off in the shower. He just got off the graveyard shift working the conveyors—that's where they take a chicken or whatever. And *whack!* Hack the little bastard to pieces. He took the cops on a chase through the men's lockers," Crayton motioned an invisible line along the building. "Got to his gun and opened fire. *Blam!* Spraying lead all over the fucking place. And *boom!* Sent a hundred Chinks screaming into the street. The Blues ran him through the whole complex, like a greased pig through a chute, until he, *bang!* Darted into the freezer. They've had him trapped in there ever since. Stark fucking naked."

They reached the front line of the deployment.

A large, low, square, unattractive building hugged the edge of the water. Anchored ships all around it had been secured, sailors forcibly disembarked. Sharpshooters crouched behind the railing on the decks of several vessels. Employees of the building stood in a separate group while officers questioned them. Enough of the peeling blue paint on the side of the structure remained to make out the name: *Cardoba Meats Cold Storage.*

"He's pinned down in the freezer *naked?*" Dutch asked.

Crayton nodded. "And he won't say shit to the negotiator. Ought to leave him in there. Let him freeze his fuckin' balls off."

Five SWAT personnel trooped to the trio's side in their signature dark blue uniforms and visored helmets. For this assault, they had on winter gloves and ski-masks to keep warm. Unprotected, sub-zero cold slowed reaction time. And that could cost lives.

"Anyone go in yet?" Bishop asked.

"No way," replied Crayton vehemently. "Finding him is going to be a bitch in that maze of meat. And he's got a street weapon. A sawed-off twelve gauge shotgun called a Kickback that can put a fucking hole right through two inches of steel."

"How the hell did he get that?" Dutch asked. It just kept getting worse.

"He pulled it out of a turkey's ass! How the hell should I know?"

Crayton sounded like a gun control advocate. Dutch was one, too. At another time and place, he would have delivered a philippic on how the Law couldn't possibly do its job if all the citizens were running around, arming themselves as if they were preparing for the winner-take-all-aftermath-of-World-War III. But now wasn't the time.

"Smell that in the air?" Crayton asked. "That's a shitstorm. Of the forty days and forty nights variety. So all I want to do's get that crazy fucking Mex outta there before it turns out to be a bigger mess than it's already shaping up to be."

Magno arrived on the double.

"Find anything?" Dutch asked.

"Yup." Magno held out a folder. Dutch waved him to just come out with it. He was not going to stop to read a profile in the middle of a possible firefight. "Manuel Briganza," Magno began. "Crazier than Captain Crunch. History of arrests. Used to be a Castro Street regular. Picked up a few times for stalking women coming out of the bars. Then he developed S&M fetishes. Played them out on hookers. Did time for cutting a Dominatrix's face with a kitchen knife."

"Sound like your man?" asked Crayton.

"Only one way to find out."

Dutch drew his 9mm and Bishop drew his .357. Crayton signaled to his five men. And just like the Wild Bunch, they strode toward the Cold Storage for a showdown.

Half a dozen uniforms covered the massive doors into the freezer. Crayton ordered a couple of them to give their bullet-proof vests to the two detectives. Dutch and Bishop donned them quickly, then grabbed the black ski-masks, gloves, and heavy overcoats from the employee lockers. Now all the men looked indistinct behind the masks and jackets. The only thing that unified them was the SWAT rollouts which hung off their backs.

Dutch watched thumbs ripple up in a successive wave, one after the other, all the way down the eight-man line. It got to him at the end. He signaled. Ready for entry. *Crash!* The massive doors sealing the meat locker hammered open. An Arctic-cold mist swirled out in a white whirlwind. The police line advanced into the icebound warehouse, measuring half a football field long and wide.

Ceiling trusses fanned out in a reinforced wingspan almost thirty feet off the ground. The enclosing walls were four feet thick, soundproof, and heavily insulated. A large thermometer over the door showed eighteen below zero. Evenly spaced, three-foot-long fluorescent tubes spread erratic green spikes of light over red slabs of meat hanging in endless rows upon rows upon rows.

The stench was overpowering. Bishop stopped and gagged. Dutch felt the bile rise in his throat, but he held on. If he puked, he'd have to take off his mask. If he did that, he might miss something. Which meant, in spite of all the heavy artillery brought in by the Special Weapons and Tactics team, he could be dead. He looked up, eyes watering, and noticed even the SWATs were fighting the same impulse.

"Don't know about you, but I'm suddenly fuckin'

hungry," Bishop grinned.

Dutch glanced over. Bishop rarely joked. He must be nervous. The breath from the team froze into white clouds. But the opposite occurred inside their bodies. The frigid conditions were quickly sensitizing their air passages. Pretty soon, every breath in and out was going to scorch. The only sound was the hum of white noise spewing out of massive air-driven coolers.

Crayton nodded wordlessly. The men diverged in a straight line, then advanced.

Screech! The rusty sound of a swinging hook scratched the silence. Everyone stopped. *Pow!* Just like that. Guns swung sharply. Fingers curled around triggers. Zero hesitation. Turned out to be a false alarm. A young SWAT kid had brushed against the hanging side of a skinned cow. Crayton glared at the youngster and they resumed their progress.

Dutch had been introduced to everyone. The young SWAT kid's name was Junior Billy. Dutch remembered because a couple of his buddies had ribbed the kid for his name, being as it was all bass-ackwards. They said he should have been called Billy *something* Jr. Junior took the joke in stride, replying Billy was his last name, so, for better or worse and to death do them part, his name was Junior Billy. The name was hardly the problem. Dutch couldn't see past his wide-eyed, buck-toothed, farm-raised-eggs-from-the-Land-of-Opportunity freshness.

This was the kid's first time on the front line of real action, and he raised his rifle and switched on the laser target like a rookie. With a shaky hand. Dutch noticed. "You okay, Junior?"

"It's just the cold, is all, sir."

Damn kids, Dutch thought. All balls and no brains. The lasers from the SWAT rifles materialized every now and then. Illuminated by patches of fog. Threads of red appeared, then vanished in the cold blasts of crisp air circulating between the suspended, fleshy remains. The beams pranced erratically, strung from the muzzles to raw carcasses. Crimson dots playing Tinkerbell. Seeking a target.

The Browning in Dutch's hand was cocked. Ready and steady. He kept his eyes trained straight ahead. Peripheral vision seeking movement. Alert. Hunting.

Something blurred past the corner of his eye.

"Down!" Bishop yelled.

Dutch dropped without hesitation. And it was a good thing, too. A heartbeat after he fell—*flash!* A yellow-red supernova bloomed. Followed by a huge roar!

Dutch realized he'd just been treated to the sight and sound of the street weapon called the Kickback. Bishop's timely warning had caused the shot to sting over his head, instead of taking it off entirely. For that, Dutch was truly thankful. Still, the damn thing nearly set his scalp on fire. He could smell the pungent aroma of burnt hair in his over-sensitized nostrils. When he patted his head, he could feel a few follicles had been singed all the way down to his scalp.

"Fuck!" he breathed. Squirming on the floor. Cheek flush against the frozen ground. Banging his skull as he pressed himself flat to avoid another close encounter.

BoomBoomBoomBoom!

Bishop and the SWATs retaliated immediately. Carpeted the space in front of them with bullets. Meat exploded everywhere in a terrific blizzard of blood and gore.

Dutch scrambled to his feet. Found himself jerking out of the way of a massive rib, hurling straight at him! It grazed the side of his face. He fired blindly, discharging his weapon again and again in the direction of the assailant. Each recoil pumped the adrenaline necessary to let off another shot. One, two, three, up to nine.

Saving the last shot, just in case.

He pulled under the 6000-pound carcass of a Brahma steer and waited. His ears were still ringing from the deafening shot of the Kickback and he felt disoriented as he tried to locate the sound of the fleeing suspect. Left, right, straight ahead, behind, he couldn't tell anymore. In an instant, his world had become a labyrinth of bullets, blood, meat, and dead, swinging cows.

Then, just as suddenly, the deafening stampede ended.

A hollow silence fell. Nobody moved.

Eight pairs of eyes and guns darted warily.

Dutch reloaded his gun. Fingers fumbling with the clip through dense cotton gloves. They'd only been in the freezer a few minutes, but his fingers were already going thick and numb with the cold. He wondered how the hell Briganza could take it. The lack of breathable oxygen was getting to him too.

Dutch saw Bishop.

His partner's breath emerged in rasping, swirling gasps as he nosed the business end of his .357 around the hollow ribs of a massive hog. His muzzle safely around, Bishop did a quick-see down the row of swine and bumped back. Didn't seem like he saw anything but he did look like he was gathering the courage to make some sort of move.

What the fuck's he doing? Dutch watched Bishop nose his way around the gargantuan sow—at least it looked like a sow to him. Dutch was no pig expert, and sows and hogs pretty much looked the same once they were cut for market. *But shit, whatever it is, it's gotta be about four hundred pounds.* He stayed floor level in an attempt to see feet and legs. However, there was just too much mist to make out anything definitive.

Dutch wanted to get Bishop's attention, so they could move together, but he couldn't speak without giving away his location. And with that cannon out there, he was forced to wait for Bishop to finish his recon and hopefully look his way. But he wasn't doing it. *Damnit.* Dutch got into a sprinter's crouch and prepared to haul ass behind Bishop so that he could back his partner up.

The shit hit the fan.

The Kickback let loose another shot. It blazed across like a comet and sounded louder than a sonic boom. An entire carcass detonated right in front of Dutch's face! Dutch staggered under the red and white storm of animal splatter. Stunned by the concussive force of the blast. He lay there shell shocked, staring at the ceiling. Numb, wet and sticky. Afraid to check for damage.

Suddenly, Bishop was over him. "You okay?"

Dutch got his courage up and looked himself over. He was covered in guts. He sat and angrily asked, "What do you think?"

"I think it's a good look for you," Bishop smiled.

Dutch tried to wipe the stuff off, but that just smeared it even more. There was too much slime. He grumbled, "Aw, shit."

The two strikes sundered the unity of the assault line. The SWATs scattered individually, losing sight and cover fire of each other. Crayton, the Team Leader, scrambled to regiment them back into a solid net. The men worked their way back quickly under his command, using only hand signals.

Lasers flashed red in the icy mist.

Nesting. Crossing. Touching. Searching. A luminous web of death.

Dutch and Bishop scrambled away separately. Quickly vanishing behind dangling flanks and setting up their own back-to-back defensive posture. The freezer went deathly quiet once more.

"Ready?" Bishop asked.

"Ready," Dutch nodded.

"But I can't hear shit," Bishop said a little too loudly. "You'll have to be the radar."

Dutch nodded. No problem. The cops carefully sidled forward, making sure not to scrape their feet across the floor. Maintaining the silence. Then he heard it.

A rubber sole turned on the ice.

He whipped left. Then right. A giant flank swung in front of him. He reacted with lightning reflexes. Finger closing around the trigger. About to fire!

Suddenly, Bishop's hand was over his gun.

It was Junior Billy, the SWAT kid, who had caused the chain to grate when they first entered. Bishop eased back off his firing stance, releasing the pressure from the trigger just in time.

"Almost had you for dinner, Junior," Dutch said, shaking his head.

This kid was scared.

"Why don't you just stay put," Bishop put an oversized hand on the lad's shoulder. "We'll check this aisle, then cut back to join the group, got it?"

Junior's head jerked in a perceptible nod. Relieved. Bishop motioned and he crouch-walked with Dutch out of view.

"Helluva introduction, Dutch," Bishop smiled wryly.

"Too damn young," Dutch growled, at once aggravated and sad.

***

Junior's breathing returned to normal. He could feel creeping beads of sweat blistering out on his forehead even in the sub-zero conditions. He pulled the knit mask back off his face and wiped the sweat with the back of his hand.

Dropping his guard.

It looked so damn easy on film at SWAT training and simulated maneuvers. *Fuck, I ain't cut out for this.* He blamed his father. A decorated cop. Junior was his only boy. The rest of 'em were all girls. Junior wanted to teach high school, but it was the Marines or the Force ever since he could walk and talk. He didn't have the guts to stand up to his father—a giant of a man.

On the other hand, this was exciting shit. It was slow going but hairy as they came. His could impress the girl he was seeing, an assistant at the Moscone Center. Maybe he'd even put in a call to his Dad in Arkansas. The old man would be proud. He paused by a 450-pound heifer, his mind racing.

So he never saw the bloody arm shoot out of its belly.

Fingers webbed with the red goo of innards. Crimson-white secretions hanging but not falling. The soaking tentacle struck with the silent swiftness of a cobra! Coiled around Junior's neck in a flash!

He opened his mouth to scream.

A second bloody arm emerged swiftly, crushing his windpipe. Junior lost his sight as fingers curled like fangs into his eyes. Gouging them. In a split second of clarity, the kid knew he was going to die. And how.

The assailant wrenched Junior's head in a single, savage jerk.

Crack! The spine just below his skull snapped.

***

Dutch and Bishop finished their run and doubled back to the spot where they left the kid. Dutch asked, "Where the fuck is he?"

"There's too much fucking space in here," replied Bishop.

Dutch crossed the aisle, about to pass on, when he noticed the rooster tails in the ice along the floor. Cut by boots dragged across the floor. Ahead, the 450- pound carcass swayed gently. It was the only one moving in the long line.

Stop! Dutch motioned urgently to Bishop. Then the two cops approached cautiously in tandem. Guns up. Muzzles trained for quick fire. In the lead position, Dutch closed in on the swaying slab. Bishop checked over each shoulder and behind. *Nothing,* he signaled.

Dutch was an arm's length away. Erratic bursts of breath pumping from his mouth, misting his vision for split seconds at a time. The riven underbelly faced the other way. Dutch couldn't see the cut, but he knew it was time to act. He reared his leg back, kicked it around and jumped into a wide-legged shooting stance. Both hands aimed the Browning for deadly fire as the meat spun. The incision swung toward him.

Shit!

"Man down! Man down! Man down!" Dutch screamed.

A nervous jitter electrified his spine. His eyes leapt about the room for the monster that could have done something so terrible. Bishop froze. The remaining SWAT team came running in formation. What they found made them turn away in horror.

The kid was stuffed inside. Hanging from the hook holding up the carcass. It's tip protruding from his gaping mouth. The stem pushed up against his nose, flaring the nostrils into wide, black ovals. Like a voodoo zombie, his eyeballs rolled back into his skull, leaving only white disks in their stead.

Dutch couldn't remember a more gruesome and appalling image of a fellow officer's death. Then he caught the kicker. *The kid's outer clothing had been stripped.*

"Briganza's wearing one of our uniforms!" Dutch barked. He grabbed his radio and repeated it for the blues outside.

Only static crackled back at him.

"They can't hear us!"

The SWATs made an urgent sprint for the door.

Dutch burst out first. A perplexed uniform stared at him.

"Did anyone come through here?" Dutch shouted. He didn't mean to yell, but the adrenaline rush and the fact his ears were still ringing caused his volume to soar.

"Just a SWAT," stammered the uniform. "Said he was feeling sick and needed to throw up."

"Goddamnit!" Dutch ripped.

"Which way did he go?!" hollered Crayton. He'd never lost one of his own.

He got the typical, lackadaisical shrug of a beat cop who didn't want the fuck-up of the city's Number One felon to fall on his shoulders. "Search me. Some guy wants to puke, I say, go puke. What do I care for where he does it?"

Dutch wanted to clock the uniform. Instead, he kicked a crate clean across the room.

Crayton raised the radio, which had begun working again, and shouted for the entire carnival to hear, "Briganza took out one of ours and is wearing his uniform!"

The army outside flurried into action. Blues, plainclothes, and other SWATs scattered, searching every inch of the wharf. Half an hour later, they didn't even turn up the uniform, let alone Briganza. He'd slipped outside the security ring and into the safety of the pier side crawl.

"Put out an APB," Dutch ordered.

The cop carnival broke up rapidly. Crayton did not even have time to mourn the loss of Junior. They had ship out to their next call—a bank robbery with multiple 207s. Heists were in vogue again all along the Golden Coast. Every couple of years saw a new spate of crimes as successive generations of felons tried to carve their own niche. The last few years had been armored cars. Before that freeway shootings. Now, it was Old West turn-of-the-century retro.

The black-and-whites dispersed as well. With a crime being perpetrated every five seconds in this city, they had their own agendas to attend. Only four cops stayed back to tape off Junior's crime scene. A CSI unit would show up as soon as one became available. The kid was already back page in everyone's minds.

Dutch and Bishop walked back to the SUV, still frustrated. They'd come so close. Bishop got over it faster and more easily than Dutch. It was just his way.

"We'll get him," Bishop said, gesturing around. "Case is too high profile." He'd been a cop long enough to realize the cliché long arm of law was no myth. It would eventually nab Briganza.

"Hope so," Dutch agreed. Still feeling sickened by the

Junior's death.

Magno caught up with them as they were getting into Dutch's SUV. "I got more on him."

"Spill it," Dutch said.

"Part time tattoo artist. Part time enforcer. His parole officer figured he was dead because he's been a no-show since he was released. No address. No phone number. No sightings. No show."

"Probably living under an alias," Dutch deduced. "Canvas every club and freak show in the city. Degenerate like this is bound to show up sooner or later. They're creatures of habit."

"Will do." Magno left Dutch and Bishop alone.

They read each other's minds.

"You think this is the guy?" asked Bishop skeptically.

"Seems too easy," replied Dutch with a similar lack of conviction.

**

"Too easy?!" Lieutenant Schiff thumped his desk angrily. "Since when did too easy become an alibi?" He extended a finger for each subsequent argument. "His name was on the list. He ran. He killed a cop." Schiff shoved the three fingers toward them. "Three strikes, you're out!"

The intercom buzzed. "Dr. Tilton is here."

"Send him in," Schiff said. He turned to Dutch and Bishop, "Tilton's an FBI profiler. He's here to help."

Dr. Tilton was around sixty-five, thin, scholarly down to his thick, black, horn-rimmed glasses. He had the no-nonsense aura of one who commanded respect by dint of sheer knowledge, encyclopedic recollection, and devotion to detail.

"Dutch, Bishop. Meet Dr. Tilton. He's an expert in deviant sexual behavior." They shook hands. Everyone found chairs.

Dr. Tilton didn't waste any time. "I have been studying

blood sports for several years. Curiously, it appeals mostly to white women. We released a report in November that showed nine out of ten Caucasian females don't like their body."

"How does cutting it up help?" Bishop asked acidly.

"It's their way of reclaiming it," answered Dr. Tilton. "Historically, bloodletting has been a widely used method of easing tension by lowering blood pressure. Women accept it more readily than men...probably because their monthly menstrual flow better prepares them for the loss of their own blood and helps them see it as a natural process. Cutting sheds only a fraction of the quantity they lose during a typical menses cycle. Also, women experience an endorphin rush with bleeding, a key reason to understanding why they prefer blood sports to sadomasochism."

"Didn't you say Nicole said her clients were all female?" Schiff recalled. Bishop and Dutch nodded and added they'd had yet to see a man under the knife at *Scars*.

"As an art form, scarification is the rage today because it is personal," Dr. Tilton continued. "It is real."

"But it's dangerous," Bishop interjected.

"That's a misconception." The FBI specialist shook his head. "Cutting is such an intimate blood sport, individuals who work on themselves rarely share instruments. In the case of partners, they generally know one another, minimizing the danger. Professionals follow the same hygiene procedures as hospitals. Still, cutting suffers the stigma associated with drugs—even though it isn't as addictive or life-threatening. Risk from the nicks and cuts are comparable to gardening, hiking, or any other outdoor physical activity."

"What about the psychological effects?" Dutch asked.

"Actually, cutting empowers," replied Dr. Tilton. "That's why women do it. It makes them feel in control." He reached into his briefcase and slid over a newsletter, *A Cut Above*. "Caters to the Self-Inflicted Violent, or SIV. Far from being a fad, women consider cutting a form of expression. Men have always made the rules on beauty. Flat stomach. Firm breasts. Flawless skin. Cutting permits women to destroy the stereotypical male fantasy of the female form and redefine it in their own image."

Dr. Tilton went on to describe the typical profile of a woman into cutting.

"They are generally single, white, of average looks, bordering on plain, twenty-five to thirty years old, and invariably, victims of one of the following—abuse, incest, failed relationships, and infidelity. These women tend to be submissive, almost too eager to please, during sex. Cutting offers a way to release their aggression by turning it inward, on their bodies. It helps alleviate their depression. And, oddly enough, calms and arouses them at the same time. In some instances, it even prevents them from taking their own lives."

"Sounds like a Pyrrhic victory to me," Bishop said.

"Perhaps," countered Dr. Tilton, "but perhaps it is the only kind their psyche will allow."

Dutch and Bishop took turns to recount self-mutilation stories of Christmas Girl, India, and Hershey Girl.

"That's one for your theory, Doc," smirked Schiff, who noticed his detectives' reservations about the clinical expert were quickly receding. They leaned forward in avid interest to what the doctor was saying.

"Those frequenting Castro Street represent barely one third of the statistics," revealed Dr. Tilton. "The majority either can't afford professionals, are too shy, or keep it secret for fear of losing respect at work or home. These women carve themselves using razors, tacks, kitchen knives, beer can lids. Anything household and sharp."

One of Dr. Tilton's case studies performed in clubs, biting herself and volunteers from the audience. "In quite remarkably imaginative crescent patterns," he added. "The less artistic would etch alphabets, names, crude pictures...but most of them just broke skin to feel the physical pain and forget that unreachable inner heartache. The scars became emotional cynosures of triumph and honor."

Once again, Dutch brought up India's ragged scars on her wrists. How proudly she had displayed them.

"Two for the good doctor," remarked Schiff.

"Whatever the motive," Dr. Tilton continued, "whether it's a superficial need to get attention, to be considered cool, to derive a neoprimitive buzz for sex, or be they more complex, such as using the body as a metaphor for rebellion—it's all about seeing, feeling, tasting, and ultimately shedding blood."

Dr. Tilton displayed a stout, 5x7 photo book that looked like a family album purchased from any ordinary drug store. Inside, the pages were filled with patients, past and present. Demonstrative cases of the Self Inflicted Violent. The pictures were Polaroids mostly. They all had the tell-tale greengage cast of fluorescent, hospital lighting. The subjects appeared more gaunt and hollow than Schiff would have imagined, after the chichi clients from *Scars*. Despite the variety of scars and cuts and abrasions left in evidence of their private obsessions, when he looked into their eyes, Schiff saw one common denominator. He said out loud, "Fear."

Tilton nodded, "The simple, universal emotion that accompanies the desperate in their penultimate effort to get help and grab a lifeline, before going over the edge, into the abyss."

Bishop skinned his lips over his teeth. "I don't see the fear so much as sorrow. These people are suffering. Pleading for attention. And when the world won't listen, they demand its notice by harming themselves. Honestly, I don't see the reclamation, doctor, I see tired, lonely people, dressed in open hospital gowns, showing the signs of their suffering, and asking for help."

"Shit," smiled Schiff wryly. "That's deep." He wasn't surprised. Bishop was well read and even better spoken.

"Blood is the essence of a person," responded Tilton.

"It's the reaffirmation of life. Particularly in this day and age. When our movies, our books, the first fifteen minutes of any newscast celebrates bloodshed. Religion tells us to drink the blood of Christ to atone for our sins. A child is born covered in blood. Most of us have bloody, violent fantasies. Cutting lets you look inside without killing. That is power. Something police officers should readily comprehend. When your finger is around that trigger, you can give or take life. In that fleeting, critical moment, you are God."

Dutch handed the book of Polaroids back to Dr. Tilton. "Yeah, but our homicide occurred *after* the cutting."

"She was killed following intercourse," Tilton interposed.

"Meaning?"

"Disapproval. When you cut someone without killing them, you're essentially marking your territory. So the killer could have been unhappy with her or her performance."

Schiff's face cleared. "Oh. So whoever cut her probably killed her. Nicole, Gillette, or both."

"Not necessarily. Anybody aroused by the sight of blood could have seen what was happening in the club, followed her to her car, and killed her there."

"Crazies," said Schiff, turning toward Dutch. "Like our meat locker man, Briganza."

Dr. Tilton cautioned, "I want to make sure you're both being factually accurate before rushing toward any conclusions. The throat laceration that caused her death looked like part of the body art. Which would point to someone familiar with cutting. The autopsy, however, revealed no semen in the vagina. So, either a condom was used, or, uh, a—"

"A dildo," Schiff cut in bluntly. Dr. Tilton nodded.

"So the killer can be a man or a woman wearing a prosthetic," said Dutch, running down the options.

Schiff noticed Bishop meet Dutch's eyes and demanded irritably, "What?"

Together, they said, "Myke the Dyke."

Seven.

"What about Myke?" Nicole asked from behind the bar.

Dutch and Bishop sat on stools facing her. Nicole looked splendid and intelligent, draped in a black Ann Taylor evening gown and low, velvet pumps. Unlike any time before, she was wearing thin, rimless spectacles with polished titanium stems. The glass was completely clear and her eyes did not appear any larger behind them, leading Dutch to believe she either needed minimal correction, or they were merely decorative.

It was early. *Scars* contained only a few solitary clusters of devotees. On stage, a bunch of girls, young, skinny, and pale enough to have walked off an Abercrombie & Fitch billboard, laughed and giggled while Myke the Dyke worked on one of their friends.

The center of attraction was a nineteen-year-old brunette with strikingly delicate bone structure and voluptuous lips. Faint markings from previous brandings dotted her shoulders. Myke continued the pattern between her blades. He removed what looked like a superheated cast iron light pen from the brazier and applied it to the girl's skin. She emitted a light scream and shucked air between her teeth. Her friends gaped wide-eyed and pushed each other a bit.

The detectives flinched.

"It's only painful to watch," assured Nicole. "She wanted delicate scars—Hamburger cuts, that's what we call them— for more ephemeral documents. After a week, they'll be so faint you'll have to look closely to see the pattern."

"He, she, whatever the fuck Myke is," said Dutch, "sleep

with any clients?

"Like Lauren? No. That's strictly prohibited."

"You have rules?" Bishop reacted as if he'd seen a cow fly.

"We like to make them up as we go," she said provocatively. "Myke liked Lauren, actually. Tried to sell her on branding. But she went with cutting, instead. After her session, on the night she died, I overheard Myke ask her to dinner and she refused."

"You never mentioned this before," Bishop asserted.

"Didn't I?" Nicole shrugged.

"Are you saying Myke may have gotten jealous?" Dutch asked.

"That's detective work, isn't it?" Nicole smiled.

Dutch realized Bishop and he wouldn't elicit much more than word play from her. Not today. Not like this. Nicole was too smart for the Mutt and Jeff routine. If pressed, she would disappear behind her high-priced attorneys in the blink of an eye. Dutch would have to do this informally, out of the public arena, and certainly away from the club. A little one on one wouldn't hurt, he thought. But then again, he couldn't be sure. Because, in complete honesty with himself, he wasn't too convinced he'd get the better of it.

Nicole invited Dutch to stick around. Catching Bishop's disapproving eyes, Dutch refused. Outside, they ran into India getting out of Nicole's candy-apple red Jaguar convertible. Her keys rattled like wind chimes from a tinkling platinum chain.

"Hiya," India approached.

"Back for more?" Dutch asked.

"Hmm," she smiled and kissed his cheek. "Hiya, Bishop."

"India."

The two men watched her walk away. Short furbelow rustling. Attractive, yet untouchable. Pristine. Not a part of the darkly sexual possessions that belonged to the club.

"How the hell does she manage to look so innocent in all this," Dutch said with a sweeping gesture.

"Dunno," Bishop remarked. "Some people just don't get touched by it, I guess."

With nightfall still an hour away, Castro Street wasn't jumping yet, with pockets of space still open on the sidewalk to stand and talk. Permitting the regulars to gather in small, concentric circles.

Dutch looked from India back to Bishop, then said, "I got an idea. Go with me on this, will you?" Then he called out, "India! Hold up a sec!" India paused, a smile flowering on her lips. Dutch turned toward Bishop, speaking sotto voce. "I was thinking. Maybe I can get something out of her about Myke the Dyke."

"You want to nail her, don't you?" Bishop said.

"I'd never compromise the case."

"Uh, huh. One problem."

"What's that?"

"You drove."

"Take my car." Dutch removed the key off the chain and handed it to Bishop.

"Ten bucks says you're looking to park your dick head-in at the pussy garage."

"Have some confidence, will you?"

"Sweet piece like that? And willing? Head-in," Bishop said, convinced. "Before midnight."

"Bring cash." Dutch walked away. Rolling up on India, he asked, "How about dinner and you show me the sights of the Street?"

"What about the club?"

"Forget the club."

India's eyes flitted from Dutch to the club entrance. "I have to give Nic her keys back—"

"Later," Dutch said, "after we eat."

"No," she said firmly and turned away.

Dutch followed her inside. Nicole was relaxing on a barstool at the counter before *Scars* started up for the night. India handed the keys to the Jag to Nicole and whispered into her ear. India confiding that he'd asked her out, Dutch figured. Nicole looked past India to Dutch and waved with smile. But the moment India turned around, Nicole's smile faded. *Jealous?*

***

They ate at *Havana*, a noisy Cuban diner. India refused to let him order his usual Miller, insisting he try a foreign lager, Negro Modelo. Not Cuban, but a close cousin. Negro Modelo was brewed and bottled in Mexico city. Rich, smooth and full-bodied. The dark ale tasted faintly of burnt hops, and Dutch had to admit, it was a helluva beer—all things considered. Out of his element, Dutch prudently submitted to her choice of dishes. India didn't even look at the menu, rattling off their order. Moments later, the waiter returned with roast pork, steamed rice, fried sweet bananas, black beans in a bowl, and onions in garlic sauce.

"This is good," Dutch said after the first mouthful. The richness of the food brought out a hunger he hadn't realized. Before he knew it, he was finished, ordering a second beer and staring into the lovely eyes and libethenite skin of the charming woman seated across from him.

India asked him a couple of cursory questions about his personal life throughout dinner, but Dutch deflected any more probing than where he was from and what his favorite pastimes were. The first was easy. Sweetwater, Texas. Just outside of Abilene, in the no man's land west of the big cities. "Not much to look at there besides sky."

As a kid, he had marveled at how the earth baked up flat, in every direction, from temperatures that soared well over 100°F in the summer. As for recreation, Dutch preferred racing. "Not Formula One," he grinned. "It's too polite."

Dutch was into NASCAR and bull riding. He was a big fan of Dale Earnhardt and Lane Frost, both killed. Dale in a high speed crash and Lane under a bull called Taking Care of Business. Those two sports appealed to him, he confessed to India, maybe because he shared their common thread of danger, living life on the edge. It went on like that throughout dinner, but as for more intimate questions, India was unable to get a firm purchase on his personal life.

She, on the other hand, had no qualms, speaking openly. The only child of well-to-do parents, her upbringing had been a sheltered one in Connecticut's white suburbia. The more she told him, the more India completed Dr. Tilton's picture of an SIV individual. She had been sexually abused by her father and remained an incest victim until eighteen, when she left home for undergraduate school at Berkeley. Convinced her mother knew, she had never been home or spoken to her parents since.

She told the story casually.

In California, she'd gone through several boyfriends, the last being the most serious. The one she hurt herself over. Now she played it safe. Sex without emotional attachment. And, of course, cutting.

"Why?" asked Dutch, testing Dr. Tilton's theories.

"I...don't know," she said, her brow clouding. "It's nothing I can sum up in words. For me, it's just, like, the ultimate turn on. I can't make love anymore without cutting. I want my partner to taste my blood. And vice versa. It completes the connection at, like, the deepest, most basic level. It's sexy." She moved closer to him. "You can see for yourself, if you want."

Dutch shrugged. Noncommittal. "And the pain?"

India's voice stayed low and dusky. "It teaches you patience. Helps you set limits. Suffering during sex makes the pleasure so much more satisfying. It gives orgasm many more layers...there are no words to describe it." Her hand stroked up his thigh to the apex. "You have to be shown."

Dutch reacted to the gentle scratch of her nail. Manicured to a sharp point beyond her finger. He stirred at once. She sensed it. Dutch suddenly felt anxious. Agitated. He broke into a cold sweat. Drawn uncontrollably into the strengthening vortex of electricity between them.

The waiter arrived with their check. She withdrew her hand. The overwhelming curiosity to enter her tantalizing world of sex and blood receded. Dutch immersed himself in the mundane, mathematical task of doubling the tax to calculate the tip.

India sat back and asked simply, "Have you ever killed anyone?"

Dutch froze.

***

Seeing his reaction, India's entire manner changed with the abruptness of a light switch. The diabolical glint left her eyes. The carnivorous blush faded from her cheeks. "I didn't mean it the way it came out. And I definitely did not kill Lauren, if that's what your thinking. Death," she added seriously, "is like pain taken beyond the brink. The ultimate. I don't know. It seems like, well, the ultimate power. The natural conclusion to cutting."

Dutch never saw a transformation as swift and chameleonic. His skin crawled when she closed her hand over his.

"I just have homicidal dreams." She tilted her head coyly. "Doesn't everybody?"

And all of a sudden, Dutch wanted to leave. He uncertainly removed his hand from under hers to reach for his wallet. He placed exact change in the tray so they wouldn't have to wait. The restaurant was packed, with a line of at least twenty people stretching from the hostess's station. It had taken the waiter fifteen minutes just to get them their check.

"How well do you know Myke the Dyke?" he asked her, when they stepped onto the sidewalk.

The night crowd had swept into the street. India grabbed Dutch's hand before they got separated. She crushed into him. She slipped her hand around his waist. He couldn't find any pretense to remove it. So, he let it stay. And she kept it there. As natural as could be. He had no choice but to reciprocate by circling an arm around her shoulder. Out in the cold night air, the strange claustrophobic feeling brought on by the unsettling nature of India's questions quietly vanished like faces in the crowd. Everything became clean and rational once more.

"Myke's quiet," she hushed into his ear. "Says little. Always alone. Has that far off quality, you know? Even when he's with others, he seems a thousand miles away." She turned to Dutch candidly, "Why? Is he a suspect?"

"No," Dutch said, trying to dismiss her suspicions, "but we have to check everyone out." Dutch turned, his lips brushing her cheek inadvertently. They were that close. When they separated, it was apparent it wasn't an unwelcome encounter. For either of them. They smiled, innocent, like school kids, until India broke the awkward moment.

"What's Myke's alibi?" she asked.

"The Necro?" Dutch said unsurely.

She recognized the name and her eyes opened just enough to reveal surprise.

"You know it?" Dutch prompted.

"It's a vampire strip club."

"Can you take me?"

"Sure. But I'm warning you, it's a shocker. I mean, it's pretty out-there."

Dutch was beginning to wonder what wasn't. "Why run when you can fly?"

They left the rush and roar of people behind. India steered Dutch down a maze of narrow, pitch-black alleys. She led the way, but held his hand fast, like a child seeking reassurance.

Occasionally, she would turn to him, look into his eyes, then look away.

It wasn't long before they found the Necro.

"The lack of lighting around the door is deliberate," she said. "Creates the creatures of the night atmosphere. Also keeps away the casual, curiosity seeker." No harm in that, Dutch thought. In a city that raked in over $3.9 billion a year in tourism, vampirism probably wouldn't be a great selling point. "The Necro practices hard core vampirism. A closed world to just a limited number of disciples." Then she grinned, "But Nicole's club offers reciprocal privileges. We won't have any trouble getting in."

The solid black door, set in the dilapidated wall, didn't carry even the solitary nameplate displayed at *Scars*. Just a lonely, featureless front. Dutch reacted to scraping feet in the blackness. He faintly discerned lurking silhouettes and his police instincts caused him to tense involuntarily.

"Security guards," India dismissed with a wave.

Dutch caught a glimpse of their tallow, lantern-shaped features and flinched. Their heads were scalped down to their marble skulls. Haunted eyes, deep-set in a sea of midnight shadow. In their hands, they carried broken slats of wood to discourage trouble. One of them even dragged his foot behind as he walked. Dutch couldn't be sure if this was an act or a genuine impairment.

When the security nodded for them to enter, Dutch saw clods of dirt smeared over their necks and faces. Embedded within the folds of their flesh. It was as if they had just awakened from the grave, and when their mouths opened, blood or worms might very well spill out. Dutch wondered if he wasn't getting in over his head. He'd hate to wind up a statistic in a place like this if anything went wrong. Though, he thought, amused, it would give credence to Elise's claims to irreconcilable differences in their marriage.

India pushed her way through the rickety door. It

squeaked open. They entered a small vestibule lit by a naked fifteen-watt bulb. Nothing else. The walls, floor, and ceiling were painted matte black. Dutch couldn't see any corners or seams. Couldn't tell where the floor ended and the walls and ceiling started. It felt as if he were standing in a free floating vault of endless space.

India waved to something, then Dutch saw it. The convex, lifeless eye of a security camera staring down at them over a second set of near-invisible doors. She was recognized. The lock buzzed. She grabbed the handle. And pushed.

The moment they stepped through, an ear-rending scream tore out of the blackness!

And swept over them like a horrible, dark-winged fury.

***

It came from a woman—called a vampire, as all Necro patrons were—on a runway stage, being held by a man, while another whipped her. The vampire's shaved labia thrust upward. Sybaritic. Pushed to the conical tip of pleasure.

"It's a hemospastic reaction," India said. "The whips help bring blood to the surface." The woman screamed again and curved upward, following the next lash. "The men are actually licensed phlebotomists. They help vampires draw and drink their own blood. It might look funky, but it's sanitary. These days you've got to be careful. But if you do it right, it's all good, clean fun."

"Yeah," Dutch could barely get the words out, "but it ain't exactly 'Leave it to Beaver.'"

He looked around, awestruck.

The music was Primrose, a Gothic/Industrial band appropriately suited to the occasion. The art and artifacts, arches and pillars, furniture and furnishings, the whole space, even the air, reeked of antiquity. On the ceiling, a sprawling image of Kali, the Indian demon goddess, dripped *real* blood along the tongue detruding from her mouth into an ornate bowl and recirculated back up through a hidden network of pipes.

Illumination came entirely from candles. Globules of wax serrated down the sides. The dancing flames created a sciography of constant motion. Of exaggerated, wildly mobile, almost Satanic, shadows. Of bright and dark niches, where a naked, half-naked and fully-clothed populace devoted themselves to extracting and ingesting blood.

A Necro employee handed India a three-tiered candelabra. The faint light became their guide through the labyrinthine abode. The Necros took their pleasure seriously. Dutch noted a painstaking efficiency that prevailed throughout. In a pocket of gloom, he saw a pale, thin couple cut each other precisely with a pair of five and one-half inch, curved, surgical tweezers, then suck the blood. The strange, stainless steel instrument was shaped like fangs and left a vampiric bite.

India knew them. Hard core vampire junkies, who lived in a basement apartment with blacked-out ventilators and no electricity. They regularly shot heroin, slowing their metabolisms and mixed preservatives in their food to retain a gaunt lemon-white appearance. On a good night, they could use jerry-built cookers, consisting of half a coke can and a butane lighter, to whip up a batch of the Real Thing. Laudanum. The coagulant noted in the *Anne Rice Vampire Chronicles*—the Gothic horror bible for followers of the undead.

"Do they sleep in coffins during the day too?" Dutch quipped satirically.

"As matter of fact, they do," India replied, entirely serious. "They work the swing shift as toll booth operators. This is their night off."

"Jesus."

"Be careful," she wagged a warning finger. "That's a forbidden word around here."

In another corner, Dutch spied a bubbling cauldron. Money exchanged hands. Dutch edged closer to the action. Something floated in the water. White, cuneal curiosities surfacing momentarily, forced up on steaming pockets of air, then falling back into the impenetrable liquid. A headsman used forceps to fish around the roiling waters, maintained at a sanitary 212°F. He pulled out one of the ghoulish floating crescents. Dutch saw one clearly for the first time.

Vampire teeth.

Not the plastic dime store variety sold for Halloween. These were utilitarian. Constructed of durable ceramic with tiny holes at the end of elongated incisors.

A woman craned her neck, offering it to a Necro employee. He placed one hand on the back of her head, the other on her breast, and bit down. She swooned. Giving herself completely to her demon lover. A trickle of blood escaped from the corner of his mouth.

"Kinky," India said, an undercurrent of fascination gilding her voice. "But it really is safe." She pointed to the cauldron. "The water's mixed with ethanol and other hospital grade disinfectants. It would do the job even in a cold solution, but they boil it just to be sure." She gestured back toward the entrance. "They take your papers at the door, for, you know, AIDS. Everyone who comes in has to have been tested negative within the last thirty days." Dutch was about to ask a question, when India answered it for him. "I told them you only liked to watch."

India took Dutch's hand and led him toward an area marked by a nictitating neon sign in a brilliant electric blue: *The Pit.* This was the main staging area. Surrounded by crumbling columns. Topped with green leafy plants bearing black, delicious berries.

Dutch reached for one. India stopped him. "Nightshade. It's poisonous."

In the center of the ring, a group of men and women cavorted in various stages of undress, striking an image of utter Roman decadence. For every vampire, there was a Necro guardian. Ensuring strict adherence to safety procedures.

Keeping a close eye on the twenty-gauge needles drawing blood from a vein of the individual's choice. The needles were sold by a petite, though extremely well-endowed Vampirella. She had waist length, sable hair that shined like glistening spiderwebs under an ashen moon. Her skin was deathly pale, its milky-white hue irresistible to the eye.

The moisture drained from Dutch's mouth as he watched her lithe, aerial movements across the open chamber. She was clad in a skin tight black latex corset and matching mini skirt that exposed her leather thong whenever she bent over to make a sale. When she turned toward Dutch, it was as if she were walking in slow motion. He could see a wide, spangled ribbon draped diagonally from her right shoulder to the left side of her waist. It was a Spanish War style bandoleer that hung loosely over the front of her form-fitting cups. Though, instead of bullets, needles for sale were nestled within each solitary tube. A short, clean patch in the center read simply: *Shots.* Dutch got it immediately. She was the equivalent of the Tequila girl in a college bar.

The Necros in the central crypt began to wail. The insulin syringes had filled with blood drawn from their supplicants. They were ready for the main event. Nodding to one another and surrounding their charge in a ragged circle, they locked eyes and nodded simultaneously, as if sharing one mind. The mind of the hive, or Dracula, Lord of the Undead. Then, all at once, they jammed down the stoppers with a single push. Fountains of red shot up and fell outward like the dying sparks of a fireworks display. The vampires opened their mouths with gleeful screams. Whatever they couldn't drink, they smeared over themselves and rubbed against one another in a mortal frenzy. A couple in the heart of the crypt, on a plastic cinnabar tarp, began having sex without inhibition.

Dutch looked away, appalled. India followed his eyes. "Not your style?"

"Not by a long shot." Dutch scanned the club, looking

for some kind of authority figure. "Who do you think could verify Myke's alibi?"

India frowned, noticing his detachment, then spotted a Necro employee she recognized and guided Dutch in her direction. He trailed submissively behind the three flames of the candelabra, holding India's hand. He couldn't believe the utter quality of the darkness. Not a single reflective surface. He was constantly bumping into things. Every now and then, sallow, vampiric faces emerged, then receded, just like the teeth in the boiling cauldron. Without the light, or her hand, Dutch would have easily become lost. Approaching the Necro that India recognized, Dutch stepped from behind the wavering flicker of the tapers and felt a surge of bile. His heart thumped powerfully and he felt suddenly sick to his stomach. "Is she doing what I think she is?"

India nodded.

A twenty-five year old, mousy vampire squatted on the tips of her toes over a porcelain bowl. She filled it with her menstrual blood. Then raised it to her mouth and drank it.

"She is discovering her own myth," explained India, her gaze riveted upon the woman. "Finding herself." Dutch had to turn away. India found his acute discomfort difficult to understand. "You're a homicide detective. You must've seen worse."

"Yeah. But it's all in the knowing. When you go to the scene of a crime, you know, generally, that whoever wound up there, didn't ask to turn out that way. This is different." Dutch couldn't explain his revulsion any better than that, and kept his back turned until it was over.

The Necro employee, a very young, very pallid, and under-nourished looking teenager, went on guard as soon as India introduced Dutch as a cop. She was cagey, to say the least. But he got just enough information to be useful, then made an excuse and got out of there as quick as he could before he threw up, or started arresting people, or both. Unlike

Scars, this place held no allure for Dutch. No enchanting, sexual élan. Just a bunch of raw and tired puppets enacting Luciferian fantasies.

When they emerged outside, the Bay wind had picked up to a nippy 20 M.P.H. Their matching stride was afflicted with the stiff, irregular gait brought on by the chill. The remainder of the night, India gave Dutch what she called free samples from the Velvet Underground boutique. Taking him to an S&M club, an androgynous bar, and a Torture salon. The common thread in all these places was the use of blood and agony as aphrodisiacs.

By sunup, Dutch had lost many of his prejudices. Still wary, but intrigued. He had become desensitized to the questions of right and wrong. Engaged instead by the moral ambiguity of the acts. In a few short hours, he saw how easy it was to fall into their world.

The other half. The darker side of being.

From his training as a police officer, he recalled the rules of progression into deviance. Take down one wall. Then another, and another, and another. Until anything imaginable appears normal. Pretty soon, the face on the other side of the mirror was unrecognizable.

Dutch was losing the first of those walls.

Even without participating, just by being there, he was taking the initial steps. Baby steps. Soon, he would no longer see the club crowd as deviant. He already began to feel these people were adventurous beyond the humdrum of normalcy. Into a realm of pure sensory perceptions. They chose pain as the conduit. At one point, he looked at India and saw a person of labyrinthine complexity. Her cutting scars were snapshots from journeys into the very heart of fear. Where soul searching began. He felt shallow, jealous pangs and hungered for the experience. But it was still too soon. He wasn't ready yet.

"I hope you had a good time," she said.

"Yes."

India kissed him innocently on the cheek. They'd been touching, teasing, all night. But she smiled her innocent smile and waved a brief goodnight, rolling her fingers the way he had seen Nicole do it. *"Ciao."*

In that moment, Dutch wanted her. He knew it was just a matter of time before he crossed the line.

And when he did, no one could know.

Eight.

"Everyone saw Myke the Dyke go in an hour before Lauren was killed. But nobody can remember Myke leaving," said Dutch.

"Then the alibi will stand," Bishop said, dejected. He held out an open palm. "My money."

Dutch shook his head. "Gentleman's night out."

"Your choice?"

"Absolutely my choice."

"Bullshit."

They were having brunch at Ghirardelli Square, where new construction clambered up alongside the old, red-brick buildings of San Francisco's most famous chocolate factory and woolen mill. The trademark Ghirardelli clock tower, with its original bright electric sign on the roof, chimed the bottom of the hour. 11:30 A.M.

After a brief early morning cloudburst, the skies had quickly cleared. The sun shone down unobstructed. A strong sea breeze inserted pleasantness into the air. Temperatures leveled off in the mid-seventies. No more rain was forecast. Fountain Plaza jumped with color, clamor, and energy. Tourists shopped at the elegant stores, took in the National Maritime Museum, and strode along the Hyde Street and Municipal Piers.

"You're wearing the same clothes," Bishop observed, putting his hand back out.

"Have to do laundry."

"Bullshit."

"Look, if you don't want to keep your end of the deal—"

"I'll treat all right, but I'm calling bullshit on your night alone thing. I mean how do you—she was *there* man—aw, just forget about it." Bishop signaled for the waiter to take their order. Within minutes, he delivered two baskets, each with an open-faced burger, sliced dill pickle, and a generous helping of thick, hand-cut fries.

After the waiter left, Dutch exhaled. "Never hit so many dead ends in an investigation. There's a code of silence around this club scene worse than the force." Dutch shook his head. "They're all so paranoid. Nobody wants their secrets coming to the surface."

Bishop didn't seem bothered. He took it all in stride. Another day. Another case. He dumped a big puddle of ketchup over his fries. "Can you pass me the salt?"

Dutch did so, absently. He was still worked up. Turning it over. Looking for the angles. The right corner to turn in the maze. "Man with a condom? Woman with a dildo? I'm telling you, I don't know if the world is getting sicker, or if we're just getting used to it by degrees."

"Both, I imagine," said Bishop, not seeming to care one way or the other. "With every new tragedy, we expect something worse. These guys out there, they're just fulfilling our expectations." He shook salt over the ketchup. "You just can't let it get too close, is all. Otherwise, you're the one who goes crazy." He put down the shaker and noticed Dutch staring with arched eyebrows of disbelief. "What? Makes the salt stick better." Then proceeded to blend the salt and ketchup with a stirring fry.

"The rest of America is trying to cut down and you're inventing ways for salt to stick better?" Dutch questioned. "You see? This is exactly the kind of sickness I've been talking about."

"Amen," Bishop laughed and took a deliberate, big bite. "Now that's a sickness I can handle."

Dutch called India from the station and thanked her for

last night.

The rest of the day was without incident. The detectives helplessly realized that each hour that went by without a break made the case that much more difficult to crack. They were into the thirty-six of the 24/24, having exceeded the key time on the back end by twelve hours. From now on, the trail would keep getting colder.

Dutch returned to his apartment with no plans for the evening. He thought he'd stay in, order pizza, maybe watch a ball game. But none were on, so he channel surfed. He paused on a celebrity reality show. Within a minute he was bored. He passed over a bunch of reruns. Stopped on sports. Given that he was from Texas, it seemed like he would be into football, but he wasn't. He never played as kid and found being a spectator even more boring. He finally shut the tube off, but kept the scanner chatter on.

His wife, soon to be ex, Elise, blamed his daily contact with violence as the cause for his refusal to let the real world go. Even briefly. Maybe she was right, he thought. He hated movies, too. Always had. Never had the patience to sit in a theater for two hours. Every report card dealing with his conduct carried a notation about his unrelenting seriousness. An intensity his teachers mistook for resentment, sullen behavior, and the typical rebellion against authority. Not true, Dutch thought, he just didn't like to be jerked around.

There was a knock at the door. Dutch got up and looked through the peephole.

No one in the hall. He got his gun and nosed the door open.

"Nicole?" Dutch asked. Surprised.

She stood in silhouette before the large bay window at the end of the corridor. Dressed to kill in a black one-piece that blossomed into a lacy bodice. Looking the full length of her body, her feet kindly nestled in open high heel pumps crisscrossed in elegant spaghetti straps. Her toe nails, fingertips, lips, all the same coordinated shade of red as the choker made of expensive corals circling her neck and ringlets hanging from her ears.

Revealing, yet demure, as always. Dutch couldn't help but smile.

"Hi, Dutch." Then she asked him out to dinner.

Dutch realized he'd been right. Nicole was jealous. This could be a knee-jerk reaction to his night out with India. But he did not believe it was. Nicole was too smart for that. Whatever, he wasn't complaining. Who would? Exceptions made the rule. Nicole and India were that and more to Dr. Tilton's profile of average looks and submissive behavior.

"I have to shower first," he said, and warned her about his apartment before letting her in. Even so, he could tell she was uncomfortable with the sprawling clutter. He cleared a spot for her on the couch. She said she preferred to stand and politely refused his offer of a drink.

Under the steaming jets, Dutch wondered what would happen. When it rains it pours, he thought. He hadn't had a woman since Elise. Now, he had two gorgeous possibilities in India and Nicole.

India had seemed hesitant. Reluctant. Maybe even too innocent, if there was such a thing anymore. And he didn't want to hurt her. But now here was Nicole. Elegant. Refined. Exhilarating. He felt himself stiffen with the very thought of her.

***

Hearing the shower turn on, Nicole busied herself accounting for the small objects and telling details that would give her some insight into the policeman in the shower. He seemed handsome, but awkward, with just enough intelligence to be gullible. He had yet to overturn that opinion. He could be equally shy and bloviate. This, she assumed, came from overcompensation. The ego that went with being a cop. Seeing himself as the thin blue line between order and chaos. She could deal with that, she supposed. As long as it was necessary.

Then she found his art on the walls.

The bleak, solitary landscapes. That's when she became confused. Before that, she had though the was just a typical, lonely cop. Tired of the streets and hookers and lowlifes. Looking for a fraction of warmth and compassion. Someone to take him in and tell him everything was going to be all right.

But these pictures were different. They didn't show isolation so much as self-imposed exile. Dutch's choice to exclude others was deliberate. If true, that made him dangerous.

"Find anything?"

Nicole jumped.

She didn't hear the hiss of the water being shut off. Now Dutch stood behind her. A towel wrapped around his waist. Droplets rolling off his tone body. Dutch worked out three times a week in the police gym. And it showed. He possessed well defined pecs, deltoids, a washboard stomach and powerful arms and legs.

Does he have any secrets? Will he trust anyone? Or is he one of my kind? A calculating hunter. Always patient. Curious. Playing the game. Waiting for the other player to make a mistake.

"Nothing," she said. That was the honest truth. "Nothing at all."

***

They drove in Nicole's Jag to Sutter Street, home to an oh-so-elegant restaurant, *Fleur-de-Lis.*

San Francisco's best French Cuisine.

Dutch felt under-dressed the moment he got out of the car. The valet, who took the keys, recognized her immediately. He'd parked her car before, but it wasn't the car he remembered. There was something about her cat-like eyes that set his motor running. He looked at Dutch, as if sizing up the competition.

Dutch looked like a plain, ordinary schmo to him. Or just another boy-toy for the blonde, who, he thought, reeked of perfection.

Walking in, Dutch felt even more out of place.

The walls were lined in sumptuous red velvet and embroidered with garlands. Formally attired, old-wealth patriarchs with their families were seated at every table—all prominent politicians and businessmen in the Bay area. Nicole recognized some and waved.

"You should have told me it was a jacket and tie affair." Dutch wore a safari shirt, Dockers, and Timberland deck shoes he'd bought on sale for $39.99 at The Boot Mart in Amarillo, Texas, three years ago.

She whispered back, "Sorry, Dutch. Sizzler's not my style."

He regarded her suspiciously. Was she trying to embarrass him? Keep him out of his element and off-guard by making him feel inferior? Maybe that way she could pump him for information about the investigation. Didn't matter. He had nothing.

"Miss Gray. Your table is ready." The maître d' recognized Nicole, but stiffened when he saw Dutch. "Is the gentleman with you?"

"Yes," she said liltingly. Adding syllables to the word. Making even that simple utterance utterly pleasant. "Can you get a jacket." Gave his ensemble a quick once-over and added, "Brown, preferably."

Dutch was about to say something but held his tongue. He wasn't going to let it become that kind of a night.

The maître d' snapped his fingers to a waiter in uniform. "A brown jacket."

He motioned to Dutch with an abrupt gesture. Dutch casually placed his palm over Nicole's open back as they followed the maître d' to their table. Dutch walked between the man and Nicole. The waiter arrived at their table at the same time bearing a size-44, Regular, nut-brown, tweed sports jacket with smoker's patches. It went remarkably well with his khaki trousers and denim banded collar.

"That's better," Nicole said, smoothing the jacket over his shoulders.

Dutch pulled the chair out for her. The maître d' tilted his nose up, just slightly enough to be a rebuke, Dutch ignored it. Where he came from, the man always pulled the chair out for his lady. After he sat down, the maître d' said with a perfectly disinterested enunciation that could be politeness or insult. "Your menu, sir."

Dutch knew where he stood with the guy. Ignored him again. He opened up the menu and his eyes widened. "Do these prices include the silverware?"

Nicole laughed. "It's my treat."

A waiter arrived at their side. "*Bon soir. Je m'appel Henri. Prennez-vous quelque chose de boir?*"

"*Un boteille du Pouille-Fuissé, s'il vous plaît,*" Nicole answered as fluently.

The waiter retreated. Dutch stared at Nicole with a somewhat aggravated appreciation. "Pardon me for saying so, but all this and the club don't exactly add up. What's the catch?"

"Simple," replied Nicole. "Middle class rebellion. My father's a plastic surgeon. And my mother—well, she's a rich man's bored housewife. As a teenager, he went ballistic when all I wanted to do was pierce my nose. Yet, he practically rebuilt Betty Crocker from scratch."

"Betty Crocker?"

"Mom." She shook her head with laugh. "Nose, breasts, ass, eyelids, you name it. There wasn't any part of her anatomy my father didn't fix. So, to spite him, I pierced my belly button. He got so pissed off, I pierced my eyebrows, nipples, tongue." She stuck her tongue out. For the first time, he saw a multi-carat diamond stud at the tip.

"I get the point."

"So did he," she said proudly. "He threw me out of the house when I was fifteen. I worked briefly as a stripper where I learned a great deal about the weaknesses of men. The money was good, but I bored quickly with the fawning faces of college boys and the Kentucky bourbon breath of panhandlers who'd raised enough cash to earn a seat."

She knew how to handle herself, Dutch gave her credit. It was as if she'd dipped her foot in mud and it came out gleaming. A class act, he figured, all the way.

"I moved in with my rich aunt, a New England dowager who *hated* my autocratic father and used her connections to enroll me in Vassar. My MBA was conferred from Columbia— minoring in psychology and entrepreneurial business—before coming out West, where my two worlds came together in *Scars.*"

The waiter returned with a bottle of Thibert Pouille-Fuissé 1997, after which Nicole ordered, *"Nous allons partager des huîtres fraiches et nous aimerions tournedeaux du veau chaque. Merci."* The waiter left. Dutch looked to her inquiringly. She smiled, "Oysters. Its an aphrodisiac."

"You just love to tease, don't you?"

"A woman's prerogative."

"It's not working."

"We'll see. But enough about me. Let's talk about you."

Dutch tossed his shoulders up and down, saying without words there wasn't much to tell and none of it worth discussing. Nicole wasn't buying. Then she surprised him, revealing she had done her homework.

"Bright but not ambitious," she smiled, "you enrolled in accelerated programs all through school—scored extremely high grades. But your somewhat dysfunctional and exclusionary approach led to a brief period of truancy. You did some time in juvy for petty theft and aggravated assault. While incarcerated, you met a Goodwill cop who turned you on to the force, where, in their 'be all you can be' academy—"

"That's the army," Dutch interrupted. "Cops protect and serve."

"Whatever."

He'd pushed a button because she sounded impatient, like she didn't care to be interrupted. Wanted his full attention and respect for her thoroughness. Having gone to a great deal of trouble to have his records pulled, she wanted him to appreciate it.

"The police academy—where you transformed all of your lost hope and lack of conviction into a force for good. A White Knight."

Dutch forced a half-impressed expression. "Do you always get this bent when you get turned down for a fuck?"

She laughed. Unoffended. Delighting in her knowledge of how he worked. What made him tick. When confronted with details of his personal life, he got defensive. Hostile. He couldn't help it. *She knows how to get to me now. How to push my buttons. Fuck.* He'd just been played and he didn't care for it.

It was too easy to lose control with her. And the harder he tried not to give anything away, the easier she took it. Power just seemed to naturally flow toward some people. Nicole was one of them. Always, effortlessly in control. *Maybe I should fuck her.* Maybe that was the way to get to her. Knock her defenses down. Have her lose control. He'd like to see that. Look behind the curtain.

Find the real Nicole Gray.

He turned the idea over briefly, then rejected it. No, that would be a mistake, too. Where most women were weak, she was strong. Nicole had mastered sex. Vulnerability. Made it into a business. Practically an art form. If anybody lost control in the bedroom, it would be him. He'd just wind up giving more away. Until, all too easily, she owned him.

Still, he thought, eyes drifting down her neckline to the voluptuous curvature of her breasts beneath the blossoming lace, he wouldn't mind. He looked up sharply. Her eyes bored into him. Challenging.

She asked, "Now who's teasing?"

The sexual tension at dinner carried over into the ride home, where she double parked outside. It was well past midnight, and being the middle of the week, every window on the street had long since gone dark. The quiet of the night enveloped them.

Nicole tilted her seat back, kicked off her shoes, and raised and rested her bare feet on the dash. Dutch's eyes drifted from the single gold anklet on her left leg, up the shapely calves, to well-exercised thighs. Her hem rode up almost to her hips. His eyes tarried on her breasts, which rose and fell, limned by the street lights.

She caught him staring. Her flinty eyes glinted in the light of a passing car. She had intelligent eyes. Inviting eyes. Like polished water, they had a wonderful liquid quality that distorted depth. Dutch had noticed at dinner, if he asked a question, particularly the wrong question, a ripple would cross the surface and the depth would disappear. Her eyes went flat. And he'd be shut out.

"Cigarette?" She produced her gold case.

Dutch accepted and lit hers.

Nicole's lips parted slightly as he brought the flame near. An inviting door, Dutch thought, but a false one. He knew he'd never get anything resembling objective truth out of her. Like a sculptor pulling an image from unformed clay, she revealed only what she wanted him to see. She cupped his hand unnecessarily and he could feel electricity passing through her fingers. *Shit. Can't even touch her without losing control.* They lit up.

Nicole leaned away, exhaling a feather of smoke out the driverside window. "I had a boyfriend in college who cheated on me. I found out and confronted him in his dorm room. We were alone and the fight got out of hand. I grabbed his Swiss Army knife and held the blade to his throat. He jerked, I cut him. There was a lot of blood."

She paused.

"He kept screaming, 'You fucking bitch, you fucking bitch, you cut me, you fucking bitch.' And I yelled, 'Go back to your whore. Get your fucking whore to help you!'" Nicole's voice faded to a whisper, "When we finally stopped shouting, I took a towel and held it to his neck. But there was so much blood it flowed onto my fingers. Then, on impulse, I licked it off."

She turned her head, looked into Dutch's eyes. "It was erotic as hell."

Dutch realized his lips were dry. His self-control edged closer to breakdown.

Nicole looked away, a light breeze blew through the window and a lock of hair curled seductively over one eye. "We didn't talk about it for a few days, but neither of us could stop thinking about it. The next time we had sex, we drank red wine because it slows coagulation. We slapped each other to accelerate circulation. Then, to really get him going, I gave him head. When he said he was ready, I jumped on top. And that's when I grabbed the knife."

"You cut him?" Dutch asked.

Nicole nodded. "And he loved it."

"Where?"

"The chest and stomach, mostly." Her fingers traced three Xs across her own body.

"What about you—"

"Sure. I did it, too. After he came, we took a breather. Drank some more wine. And when I was really drunk, he turned me over. He cut my back and I felt just enough of the burn to have the best climax of my life."

Dutch couldn't believe what he was hearing.

"With cutting," Nicole continued, looking deep into his eyes, "the connection you feel with your partner is complete, pure, unadulterated. Your lives are totally in each other's hands. It's like...love. There's no other word to describe it."

India had said the *exact* same thing.

"You have to be shown," said Nicole.

That, too.

The heat in her stare was undeniable. The invitation left hanging in the thin space between them. Nicole raised herself, and like a reflection in the mirror, so did he. Hypnotically drawn by her rose-petal lips. Redolent breath. She was irresistible. *Damn, here we go.* The V of her bodice folded open.

He could see the arousal of her breasts. Her legs still rested on the dash, moving from side to side, naturally bent at the knees. The short dress bunched up around her waist. Exposing black lace panties. She made no move to cover them. Instead, her hand slipped behind his head, the fingers knotting his hair.

Dutch felt his scalp tingle.

His erection grew with the pressure of her touch, which mounted, as she pulled his face down toward hers. She opened her mouth, white teeth shining, lips seeking his. Inches away, she closed her eyes. At the last moment, Dutch turned his face.

The kiss planted firmly on his cheek.

"Thanks for an interesting evening," he said.

Nicole opened her eyes, stunned. She'd probably never been rejected. Dutch relished the moment. By getting a hold of himself at the last instant, he'd maintained equal ground. It was a victory, to be sure, but that didn't solve his dilemma. She was no less vulnerable and he hadn't gotten any concrete details that would help him on the case.

She was still an enigma.

Dutch got out of the car without another word. He shut the door and leaned down. "Goodnight."

"Aren't you to going to ask me up?" she asked. A touch

plaintive.

"Man's prerogative."

If she was disappointed, she didn't show it. She just tilted her head, raised her eyebrows, and blew him a kiss. "Next time."

Gratified by the recollection that she had immediately bristled when he pulled away, he smiled, "We'll see."

She drove away with a punctuating rev of the engine.

***

Around the corner, Nicole's brake lights glowed. Gillette dogtrotted out of the shadows and climbed in.

"The man lives like a pig—" began Gillette.

"Later," Nicole cut him off. "I'm wet." She pulled up at the stop sign. Gillette's insistent hand raced over her body. He pulled the top of her dress down and began sucking her nipples. Driving her passion up another notch.

She pushed his head away.

"Let's go to India's."

***

Dutch flopped onto the couch, thinking of what might have been if he'd said yes to Nicole. He turned on the TV. Flipped through the usual 11 P.M. soft core fare. That didn't make it any easier. He turned off the set and tried to listen to the monotonous, static-ridden chatter of the police scanner. That helped. A little. The buzz in his head eased and the bulge in his crotch subsided. Dutch grabbed a half-empty beer from the end table. Stuck to the bottom was the crumpled napkin from *Scars.* He plucked it off and read the single line of unfamiliar script.

India's address and phone number.

***

Stretching from Buena Vista to Golden Gate Park,

Haight-Ashbury provided an escape from downtown San Francisco in 1880. Eight decades of suburban middle-class occupation followed. The demographics changed abruptly in the 1960s, when thousands of hippies moved into the late Victorian homes. Ever since, this neighborhood strove to maintain its unconventional image, with a residential and commercial mix that could only be called eclectic.

India fit in perfectly.

She lived in a fourplex, one of the many ornate homes built on the steep gradient of Masonic Avenue. She'd decorated her one-bedroom, ground floor apartment to the left of the entry way in the same style as her art. Japanese. Spare, light, and airy. Utilizing large mirrors cleverly, she made the space seem larger than its four hundred and fifty square feet.

As late as it was, India worked with deep concentration. She had just finished carving an intricate figure on the side of a small wooden block—a woman stepping into a bath, kimono falling from her shoulders.

India's dark hair swayed at her waist, gathered into a single bale by an oxblood ribbon. Every now and then, she blew forelocks from her eyes as she carved the Kento guide marks around the four corners. This was designed to be a polychromatic print, so she had to make sure the color dyes registered in proper position. India picked up a brush to dust off the shavings, then adjusted her reading glasses to appraise what she'd accomplished. The print was traditional, exemplifying the same loving devotion to the form and detail of the human anatomy that reached its height in the Ukiyoe school of the Kansei era from 1789-1801.

Nodding satisfaction, she looked up at the clock and winced. She didn't realize it was so late. She had an early art workshop tomorrow and would apply the ink in class. She stood straight up from a cross-legged sitting position. The short, peppermint blue robe rustling briefly at the tops of her legs. Stretching her arms over her head, she rose to the tips of her toes. A tired purr escaped her throat.

The doorbell chimed softly.

India dropped her arms. *Who can it be at this hour?* It chimed again. Insistently. The tinkling of fluted wind. She padded barefoot across the living room and put her eye against the peephole. Her shoulders relaxed. She drew back the dead bolt, undid the night latch, and opened the door. Her face broke into a smile.

"This is a surprise."

Nine.

The delivery truck pulled up with a whine of brakes. The driver, youthful, Hispanic, hopped out, went to the back, and heaved the box of art supplies onto the dolly. It was addressed to: *India Algieri.* He knew India. She was a regular customer. And he suffered from a huge crush on her. He always timed his route around her workshop to be sure she would be home to sign for her deliveries. He wheeled the parcel up the brick path to her front door. He smoothed down his hair with the flat of his hand, cleared his throat, and knocked.

The door swung open a crack.

He peered in apprehensively. It offered only a narrow view and he didn't want to press it open any further in case she had accidentally left it open. He couldn't see anything. Just a long, empty hallway with a guest chair and a few pieces of her original art hanging on the clean, white walls.

He stayed beyond the threshold and hollered, "India!"

No answer.

He listened closely. He thought he heard something inside. A man's voice? He set the dolly down and walked to the side of the house. There was a small, divided French window, where, if he stood on his toes, he could see into the kitchen. He raised up on rough worker's boots and looked inside.

Suddenly, something flashed across the window!

He jumped back and nearly fell over, before realizing it was only her cat. A gray and black striped tabby. He'd always found it unsociable. It usually hissed at him when he made deliveries. But today, it jumped on the kitchen counter and looked at him curiously.

After a second, it began to mewl.

"*Buenos dìas, loco,*" he said tapping on the glass.

The tabby rubbed its head against the clear window pane. He took the opportunity to peer inside once more and this time he could just make out the man's voice. "...Coltrane for you on a sunny Monday morning. Coming up next, we've got Miles Davis, Dexter Gordon, and the vocal stylings of the inimitable Ella Fitzgerald."

The Monday morning Jazz hour on National Public Radio. He backed away from the window. Not wanting to be mistaken for a peeping tom. He hoofed it back to the front door and knocked again.

"India!"

Still no answer.

The second knock forced the heavy door open a little more. This time, he noticed that a second guest chair at the end of the long corridor was upturned. Four legs skyward. Helpless. Like an overturned beetle. One of the legs broken. He began to sweat. He checked the street to see if anyone was looking, then he took one step inside her apartment.

"Miss India!? *Està aquì?*"

There was blood on the hardwood floor.

"Jesus," he said, and immediately crossed himself.

Rather than going in any further, he quickly retreated back outside. He had to think fast. He knew what happened when bad shit went down and he didn't want to be arrested just because he was the first Hispanic on the scene. He had a mother and sister in Los Mochis, who counted on him for money. He couldn't let the death of some gringa screw it up. Still, if he didn't do something, that might turn out to be worse. He wiped his brow with a handkerchief. He was about to pull the door closed and get the hell out of there, when he saw something.

Mud. On the floor. He must have tracked it in from the

side of the house.

Now he really was screwed. Holding the handkerchief, he got an idea. He looked around quickly, got on his hands and knees, and crawled inside. Ahead, just below eye level, he could see where the dried blood had spilled. He swabbed up the mud in the handkerchief, making sure his boots did not touch the floor, and backed out carefully.

If someone saw him...

Fortunately, her front door was semi-cloistered because of the narrow brick walkway and trellised hedges covered in bougainvillea. His eyes scanned the street. Still clear. He knocked the dirt from the cloth over the garden plants and made sure it was clean. Then he turned it over and rubbed the door handles inside and out, erasing his fingerprints.

That should do it.

He pushed the door open, so he could clearly see the overturned chair and blood from the entryway, left the dolly where it was, and broke into a furious run. Leaping aboard his truck, he grabbed the radio in the cab and asked his dispatcher to call 911.

***

Dutch and Bishop walked in.

Their drive over had been quiet. When the call came in, they'd been reviewing the case. Bishop saw Dutch go still, close his eyes, and when he opened them, the brief shadow of emotion had passed. Dutch waved off the condolence forming on Bishop's lips. He just stood up, grabbed his coat and gun, and made for the door. Bishop felt obliged to show some kind of sympathy, but he also respected Dutch's silence.

The police had found India on her back in bed. Naked.

"Should have the TOD soon," Dr. Pease, the jocular medical examiner, looked up, seeing the detectives. Time of death. He was bent over her body. Dry blood smeared her breasts, belly, and legs. Except for badly cut knees and palms, he found no wounds. He looked at her curiously, slipped on a pair of latex gloves, and turned the body on its side.

Bishop pursed his lips. Hundreds of tiny cuts zigzagged along her back. Pieces of glass protruded from several shallow punctures. Unlike Lauren Piolene, the previous victim, Bishop saw no discernible pattern. Dutch kneeled beside the ME, pushed her hair back, and checked her neck.

India's throat was cut in the same signature as Lauren's.

"Hair follicles in the back of her skull are uprooted," said Dr. Pease. "There's evidence of subcutaneous hemorrhaging."

Bishop moved on. A police photographer flashed off evidence pictures. Techs and forensics teemed like ants all over the apartment. Magno was there. Kim Lee, too. Bishop stopped beside Lee, who knelt beside a wide swath of red streaked across the floor at the end of the entryway. This was the blood the driver had spotted. They were busy questioning him outside and the kid looked scared. Too scared. Bishop figured right away he didn't do it. But they could still charge him for destroying evidence. His panic-stricken wipe down may have cleaned off the killer's prints or other clues.

"Hi, guys," greeted Lee. "You'd think we'd find a set of prints in all this blood." He shook his head. "*Nada.*"

"Spanish for none," translated Bishop.

"Thank you," Dutch replied curtly, walking up. "You're keen as a Chinaman." He turned to Lee, "No offense."

"None taken, I'm Korean," he said.

"Was she killed here?" Bishop asked.

"A lot of fucking happened here, that's for sure," said Lee, nodding to the floor, then the chair, coffee table, rug, and finally couch, where extensive bleeding had dried and wrinkled the fabric over the cushions. The police photographer's camera flash highlighted shards of glass.

"What's with the glass?" Bishop asked.

"It's from that table lamp." Lee pointed to a shade and pedestal rolling separately on the floor nearby, "They broke the bulb, then laid on top of it."

"You're kidding me?" Bishop said.

"I couldn't be kidding you less," Lee replied.

"What about the murder?" Dutch asked.

Lee nodded to the bedroom. Dr. Pease was still hunched over the corpse. Behind him, a pair of miniature bonsai trees stood symmetrically at either end of the ledge inside the windows. Damask curtains fluttered in dense pleats and cut off visibility from the outside, where neighbors in the adjacent building loitered curiously. Directly over the bed, a square Japanese lantern hung low, encasing a red bulb that still burned dimly.

Magno emerged from the adjoining bathroom. "Dutch. Can I see you for a second?"

Bishop and Dutch walked over and stopped in the doorway. Linoleum covered the floor. A sink stood behind the entry. The mirrored shutter of the medicine cabinet gaped open, the contents already examined and tagged. Next to the sink was the toilet. Magno had put the seat down and shut the lid to lay his kit on it. A scented candle sat on the porcelain top of the flush tank. He'd clipped a 'Police Do Not Touch' marker to the curtain.

Bishop walked in but Dutch lingered at the door.

Magno knelt by the bath tub, which doubled as a shower and stretched from wall to wall across the width of the bathroom at the far end. "Got some hair fibers that don't belong to the vic," said Magno, holding one between forceps. "Caucasian, at first glance."

"Eliminates the driver," Bishop said.

"The drains are testing positive for blood. It's like our killer didn't just wash, but took a shower and—" Magno's voice trailed off.

"And what?" Dutch asked sharply.

"Shaved."

Bishop returned to bedroom.

"No semen," Dr. Pease pronounced as he walked by. The ME peeled off his latex gloves and placing them in an evidence bag with a blue tag. "Same M.O. as the previous victim, but instead of cutting with a razor, we have glass doing more or less the same thing. There was no art to it this time, no premeditation to the design. They shattered the bulb, rolled around on top of it, and Ba-da-boom! Ba-da-bing!" Dr. Pease punched his open palm for emphasis. "Nirvana."

Bishop stopped listening. He saw Dutch in the mirror glare over at the ME.

"What?" Dr. Pease shrugged defensively.

His partner seemed in no mood for hangman's humor. In fact, Bishop saw Dutch's features soften for the first time, like something inside him was breaking up. India looked so innocent. So lovely. They'd been out on date just a couple of days ago. Maybe the realization of what had happened to her was overwhelming him.

Dr. Pease pointed to India's cut knees and palms. "The last act was anal sex. That's probably when the murderer pulled her hair back and, well, you know." He pointed to a cater-cornered line across her throat. "Ended it. Similar position, similar act to the companion case in the car. But, whoever did this, didn't wait until after intercourse—"

Bishop's eyes sharpened suddenly. He approached the mirror on the wall facing the bed. Placed exactly in the center opposite the four-poster, it offered a clear view of the sheets, mattress, and India's body. There was no question in his mind that it had been positioned there to enhance sex. Bishop reached out and touched the glass surface with his index finger. A distinct *space* showed between his finger and the reflection of his finger in the mirror.

Bishop stepped closer.

Traced his finger up the mirror. Just above the center, the finger shadow vanished. Bishop's brow crinkled. His finger and the mirror finger now touched. "Son of a bitch," he muttered, then shouted, "Got something!"

He glimpsed Dutch's reflection reacting sharply as he slid the mirror aside, revealing a hidden compartment. Within, a revolving base plate supported a hand-held, portable, hi-def, *video camera.* Its lifeless lens stared directly at the bed in one direction and the living room in the other.

"A camera?" Dutch asked tensely.

Bishop gave it a close once-over. "This isn't just any camera. Motion sensitive. Turns on automatically. HD, IR, low light, this shit is the cat's meow."

"You're fuckin' kidding me." Dutch loped over.

"Probably taped whatever happened both in the living room and out here," Bishop said excitedly, hoping his discovery could tie up the case before lunch. He tried to lift the camera out, but the base plate was bolted down. He saw twin release levers and depressed them. The camera came off the plate. It was so small, it fit in the palm of his hand. He saw an icon and recognized it. "Oh, yeah."

"What?" Dutch asked, his brow furrowing.

"We may have something here." Bishop pointed to the icon. "This baby goes below the visual spectrum and sees heat. It then recreates color by measuring wavelengths of temperature. If we're lucky, we can get a false-color positive off the tape." He grinned, "Even in the dark, we don't all look alike."

Dutch went quiet as Bishop pressed the eject button to pop the tape. There was a short whine and the mechanical grinding of tiny gears. The cassette door opened.

Bishop looked up. Disappointed. "No tape."

Almost on cue, a uniform ran into the bedroom and exclaimed breathlessly, "We've got an eyewitness!"

***

The line-up hall. Nothing intimidated a criminal more than being led into one, which, in any station, was quite non-threatening and plain. A drab, featureless, windowless rectangle, it usually comprised of a long, blank wall that ran parallel to the waist-to-ceiling, one-way glass. The bright green-white illumination from an egg-carton fluorescent cluster revealed more than it flattered.

That was the point, Schiff felt. Even someone as ravishing and self-confident as Nicole looked plain and frightened. Through her unease, he'd noticed her spare Bishop, Dutch, and he a withering glare as she'd walked by them earlier. When he issued the warrant, Schiff specifically instructed the arresting officers to refuse to let her change. So, when she came in, she didn't have on a lick of make-up. She looked angry.

Schiff knew the look well. He was going to catch hell if it didn't pan out because he'd let it leak to the media that they had a suspect. There were cameras outside waiting for his statement.

Nicole stood next to a couple of hookers with similar body type and features. Staring straight ahead. The unflattering light robbed her of her polish and sophistication. Her mouth lost its seductive pout without lipstick, compressed instead into a thin, unattractive line. She blinked frequently, betraying an uneasiness that bordered on fear. It was worse for her, Schiff thought, than if she'd been stripped naked.

Schiff sipped his coffee, peering at Dutch over the steam rising from the small Styrofoam cup. His detective had that look. Like he didn't want Nicole to be involved. Schiff couldn't blame Dutch. She was smokin'. But Schiff was running out of patience. She and Gillette were the prime suspects. He kept his fingers crossed and hoped for a positive ID.

Next down the line was that transsexual or cross-dresser or whatever the fuck he/she was—Myke the Dyke. Beside him/her a pale Caucasian two-time-loser-turned-informant named Larry, who Schiff had pulled out the cell, then Gillette, and a couple of female cons waiting for transfer to County.

Gillette hadn't bothered to hide his murderous

expression either as he'd passed the cops. Unlike Nicole, whose apprehension had occurred behind a tall fence, out of public view, Gillette had suffered the indignity of being escorted out of his apartment in broad daylight. His front door opened directly to the street, so his affluent neighbors had watched the policemen hustle him into the waiting squad car. Lightband prominently flashing. It was a circus. Schiff had a feeling the other tenants had no idea what he did for a living, but he could be sure, when he got back, the reception from the condo committee would be appropriately frigid. There would be questions and probably some kind of internal investigation. Innocent until proven guilty was how the system looked at things, not individuals. If there was a foul odor in the air, there was a dead body. Gillette knew he was already convicted in the court of public opinion whether he liked it or not. Police, after all, didn't go around arresting innocent people. There had to be something categorically wrong with the man getting his head forced down into the back of the patrol car. And when they found out about *Scars,* Gillette was as good as gone.

An officer entered the line-up hall, shut the door, and began to instruct them on the rules of the line-up hall.

"Looks like we got all our ducks in a row," Schiff said smiling. "Let's do it."

"This line-up is too soon," Dutch continued his protest. "We don't have Briganza—"

"He is *a* suspect, not *the* suspect," dismissed Schiff. *Snap!* The hard-nosed heavy. "You didn't think Briganza was the killer anyway. So look at it this way. Now he won't be a distraction. Besides, you've always zeroed in on Nicole and Ginzu."

"Gillette," Bishop corrected.

Snap! Schiff rolled his eyes. "I know. I was making a joke. The guy's a perv. Now we're gonna nail his ass." If Gillette was guilty, Nicole likely was in on it, too. Schiff wondered how Dutch would take that.

The officer came out of the line-up hall. He stepped over confidentially. "Lieutenant, we need one more white guy to play it fair."

"Play it fair?" Dutch asked incredulously.

"Yeah," Schiff said. "Since we don't know what the fuck Myke the Dyke is, we only got one white guy in the whole bunch besides Razor Burn. If the kid is leaning toward a Caucasian male, it will look like we set one or both of them up. Then Nicole and her high-priced attorneys will make sure the press is all over this like ten dogs shittin' in a one dog yard. I don't want any of their smartass legal analysts playing that into a race issue."

"It's a white guy," said Bishop. "What are they gonna do? Burn a Bentley in Pacific Heights?"

"Hey, that race card shit cuts both ways."

"No way a minority can be racist," Bishop disagreed. "It goes against the definition."

"What definition is that?"

"The race in power discriminates against those not in power."

"Fuck that. Anybody can be racist. It's an attitude, not a social class." Schiff surveyed the near-empty squad room. Between shifts, few cops stuck around, none male and Caucasian. He turned to Dutch. "I guess it's you."

"You're kidding?"

"You see me kidding? You see any other white guys in here?!" *Snap!* Schiff went off the scale. "What is it with everyone in this precinct? Does nobody listen?" He made a mental note to tighten up the discipline a notch. "You see Dutch? This is what we call sucks-to-be-you. Now get your narrow ass in there before you start emptying parking meters."

"Great," Dutch grumbled. "Now I'm the minority."

"That's right, Dutch. The federal prison system is sixty-six percent other. You are the minority. So go in there and help out your poor white brother." Schiff shoved Dutch between the shoulders toward the ajar door of the line-up hall.

"I don't fucking believe this," Dutch complained and went in.

The officer shut the door, locked it, and stood guard outside. His hand rested conspicuously on the unbuttoned hip holster of his sidearm. Upon positive ID, suspects had been known to make break for it. Not today.

Schiff and Bishop entered the adjoining identification room behind the two-way glass. It looked like a luxury box by comparison. The lights worked off a dimmer. There were chairs, a table, water cooler, and a telephone. The wall-mounted microphone blared instructions to the perps under scrutiny from an aging speaker above the suspects' heads.

Schiff turned toward the eyewitness.

Alex Teiss. A kid, maybe twelve years old.

Schiff frowned. Kids didn't make for reliable witnesses and he was pinning his hopes of a conviction on this one. A tough call by any standards. Add to that, the kid wore a pair of glasses that would lead the blind to see, and Schiff's job was that much worse. *Snap!* The picture of hospitality.

"Whenever you're ready," said Schiff encouragingly.

The kid looked at his father, who nodded approval, and slowly stepped up to the pane glass window.

"Brave kid," Bishop whispered to Schiff.

"Yeah, yeah," muttered Schiff impatiently. He couldn't wait to go before the cameras. He'd even had a haircut and pulled out the suit he wore only to the Governor's annual police dinner. Schiff approached the kid, sifting through the meandering statement they'd gotten out of him.

A paper boy for the *Chronicle*. He had been riding his bike, an original Schwinn Excelsior with a coaster brake and skinwall tires, on his 4 A.M. route, when he came across the scene of the crime.

The morning had been cold. In his statement, Alex remembered his fingers being numb from racing up and down the wildly sloping streets. He'd wanted to get an early start because he had to finish homework for Western Civilization that he hadn't completed the night before. The trees were bare. Leaves damp and scattered. The kid knew his details. And had vocabulary too, calling the sky a dull anvil. He'd turned off Sparrow onto Caledonia to make his first run. The saddle bags were full, heavy ballast on either side, as he pulled the first paper and tossed it. A perfect pitch all the way to the porch. *Thump!* Landing right before the door without striking it. He made his way down the street, braking occasionally.

That's when he heard a muted scream.

He hit the skids in front of India's house and waited. He thought he saw a faint red light from the side of the house and parked along the hedge. The bike was large and the heavy bags made it unwieldy. Difficult to disguise. He pushed it as far as he could into the bushes, still damp with morning dew, and pulled his shirt up over his face to hide his visible breath.

"I waited for what seemed like an eternity," he told the cops. Heart thumping, creeping up out of his chest, into his throat. Making it difficult to breathe. Or hear. Or think clearly. Glass broke or was shattered. He heard the solid rush of footsteps...how many, he couldn't be sure.

Then *someone* opened the back door.

Alex's eyes wavered behind the thick lenses. Cerulean. Uncertain. Flanking either side, Schiff and Bishop stared with him through the two-way glass. Schiff dimmed the lights. All three of their reflections vanished, allowing a clear view of the men in the line-up.

"Don't worry, Alex," Schiff said. "They can't see us. We can see them, but they can't see us, okay?"

Alex bobbed his head. Schiff watched Dutch fall in stiffly beside Gillette. The cutter flung Dutch a baleful glance, but when his head turned forward to face the icy, reflective glass, his eyes flickered with apprehension. The room was cold and boxy and he felt like a bug being pinned in a display case.

Schiff noticed Dutch fidget. Look down the line. The lieutenant followed Dutch's eyes to Myke the Dyke, whose face was sculpted in stone. A still, geodesic expression. Gone were the slinking, feline qualities. Myke resembled an ugly, menacing transvestite caught in the middle of transformation, but the direction of sexual change remained unclear.

The kid looked at Bishop and faltered, "There could have been a second person, I guess. He looked back, like I said, you know, but, I...well, got scared when he looked back, and I..." Bishop waited patiently. Schiff twitched restlessly. Alex added, embarrassed, "closed my eyes."

"That's all right," Bishop assured him. "You were scared. People do that when they're scared." They really did. Just like an ostrich. They closed their eyes and thought they could hide.

Schiff shifted his weight irritably from one foot to the other. *Snap!* A low growl entered his voice. "Just look closely. Try to remember." He pointed stiffly. "Do you recognize anybody in that line-up?"

Hearing the change in the lieutenant's tone, his father took a protective step closer. Alex squinted. Moving his entire head as he traveled face to face, left to right. Dutch. Gillette. All the way to Myke, who he gazed at interminably. Just when Schiff and Bishop thought they'd nailed him, Alex shifted to Gillette and scrutinized him just as long. Came back to Larry. Then breezed across the line to Dutch.

This was going no-fucking-where. Schiff knew if he wanted his case to stick with the kid as the only witness, an immediate and unequivocal ID was going to be his strongest ally. He barked, "Is it any one of them?"

The kid's father stepped closer, about to intervene. Schiff raised a cautionary hand. The father's eyes narrowed in rebuke. Schiff didn't care. With the fiasco down at the wharf, if the kid came up empty, he might as well go outside and puke on himself in front of the media.

Alex was anxious and would not be hurried. He shuffled

and adjusted the coke bottle glasses on the bridge of his nose, which almost touched the glass.

Schiff could practically hear the defense attorney shouting 'Objection!' to the very idea of tendering this legally blind kid as an eyewitness. Alex peered closely again at Gillette, then Myke the Dyke, then to Gillette one last time. Finally, Alex raised a shaking finger. "That's him."

Schiff rolled his eyes. "Are you sure?"

"You saying it can't be him?" asked the kid's father, butting in, as if Alex was doing them a favor just by being there, and he wasn't going to let his boy be pushed around.

Schiff had enough from the father and he didn't like his overprotective attitude. This was a fucking homicide. He waved for Bishop to quiet the father down, then huddled in front of Alex, blocking his line of sight. "Just take it easy, okay, son? We want to do this right, don't we?" Alex nodded. "So I want you to think about it. Think real hard. Everything's going to be okay. Just try to remember. Is that the man you saw?" The kid tried to get a look at his father, but Schiff stayed in the way. "Out there, Alex, not in here. Look out there now. At the line up."

Alex's eyes darted from the cops to the line-up. Lips trembling. Searching for words his brain couldn't piece together. He looked diffident. Uncertain. He tried to get a glimpse of his dad.

Snap! Schiff lost it. "Is it?!"

"Hey!" interjected the kid's father.

Bishop shook his head. A quick warning. Schiff glared over. This was how it was done. Switching tactics. If the kid was going to crack, he'd better do it now. Not in front of a jury. That would blow their case wide open.

The kid stammered, "D-Dad?"

"Not to him. To me," Schiff insisted.

"I-I'm pret-ty su-sure. It was still kind of dark and all. I-I only saw him for a second—"

"Alex. Is it him or not?"

"Y-yes, sir." Then he said it firmly, "Yes, that's him."

"Point him out again," Schiff said, "just to be sure."

The kid's entire arm trembled from shoulder to fingertip.

Schiff lowered his eyes in disappointment.

Alex aimed unmistakably at Dutch.

***

Schiff slammed the door! The entire partition rattled like pebbles rolling down a rooftop. Sound vanished from the squad room. Phones, printers, radios, everything seemed bound in a state of suspended animation. All eyes and ears were focused in the same direction.

The lieutenant's office.

Inside, Schiff and Bishop stood unified beside the desk. Dutch stood across from them. Alone.

"You fucked her!" Schiff exploded. "I can't believe you fucked her!"

Dutch didn't react. He seemed immune. Patiently waiting.

"I can believe it, but I can't fucking believe it," Bishop murmured unobtrusively. Already accepting it as a matter of course, but doubting its internal logic. Schiff stared at him until he lost his enthusiasm to speak. Bishop concluded quickly, "If you know what I mean."

"Why the fuck didn't you tell us?!" Schiff shouted. His voice carried readily to the attentive ears outside. "Were you hoping we wouldn't find out? This ain't the military, Dutch. This ain't don't-ask-don't-tell."

Dutch broke his silence. "I didn't do it."

"Didn't do what? Kill her?!" Schiff asked at the top of his voice. "Because we already know you fucked her! We know all about that!"

"I didn't kill her," Dutch said firmly.

But not firmly enough, Schiff felt. He leaned forward

and placed his hand behind his ear. "Say it again, Dutch. Tell me how you didn't kill her one more time. I want to hear bells. Saintly fucking bells that ring of holy truth."

"I didn't kill her," Dutch repeated.

Anger burning on a short fuse, Schiff recognized. He wanted his detective to lose it. That's when perps talked without thinking. Bared what they'd buried in their subconscious. So, Schiff erupted, "Goddamnit! This is Houston all over again!"

"What's Houston got to do with this?"

Schiff watched Dutch's fuse burn off a little more. *Come on, come on.* Schiff asked rhetorically. "How long do you think it's going to take for the media to pull your file?"

"I was cleared."

"With more questions than answers!" Schiff sat down on the edge of his desk, completely exasperated. "You come here. I give you a fresh start." He shook his head, "I'm pulling you off this case."

"What?!" snapped Dutch.

"It's your prints, your hair, all over the apartment! Isn't it? Shit. Don't even answer that." He stood up again just as quickly. "Then we're all fucked." Pacing like a tiger in a cage. "Consider yourself lucky I'm not arresting your ass right now!"

"What about the first victim? I didn't—"

"Nobody's shown me anything that suggests the two murders are connected."

"What the—" Dutch's expression hardened.

Schiff leaned forward. *The burn is near the end of his fuse.* A spark away from flaring up.

"Fucking perfect! Nicole and Gillette set me up."

Schiff wagged a warning finger. "Don't stretch your neck too far, Dutch. You got just about enough rope to hang yourself."

Flashpoint! *Here he goes.*

"Fucking bullshit! This is fucking bullshit and you

know it!" Dutch slammed a fist into Schiff's desk and turned to leave. Without breaking stride, he snarled at Bishop. "You could've jumped in any time, you know. You're supposed to be my fucking partner!"

Dutch pulled the door open, stepped out, and blasted it shut with even more ferocity than Schiff had done.

Fuckfuckfuckfuck! He's innocent or too damn clever. The wood and glass finally stopped shaking. Schiff looked at the scattered pencils, pens, and spilled coffee. "Now who's going to clean this shit up?"

"Don't look at me," Bishop said. "My people are done with that."

"Are you trying to be funny?" *Snap!* The lieutenant flopped into his chair with a heavy sigh. "I give up."

Bishop pulled up a chair and sat down. "You don't really think he did it, do you?"

Schiff tossed a plain, padded, brown envelope across his desk. "His confidential IAD file from Houston. Came in today. No postmarks. No prints. Hand delivered. Read it."

Bishop looked the anonymous envelope over. Pulled out the stapled sheets. Skimmed down the page. Flipped it over. And over. And over.

"This goes back to when he first joined the force," said Schiff, motioned toward the pages. "A couple of years after he entered Robbery/Homicide, a stripper was beheaded. Dutch was the lead detective. Fucked her friend. She turned up dead."

Bishop looked at the report. "Beheaded."

"Three years ago, some hobo was killing whores at train stations. Strangling them with bootlaces. Dutch got the case. Put the hobo away, but the DA couldn't pin one of the victims on the hobo."

Bishop skimmed the pages. "Dutch was with her the night before."

"I'd like to think it's a dick thing, but I think it's a Dutch thing."

"I see your point, but let's get real. Serial killers aren't that patient. They're obsessive. Even a copycatter. They're not going to wait ten years to strike again."

Schiff shrugged.

Bishop added, "Or maybe it's just bad luck. Dutch slept with a stripper. She got murdered. Nailed a whore. She got whacked. That's unfortunate, but it's not uncommon. In the real world, it ain't *Pretty Woman*. Strippers and whores eat kibbles and bits for breakfast. They do coke, smack, get beat up, raped, and sometimes die. It doesn't sell tickets, but it happens."

Schiff wasn't convinced. "One's an accident. Two's a coincidence. Three's a fucking pattern."

Ten.

The telephone was ringing when Dutch let himself into his attic apartment. He hurried across the brown shag carpet and grabbed the phone. "Yeah?"

"Hi." It was Nicole. She lay sprawled on the plush couch of her office at *Scars*. Alone. "Are you okay?"

"Why wouldn't I be?" Dutch answered curtly.

"First, the kid fingers you," she said, almost sounding amused that the tables had turned. "Then you lose your badge—"

"What do you want?" Dutch cut her off. After the line-up, he expected retaliation. The coy undercurrent to her voice was taking him for a spin and he wanted it to stop.

"Maybe I don't want anything *from* you," she said, sounding hurt.

Dutch shut his eyes and composed himself. His predicament was his own doing. No fault of hers. If Gillette was in on it, or Myke for that matter, maybe she wasn't. Maybe he was getting it all wrong. He felt confused. Muddled. Pressure closing in on all sides.

"Maybe I just want...you," she added seductively.

Shit. Why this? Why now? "I'm sorry, Nic." He realized after he said it that he'd never abbreviated her name before. Was he feeling that close to her? Or was he figuring a way out of the fire by going back in. He couldn't be sure. It was getting to be too much.

"Why don't you come over to the house?" she asked invitingly.

"Look, India's dead."

"Yes. That's sad." Almost sounding it.

"I don't know if it's such a good idea."

"Oh, come on," she purred. When Dutch didn't answer, she asked, "What if I said the magic word?"

"Please?"

"Jacuzzi."

Half an hour later, headlights blazing, his SUV appeared out of the light drizzle weeping down and passed through tall wrought-iron gates leading to her luxurious seven million dollar estate. The curving driveway climbed under a canopy of spectacular hemlock trees bathing in the rain.

She'd told him *Scars* wasn't open on Mondays and she could be home in an hour. Dutch decided to go, not out of any need to be with someone in his current depression. No. He always handled crises alone. But he realized more and more that his career depended on solving this case. To exonerate himself from the unanswered questions about his past.

Needles showered and fell on the road, giving his wheels a soft, blanketed ride up her driveway. The obscuring foliage held him in suspense until the very last moment. Then the natural cover broke away in a dramatic reveal.

A three-storied mansion sat atop the tallest, most imposing residential hill in the Bay area. Circumventing balconies under castellated pinnacles offered commanding, panoramic views of San Francisco in all four directions.

Dutch drove under the porte-cochere, wide enough to hold two cars, and supported by magnificent marble Ionic columns, which stretched a full twenty feet high. He thought the house was very much like Nicole—authoritative, discerning, bold, tasteful, and inviting. But not easily approached. Nicole's Jaguar was parked against the steps sweeping up toward the tall, solid oak, front entrance. The four-car garage was open. Deliberately? To show off a Ferrari, an Aston Martin, and a Bentley.

When he climbed out of his car, Nicole was waiting. She stood at the door in a long, white shirt, with her monogram neatly embroidered on the pocket. The light behind her, from inside the house, rendered the fabric translucent and silhouetted her body within.

"So glad you could come," she said.

Dutch climbed the steps. Just seeing her left him a little dizzy. His feet felt unsure. Ground slipping beneath him, as if a hole was opening and he was falling like sand in an hour glass from one part of her into another. She took his hand and led him inside. Her bare feet padded lightly, almost delicately, beside the thump of his boots.

The house met and exceeded the palatial expectations promised by the exterior. Like her office at *Scars,* the flooring consisted of the seamless, continuous-grain marble. Obviously a fan of white, the walls were pure snow all the way to ceiling, which in the living room, extended the full three floors and curved inward to create the illusion of a cathedral dome. A grand, crystal chandelier, suspended from the intersecting arches, glittered like diamonds from the countless bulbs within. Art on the walls consisted of modern canvases. Lichtenstein, Rodrique, Haring. The furniture minimal, expensive.

Nicole put him at ease with personal intimacy, drawing his attention to her, rather than the fabulous architecture. She walked over to the bar and mixed drinks. "Manhattan?"

"Sure."

She took a bottle of Maker's Mark from the top shelf of a double-door glass enclosure above the wet bar, then paused. "I thought you didn't like mixed drinks?"

"Tonight, I'll make an exception."

Nicole poured a finger of bourbon from the squat, tubby bottle into a heavy-bottomed drinking glass, took out a bottle of Martini & Rossi vermouth, sweet, and dumped a thimble full in after it. Dutch saw her in the mirror looking at him. She smiled.

The heat had been there from the moment he saw her at the top of the steps. She's thinking how transparent men could be, he guessed. Especially before a beautiful woman, especially before a beautiful woman who knew she was beautiful. He watched her add a dash of bitters and turn. Her fingers brushed his as the glass exchanged hands.

"What's the difference between a man and a woman?" she asked.

"Is that what this is?" Dutch took his first sip. The liquor went down smooth and warmed its way up.

"Just answer the question."

"Now you're beginning to sound like a judge I know." Dutch rounded the bar and moved closer to her.

"Are you always this difficult?"

"Only superficially." He could smell her heady perfume. Practically feel her body heat.

"All right, I'll tell you. On a date, a man wonders if he's going to get lucky. A woman knows the answer." Nicole touched the glass to her lips and took a sip. "Now, how about that dip?"

Nicole led Dutch onto the terrace, walled and roofed-in with inch-thick soundproof glass. The Jacuzzi was twelve feet in diameter, underlit, and immured by granite rock excavated from the headlands of the Pacific Ocean. Bubbles the color of limestone stormed to the surface. The conversation took a seductive turn.

"You can change in the guest bath if you'd like." She motioned to a tall, slatted, cedar door next to the one they'd entered. Everything about the room, the house, the space, was distinctive.

"No, thank you." Dutch was half way through his drink. "I'm just beginning to relax. If I get in there with you, all that could change."

"Mind if I do?"

"Go ahead."

He anticipated her next move and still found himself startled by her lack of inhibition. Nicole undid the two top buttons and let her shirt slip from her shoulders. She was completely nude. Even with the alcohol swirling in his mouth, it still felt dry. She was all that he'd imagined, and much, much more. He realized there was a limit to his self-control. And it cost Dutch every bit not to stop his drink in mid-air.

"Sure you don't want to get in?" she asked.

Dutch nodded, outwardly casual, but he couldn't take his eyes off her. She smiled an alluring, mischievous smile, then turned away, and climbed into the Jacuzzi. Tendrils of steam rose, twining up her calves, legs, and the undulating muscles of her heart-shaped ass before her body sank into the opalescent waters.

Dutch had never really noticed the way she carried herself until now. A combination of feline grace and reptilian smooth movements. Everything about her provoked, teased, and enticed. He took a seat on a rocky outcropping of the lip, kicked off his boots, and peeled off his socks. Swinging his legs over, he dipped his all-too-white feet in the invigorating water. He flinched. It was blistering hot. Soon, the warmth became a comforting blanket halfway up his ankles.

"How did you walk in just like that?"

"You get used to it," she replied. "It's all a matter of degrees." The water hovered just above 107°F.

They locked eyes. Neither speaking. Each seeking a telling movement or sign from the other to determine the direction the evening would take. She had laid out the ground work—mixed drinks, brought him to the Jacuzzi, disrobed.

But Dutch remained indecisive. He'd gotten himself in way over his head with India and he still didn't know if he could trust Nicole. As far as he was aware, she could be in on it with Gillette, or Myke, or Briganza. If she wasn't the killer, she was most likely an accessory to murder. And there wasn't much of a future in that.

"Gillette and I watched you with India on the broken glass," she said casually, sipping her drink.

Dutch went stock-still.

***

He studied Nicole's face intently. Tracking her reactions. But her face was meditative, if anything. Her eyes flat and inscrutable. He didn't speak for a moment. Letting his voice modulate evenly so that he could speak without a tremor.

"You knew about the mirror?"

"Mirror?" she asked, puzzled, rolling her back against the massage of the powerful jets.

"Yeah, behind—" Dutch broke off. "Forget it." If she didn't know, all the better. "Where were you?"

"Outside. Looking in."

"Did India know?"

"Of course. She liked that." Then Nicole paused. "You like to watch too, don't you?"

Dutch skipped giving an answer. "What did you see?"

"Enough." She waded to him. A sultry aquacade of legs and limbs, breasts and sex, all indistinct and alluring, just below the surface. Like Nicole, what she meant. Everything just below the surface. Out of reach.

"Enough?" he asked, anxious.

"Enough to know you loved it more than any first timer I've ever seen." She surfaced right next to him. Rubbing her hands over her face and tightly down the back of her hair. She straightened. Firm breasts above agitated water. Gathering in semi-circles around her. Clinging and leaping at her flesh. She put a hand on his inner thigh. The wetness left a palm print on his jeans. She leaned forward and compressed her breasts against his knees. "Do I make you nervous?"

"No. But I can see how you would have that effect on some people."

"But not on you?"

"No."

"Because you're a tough cop?"

"Because I know your type."

Nicole pulled away and arched her shoulders back, exposing her breasts to the cool air. The nipples hardened instantly. Dutch took in the wonder of it all. They were fucking beautiful. He bit his lower lip. Her body below—a fluid silhouette that changed shape in the bubbling waters that welled up around her—tantalized his imagination.

"Be careful, detective, your horns are showing."

Fuck. Dutch looked down.

She swept back between his knees, advancing confidently. A finger traced upward along a radiating crease in his jeans to its origin at the base of his fly. She locked eyes with him all the while. Dutch held his breath. Nicole dropped her eyes to the bulge in his jeans. Ran her hand over it. Dutch throbbed and stiffened.

"That's an impressive piece, detective."

Fuckfuck, Dutch thought. *It's going too far. She's a suspect.* He set his drink down and felt the first buzz from the liquor. He looked back as she ran both hands over him in broad, sweeping strokes. *A hot fucking suspect with a hot fucking mouth.* His eyes rolled back as the fire inside began to consume him and he felt himself giving over.

He heard the low, metallic tear of his zipper coming down. She slipped her hand inside.

He wanted to stop her, but he didn't. She closed her hand around him and began to slide her hand up and down. His head lifted. His fingers tightened around the stem of his glass.

She leaned forward to take him in her mouth. But did not. Her tongue emerged, touched the swollen head of his penis. Pleasure rippled like an electric shock through his body. He grit his teeth. The she took him in his mouth. Her felt the rake of her teeth just ahead of the soft caress of her tongue. Up and down. Up and down. His balls swelled up. He had to put a stop to this. *Now. No…maybe, just a little longer.*

He was going to explode.

"No!" he snapped. Placed his hand on her forehead. Pushed her back.

"No?" Nicole didn't seem hurt or surprised. She smiled crookedly, running a fingernail up and down. "Sure?"

Dutch clutched her hand. Pulled the finger away. Nodded. "Yeah."

"What will it take for you to trust me?" Nicole's voice softened into a plea.

"How about a confession?"

She deftly slipped her fingers into his. "I didn't kill anybody." She closed her other hand over their entwined fingers. "It's the truth, Dutch."

"Is it?" He continued to resist.

Nicole took his hand to her lips and kissed it, raising herself higher in the tub. Her entire manner suffused with a supple gentleness. The water fell halfway down to her thighs. He lost control of his eyes, which traveled down, following the water sheeting down her incredible body. Wet, naked, and completely exposed. She looked vulnerable. Almost, he warned himself at once.

"I'm willing to take your word. Why don't you take mine?"

Dutch weakened against the mounting heat. "What if I have to turn you in?"

She cupped his face between her dripping hands and kissed him. Each move unhurried, giving Dutch ample time to stop her. Once again, he didn't. *Couldn't.* He responded to the insistent texture of the diamond stud on her tongue. The full press of her breasts against his chest. His hands explored the curves of her body in whirlpool motions. Lowering in circles. Each ring lower. Firmer. He cupped her cheeks powerfully.

Her back arched. The slow sighs quickened to embattled groans. Nicole's fingers drove into his scalp. She was in control. He knew it. And tamely submitted.

She reached down to guide him into her, and as she did, she uncoupled her lips from his to ask, "What if I have to turn *you* in?"

He felt the tip of his penis touch the lips of her clit. Desire sparked like a high voltage shock. But he broke out of her spell. Pulling her hand off, he leaned away from all contact with a loud catch of breath. *That was close. Too close.* What the fuck was wrong with him? He had almost blown it. He stood up abruptly, adjusting his trousers, where he didn't subside as fast as he would have liked.

"Be seeing you." He left without a backward glance.

Dutch gunned the SUV along the winding driveway leading away from Nicole's mansion. The rain had ceased, but thunder still chased after lightning, both pursued by a strong, blustery wind.

He was smiling.

He had Nicole exactly where he wanted her.

***

Nicole pensively twirled a nipple. She lay her head back on the lip of the Jacuzzi and called out, "Hey."

Gillette entered from the outdoor balcony. She'd asked him to wait behind the tempered glass. Just in case. Obscured by the steam rising from the water. Dressed in a lush, all-white, cotton bath towel and Bermuda swim trunks with a Hawaiian print, he practically danced over to Nicole. She waited with her arms outstretched. A smile played on her lips, partly from the pleasure of Gillette entering her and satiating her unsatisfied wetness, but mostly from what she had accomplished.

She had Dutch exactly where she wanted him.

***

Knock! Knock! Powerful knuckles rapped at the door. *Knock! Knock!*

Dutch threw back the sheets, daylight forcing his eyes into a pointed squint. He was hung over and looked like hell. After leaving Nicole's, he had found a bar and gotten drunk. Even then, he couldn't sleep when he got home, tossing and turning. Unable to get her out of his mind. He wanted to sleep with her, but he kept coming up with the same answer over and over. He would be falling into the same trap. Thickening the incriminating cloud over his head, instead of dispersing it.

Knock! Knock!

"Coming!" he shouted irascibly, then clutched his head from the painful throb of his own voice.

He must have fallen asleep sometime before dawn. The last time he remembered looking at his watch was at 4 A.M. He clambered out of bed to the door. Treading gingerly. Even so, each footstep forced a jolt up his spine, where it drove like a hammer into the base of his skull. Ringing his bell. He leaned forward carefully to look through the peephole. Little bells ringing all the while. Dutch twisted the tumbler and opened the door.

Bishop stood outside.

"What the fuck are you doing here?" asked Dutch gruffly.

Bishop, who'd been in the apartment once previously, when he'd helped Dutch move in, recoiled at the smell of stale beer. "Smells like piss in here."

"Who are you?" Dutch gruffed. "Mr. Clean?"

"Wash up," ordered Bishop.

"What for?"

"Breakfast. My tab."

Bishop became aware of the ceaseless crime reports from dispatch over the police scanner. "That your sound system?"

"Beats KYLD," Dutch said, referring to San Francisco's Contemporary Hits radio station.

"You know, it ain't normal to keep a thing like that on all the time."

"Different folks, different strokes," Dutch grumbled.

Under Bishop's nagging supervision, Dutch shaved, showered, and dressed. Then they took the short walk to the corner coffee shop. The sun was out. Bright. Bestowing a cheerfulness to the entire city. Except Dutch. He remained morose, chin slung low. The waitress brought their coffee.

"We're ready to order,'" said Bishop.

They selected from the list of eye-opener brunch specials. Dutch took Bishop's menu and handed them back to her. She looked like she'd been doing the job twenty years too long.

Bishop sipped his coffee. "All the blood in India's shower belonged to the victim," said Bishop after she left. "DNA match came in on the hair sample. Yours."

"Now I'm a *prime* suspect?" Dutch didn't care about anything else.

"Of course not. Look. The Lieutenant was just blowing off steam because he'd planned on telling the cameras we had a lead." Dutch dumped some sugar into his coffee.

Bishop grimaced. "Come on, coffee's meant to be consumed clean."

"This from a guy who rains salt on fries like a panhandle hurricane."

"Coffee's different. Gotta drink it pure. Black. No sugar. No cream. And sure as hell no Sweet and Low. I dislike substitutes of any kind. Fake breasts, fake and bake tans, eyelashes, nails, collagen implants—I like my women, as well as my food, au naturel."

"Good to know," Dutch raised his brows blandly.

Resting his elbows on the table, Bishop tilted his head forward. "We got a little problem."

"What kind of problem?"

"Appears the loot got your confidential IAD file from Houston. Anonymously."

Dutch was surprised at first. Curious. Then cautious. "What do you mean?"

"I don't know, but it looks to me like someone's out to

nail you and has picked this case to do it."

Dutch looked out the window. Seeing but not registering the traffic and people hustling past. Tell-tale puddles remained where the asphalt met the curb. The silence between the two detectives stretched to the end of the tracks. Then Bishop started laying some new ones as he took another sip from his coffee and waited for Dutch to speak first. His morning meditations had taught him to be patient. He was an expert at the waiting game. Dutch realized he better say something. He knew how Bishop was when he was like this. Dutch had to be the first to speak. Even if he didn't feel like it. He shouldn't have to defend himself, but silence wasn't going to cut it. Bishop had to hear it from his lips.

Dutch turned from the window and enunciated clearly, "I'm not a copycat killer."

The waitress arrived with their breakfast. She grabbed the ketchup, salt, and pepper from the next table, then walked out of earshot.

"Fucking on glass?" Bishop asked quietly. Dutch glanced away, embarrassed. "Not too bright, Dutch." Before Dutch could defend himself, Bishop launched into the megillah he'd been holding back, "We got beat cops out there every day afraid to touch winos, even when they're wearing gloves, for chrissakes, because of AIDS and shit. And what are you doing? You're out fucking a total stranger with seriously deviant sexual behavior on broken glass?"

"I used a condom," Dutch argued weakly.

"Next time try a space suit."

Dutch poked at his ham and eggs, sunny side up. He dipped his toast in, breaking the yolk. Watching it bleed across the plate. He chewed and swallowed a mouthful. "What's the lieutenant think of you asking me back on the case?"

"He doesn't know," Bishop replied.

***

Then, all the way back to the station, Bishop hated himself for lying.

Walking into the squad room, Bishop saw Schiff behind the venetian blinds of his office. Clearly, he was waiting for Bishop's arrival. Seeing the black detective, Schiff crooked his finger. Come into my office. And snapped the slats shut. Bishop noticed a dip in the noise level. Cautiously quiet, but not entirely silent. He read the change and knew what to expect before he entered the lieutenant's office.

Feds.

"Agents Jett and Russell," Schiff introduced. "I called them in. "

He stood between the two men, both wearing the signature suit and tie of the Federal Bureau of Investigation. Lean and sinewy, little separated them, apart from the thin line of a mustache on Jett and the pale, boyish, scrub-apple complexion of Russell. They looked like factory products rolled out by the FBI assembly line in Quantico, Virginia. High on procedure and skepticism. Low on emotion and benefit of the doubt. Uniformly unlikable.

"They're from the Serial Crime Division," Schiff continued. "Dr. Tilton's pre-briefed them and I brought them up to speed on where we are. You'll be working with them on Dutch."

Bishop nodded. They nodded back. No pleasantries solicited, none uttered.

"How'd it go at breakfast?" asked Russell straight away.

"He bought it," Bishop said. "Thinks he's back on the case." Bishop did not hide the fact he was an unwilling participant, who objected to how they were going about what he considered was unfair entrapment of a fellow officer. Bishop decided he should draw the line and place himself on the other side of it. "I don't think he's guilty."

"That's what we're all hoping," said Jett without any conviction.

Eleven.

Elise sat with two lawyers. Across the aisle, Dutch was alone. Both had taken the day off from work.

The courtroom in the San Francisco Civil Courts building did not have visitors' benches since divorces were private proceedings, closed to the press and public. A few derelict chairs were stacked one on top of the other if for some unlikely reason more seating became necessary.

Dutch wore a dark blue suit and a conservative carmine tie over a pin-striped dress shirt. Remarkably spic-and-span in comparison to his usual attire. He noticed the effect wasn't lost on Elise. Walking into court earlier, he caught her staring at him. He looked damned handsome this morning in more formal clothes. As for herself, she wore a chic business suit with a stylishly short hemline, revealing slightly fleshy thighs and rounded calves.

Dutch noticed she'd put on some weight since she'd starting working at the office. What they called the secretary spread. Too many sweets and too many hours in a comfortable chair. She had always been nervous and timid, with a loss in appetite that resulted in too narrow hips and a stomach where Dutch could count the ribs. She looked more like a woman now, and Dutch found the fullness absolutely fetching. It gave her a healthy glow. He liked the way she filled out her dress. Her curves diminished her waif-like fragility and endowed her with a more commanding presence and a determined stride that reminded Dutch a little bit of…Nicole.

Judge Sara Wellington, with distinguished streaks of gray in her dark nested hair, looked from Elise to Dutch. "Mr. Holland, you are no longer contesting this divorce filing?"

Dutch glanced over at Elise, who turned her head a fraction and moved forward just beyond her lawyers. After momentary eye contact, which she broke, Dutch addressed the judge, "That's right, your honor."

"Even though you have previously expressed—" she paused to examine the file before her. "Strong reservations?"

"Yes, your honor, that is correct."

"Would you care to offer any explanations for sudden change of heart, Mr. Holland?"

"No, you honor," Dutch submitted respectfully.

Judge Wellington didn't pursue his reasons any further. She had a full docket and only four hours left in the afternoon session. "In that case, it is the ruling of this court that the petition of Elise May-Holland for a dissolution of marriage from Jeffrey Daniel Holland be granted according the terms of the parties' stipulation."

The judge read the terms and conditions of the divorce, division of property and money, including the one exception requested by Elise. She wanted no alimony, seeking to sever ties with her husband in a manner that left no reason for them to contact one another. Ever again.

Dutch's shoulders drooped. He stared blankly in front of him, tuning out the finality in every word of the legal language. One hundred and ninety-three dollars and a single pound of the judge's gavel was all it had taken to bring his marriage to an end.

In the corridor, afterwards, the lawyers hurried off to other courts, other cases. Dutch found himself with Elise at the elevator.

"That was painless," she said out of a polite need to make conversation.

"For you, maybe," Dutch responded. He noticed she

almost apologized, then checked herself. Glanced away. His stomach contracted with pangs of hurt and frustration.

The silence hit home.

In that moment, Dutch knew she was free. Of him. From him. Forever.

***

Elise felt it. The hair began to rise on the back of her neck. She knew as well as anyone how he hated losing. It *enraged* him. She tried not to move. Afraid the slightest gesture would set him off. But she couldn't help but feel sorry for him either.

He looked so alone

Ting! Elise was relieved the elevator did not arrive empty. The doors opened, revealing a lunch crowd inside. They joined the group and pressed their way in just as the doors closed. At the last moment, a red pump at the end of a long, slender leg blocked the closing doors.

***

An ominous foreboding swept through Dutch. Hoping he was wrong, knowing he was not. Dutch followed the red heels up firm calves and thighs that undulated with tone musculature. Short skirt. Bodice flaring over ample breasts. Pale, languid throat. Full lips. Bright, mischievous eyes.

Nicole.

The doors reopened with a disturbing clang of metal.

"Dutch!" Nicole gleamed. "What a surprise." The men in the elevator turned unanimously in her direction. Gillette followed Nicole into the elevator. The doors closed. The elevator descended.

Dutch gestured toward Elise. "Nicole, Gillette. Elise. My wife."

"Ex-wife," corrected Elise.

Edging between the divorced couple, Nicole frankly appraised Elise. Dutch recognized the same aggressive, predatory delight from their first encounter in *Scars*.

"Hi." Nicole smiled with her lips, not her eyes.

***

Elise's face went flush. Piqued not because this refined demon greeted her ex-husband with an air of intimacy, but because Elise, the court clerks, and female assistants, all seemed to vanish in a way women did when a beauty like Nicole walked in.

The doors closed with another *ting!* It was as if a boxing match started. And the lunch crowd had front row seats.

Elise took one look at the three-dimensional flesh sculpture of the leaping fish between Nicole's breasts like a pendant for the pearls around her neck and wrote her off as a high-priced call girl. Then Gillette stepped close, obscuring her view of Dutch and Nicole.

Ting! The elevator opened on the next lower floor. Nicole squeezed Dutch back into the corner, allowing three women, who climbed in, to form a human wall between them. Gillette nudged Elise into the opposite corner.

He shocked her by taking her hand and introducing himself, "Hi."

"Gillette. That's an unusual name," she remarked politely and shook his hand. When they disengaged, Gillette turned her palm over and caressed her hand. "Interesting."

"Are you a palmist?" she asked.

"You might say I'm a connoisseur of the female form."

"Most men would like to think so."

Gillette laughed. "Well, I am. I do body art. And I find your skin absolutely breathtaking. Flawless."

A brief flutter ran through Elise. She always thought of herself as plain, rarely meeting a man who showed any interest in her. She wondered what he saw. At best, her features were 'attractive.' Nevertheless, on some level, she was flattered by his remarks.

He leaned into her ear and whispered, "Have you ever been cut?"

***

In the opposite corner, Nicole pressed into Dutch, casually circling her arm around his waist. Her white teeth flashed like a tigress. "She's nice, if you like heavy." Nicole's lips touched Dutch's ear like a brush stroke. "Officially single?"

Then, without warning, using her body as a shield, she slid her hand down his fly to take a firm grip. Dutch's eyes popped wide open, caught completely off guard.

"I miss you," she exhaled, voice rich as morning dew.

***

Elise flinched from Gillette's fingers dancing up and down her forearm. He edged closer, casually draping his other hand around her shoulder. They looked like lovers in a clinch. Elise didn't know what to do. She wanted to pull away, but she couldn't.

"Your skin is rich in melanin," he said, "perfect for creating keloids—permanent scars. Come on down to our club sometime. I'll do you for free."

"I don't think so, really—"

"Hold on." Gillette reached into his back pocket, and as he did so, pressed his hips into hers because there wasn't enough room.

Elise hadn't slept with anyone since Dutch and she had parted ways. Elise felt Gillette through the expensive fabric of his trousers. He wasn't wearing any underwear. Gillette radiated sexuality. She tried to distract herself, looking at his hands. It didn't help. He had the good, strong hands of a craftsman. From the way he'd touched her palm, she couldn't help wonder how they would feel on her body.

His powerful shoulders abruptly shifted under his tight fitting shirt. He drew his hips away from hers. The contact ended. He handed her an eye-catching wafer of silver and gold. Elise felt like fool, realizing the seduction was all in her head. Hers alone.

"My card," he said, and smiled. "For you, I'll even make a house call."

***

Dutch looked down at Nicole's hand, then furtively around. Nobody looked in their direction. "I know it's hard to let go, Dutch," said Nicole, teasing him with the double entendre. "But you have to. She doesn't love you anymore. Trust me."

Ting! The doors opened in the lobby. Nicole released him. Dutch shifted and tried to compose himself. They were the last ones out.

"Bye, Dutch," Nicole said, eyes flashing. "Oh, and you, too, Elise. I'm sure now that you're single, you will be very happy."

Gillette threw her a flying kiss with both hands. "You're beautiful."

"Thank you," Elise replied.

"Call me."

Dutch was curious, but held his tongue. As they took successive sections of the revolving door outside, he caught Elise's eye. He knew she sensed his jealously and her lips curled spitefully as she emerged outside. She turned back, waited for Gillette, who came out after Dutch, and waved. *Just to get my goat.*

Gillette returned a spectacular smile. "Be seeing you!"

Dutch composed himself and walked Elise to her car, a Chevy Cavalier. Elise unlocked the door and Dutch held it open.

"I have packed up the rest of your things," she said. "I can have them sent—"

"That's okay," interrupted Dutch. "I'll come by."

"Dutch, I don't—"

"Friday night?" he asked. Elise hesitated. He pecked her lightly on the cheek. "Okay? See you then."

He jogged off. Reaching his SUV, he looked back up at the courthouse steps.

Nicole stared down.

***

"Why the fuck are we watching them?" Gillette asked.

Eyes attenuated to cruel pinholes, Nicole said, "I don't like competition."

***

Between midnight and the swing shift was the Morphean hour. The squad room became deserted because those going home were more punctual leaving than their replacements coming in. Hence, a gap in manpower. Bishop told Dutch to choose the lag time to come in and catch up on the case.

"What's wrong, partner?" Dutch asked, pulling up a chair.

"Long days," Bishop replied, acknowledging the prevailing distance between them.

The truth was he felt twisted and wrung out. He didn't like lying to Dutch and it was getting under his skin. Disturbing his placid equilibrium. As a matter of course, Bishop had led Dutch to believe that he was getting the real deal. Still on the case, though not officially. But Dutch was the case. Bishop was acting with the full knowledge, approval, and urging of Lt. Schiff and FBI Agents, Jett and Russell.

Dutch flipped a chair about face and sat beside Bishop, who pecked at the keyboard using the Columbus approach. Two fingers, sight and land. Bishop displayed the tentative naiveté of the triplicate pen and ink generation which still distrusted the roadless reliquary of cyberspace. Satisfied with his keystrokes, Bishop sat back as if he'd completed a

Herculean act and hit the ENTER key. The screen went blank. Thanks to the paranoia surrounding computer viruses, Bishop fearfully held his breath until 'SEARCHING' appeared inside a rectangular, flashing box.

"This should be it," Bishop exhaled.

"Think we got her?"

"Hope so." Bishop paused. "Have you?"

"Have I what?"

"Fucked her?"

"Nicole?" Dutch scoffed. "What the hell is the matter with you? I don't have sex with every woman I meet."

"But you'd like to, right? You're into her?"

"Well...sure..."

"So, what's stopping you?"

"One thing," replied Dutch, then didn't elaborate.

"She's a he?" Bishop prompted.

"Trust."

Bishop stopped, looked, and listened. Dutch actually sounded sincere. That, above most other things, made him throw his head back and laugh.

"What?" Dutch asked, sounding hurt.

"Oh! So what you're actually telling me here is that if she's innocent, you'll fuck her."

"Hey, come on, I didn't mean it that way—"

"That's very advanced of you, Dutch. Hey! Maybe if she is guilty, but she plea bargains, you can work an arrangement into her acquittal: Three years probation with a taste of pretty in pink every six weeks for Detective Holland."

Dutch shook his head. "Do you have to profane everything?"

"Excuse me," Bishop chopped. "Just because you get down on your knees for pussy doesn't make it sacred."

Dutch frowned defensively.

Bishop knew right then and there that his partner was beginning to have feelings for Nicole. Feelings Dutch knew better than to express.

Beeeeep! Bishop and Dutch lifted their eyes in unison toward the computer screen. A message flashed.

"Access denied?" Bishop read it like an absurd question.

"To Nicole's file?" Dutch sounded just as baffled.

***

It was 2 A.M. when they got to *Scars*. Dutch easily found a parking spot, one of many rapidly becoming vacant. Castro Street, its side roads and alleys, emptied of patrons reluctantly returning home to the mundane—apartments, Empty-V, and the late night news.

Dutch and Bishop walked through *Scars*'s inconspicuous door and entered the downturn hour. Most patrons had long gone. Others showered in private stalls in the men's and ladies' rooms, hosing off before the long walk home. Employees stacked chairs on tables. The door hostess looked for belongings people had left behind and dropped them into an aseptic-looking trash can with wheels on it and rolled them away. The clean-up crew wore signature yellow latex gloves and non-slip lug-soled boots. Rock music blared over the speakers with none of earlier seductive subtlety.

Hell, that's showbiz, where even the wrap is another production. Two men and a woman. They pushed brooms. Mopped the blood off center stage. And sprayed the hitching post with a disinfectant. Dutch recognized the label as hospital grade.

They scanned the room. There was no sign of Gillette, but Nicole sat on a barstool, smoking a thin, filtered cigarette, and tallying the evening's receipts. The platinum blonde bartender, now in a tied-off Super Girl tee-shirt, counted the cash in the register and called off the number of 1s, 5s, 10s, 20s, 50s, and 100s to Nicole. Sounded like a good night to Dutch. Nicole didn't seem to swing one way or the other. Super Girl saw the cops and tapped the bar with a long, pointed nail.

Nicole followed her eyes toward the two detectives. "Dutch?" She did not even acknowledge Bishop. "What a nice surprise."

Bishop's face tightened. He stepped in front of Dutch. "Could you tell us why your personal records are sealed?"

"I could."

They waited. She didn't speak. Instead, Nicole returned to her tally and took a drag off her cigarette. The detectives looked at one another. Dutch shrugged. Two can play this game, he thought, deciding to nip this mine's-bigger-than-yours contest Bishop had kicked off before it got any further.

"Why?" asked Dutch impatiently.

Nicole closed the box of receipts and exhaled a shroud of smoke straight up into the lights over the bar, creating a soft nimbus of light that gathered like a skirt around the dim lamps. "One of the benefits of being a blue blood."

Dutch didn't get it. Looked over. Neither did Bishop.

Nicole nodded to Super Girl. "Time to go home." The blonde smiled and bounced off like a bunny. Out of the corner of his eye, Dutch noticed that this time it was Bishop's eyes that tarried. Super Girl had a super ass. After she receded out of earshot, Nicole said, "Part of my father's plastic surgery practice supports the witness protection program. Removing identifying marks, altering appearances, you know, putting new faces on old problems. It's standard procedure for the FBI to keep the whole family anonymous."

Dutch could only shake his head. This case was taking the more twists and turns than a New York cabbie's route.

"How's the investigation coming?" Nicole asked, once again honing in on Dutch.

"Pretty good. We've ruled out a shark attack."

Nicole laughed. A crisp, throaty laugh that spilled out like a waterfall and had a way of making a man feel special. "Any sign of Briganza?"

"Nope," replied Dutch. "Not since the Cordoba Meat

shootout."

"You worried, or just curious?" Bishop asked.

Nicole turned on Bishop. "Did you ever consider the killer might have mistaken Lauren for me?"

"Why would someone be after you?" Dutch asked, interested.

"Why would someone be after anybody?"

"Love," offered Dutch.

"Revenge," Bishop suggested.

"Money." Nicole lifted her cash box, stepped behind the bar, took out a plastic card, and swiped it across a Safelok security case. She waited for the red light of the electromagnetic lock to flash green and then placed the cash inside. Then she turned to Dutch, "Love? Now there's an interesting choice. I wonder. Out of all your women, did you ever love any?"

Bishop's eyes slid to his partner, flashing Dutch a silent warning. Dutch caught it and let the question go.

"Say, you're not gay, are you?" She looked at Dutch, then Bishop, then Dutch.

"Because you seem to me remarkably...uninterested," Nicole persisted.

"Thanks for your time." Dutch stood up. He'd gotten himself in enough trouble lately, almost lost it the other night. Now was no time for a rematch.

"You're always walking out on me," Nicole smiled.

"Doesn't everyone?" he came right back. He realized she was tugging at his fraying edge, hoping he'd unravel.

"Sooner or later," she agreed. "Sweet dreams." Nicole blew smoke rings as the men stood up.

Dutch and Bishop climbed into the SUV. The interior light went dark. Dutch clicked his seat belt and reached for the steering column. He was about to turn the key in the ignition when he caught a movement in his peripheral vision. He paused.

"Step on it, will you?" Bishop said impatient. "I'm

tire—"

Dutch raised a silencing hand. Bishop followed Dutch's eyes to a silver, expensive, top-of-the-line hotrod. Its twin, oval eyes glimmered in the darkness. The contrasting front and rear bumpers, black cloth convertible top, menacing grille, and extended mobility tires set it apart, just as the 3.5 liter, 24-valve V8 engine ran louder than most other automobiles. It was the kind of high-profile giveaway that cops liked when trailing a suspect.

"Gillette," said Dutch.

The cutter ground to a noisy idle at the corner, where the alley behind *Scars* fed into Castro Street. He looked left and right. A fugitive search. He didn't see the detectives. The SUV's black paint blended it into the darkness. But the street lamp clearly illuminated Gillette as he sniffed white powder off his knuckles, licked them clean, and reset his grip on the leather-wrapped steering wheel. The music from hotrod was so loud it reached the detectives. Gillette suddenly howled like a lonely wolf.

"Crazy motherfucker," said Bishop. "Everest high."

Dutch looked at Bishop. "He made some bad investments, he said."

"A coke habit is the worst there is," Bishop echoed.

They heard Gillette jerk the stick shift and tested the car for guts. The rear, 20-inch, cast-aluminum wheels turned and burned. Dual exhausts belched tornadoes of smoke.

Gillette then burned it flat out. Let the hotrod go. It careened toward the detectives like a racing car out of the starting grid. Dutch and Bishop ducked in a hurry before the quad projector beams circled around and exposed them. After it roared by, Dutch fired the SUV and followed. There were no cars in-between, so he maintained a safe distance.

The traffic signal on 18th Street turned yellow. Gillette sped across. Dutch ran a red light. Luckily there was no cross traffic and no cops to mess things up by drawing attention to the covert pursuit.

"Surviving partner gets the club," Dutch said. "But mebbe Briganza whacks the wrong woman."

"That doesn't make sense," Bishop argued. "Lauren knew Briganza. His name was on her computer."

"Gillette could've put it in the computer. He's got a degree, remember?"

"That's thin."

The cars raced past the landmark Castro Theater. In quick succession, the brightly lit neon marquee of San Francisco's best preserved film palace washed fluidly over the silver hotrod, then the black SUV. Gillette's V8 grabbed all the sound, which was great because the SUV seemed nonexistent. They approached Market Street. Gillette swung toward the curb, slowed at the intersection, signaled at the last moment, and turned. He took off like a rocket. Dutch pushed it up to 70 M.P.H. and was still falling behind. Gillette was doing close to ninety. Dutch floored the gas pedal.

"Then why was India killed?" Bishop asked.

"Confuse the investigation?" Dutch suggested.

"Thin and getting thinner."

They blasted by the NAMES Project gallery, which housed the AIDS Memorial Quilt. During the day, tourists thronged to see the handwork of friends and relatives commemorating a person lost to the disease. At this hour, there wasn't a soul in sight.

"He sure is in a hurry to get some place," Dutch said.

Bishop's eyes swung ahead. The light at the upcoming intersection of 16th, Noe and Market was red. Gillette showed no indication of slowing. *Has he made us?*

Five yards from the crossroads, the light turned green. The hotrod, whose revs continued to tear the night air with a staccato growl, snarled even louder as he barreled across the intersection. The low control arms of the front suspension barely cleared the crest following the dip in the road. The independent rear flew out, lifting the wheels into the air.

"Son of a bitch is a speed freak," Dutch complained.

"Fast cars, fast livin'." Bishop shook his head. "It's the American way."

The SUV stood so high off the ground, all four wheels bounced airborne when they hit the dip. The speed sent the two detectives rocketing forward. Their seat belts snapped taut. Stopping them an inch shy of shattering the windshield. The tires banged back down on the asphalt. Dutch and Bishop slammed back into their seats.

Lights at 15th, Sanchez and Market were green. The two cars bulleted across.

At 14th, Church and Market the signals turned red. Gillette didn't ease up until fifteen yards from the intersection, when he realized the green wasn't coming. The four-wheel Vented Disc brakes easily reined in the hotrod's 214 horses. By the time Gillette came to a standstill, the hotrod nosed halfway into the zebra stripes of the crosswalk. He had pulled alongside a bus disgorging two passengers at the stop.

Seeing his brake lights heat up, Dutch slowed, allowing a Honda Civic in front of him. He could see the hotrod over the top of the tiny hatchback.

"You got a better theory?" he asked.

Bishop took a shot. "Lauren was a mob realtor. She was in business with Nicole and Gillette. But something went bad. An investment, maybe. Nicole and Gillette choose the night of her cutting to end it. Call in Briganza, a part-time enforcer. They throw his name on Lauren's computer to frame him. Or maybe it was there already from before when they used him as muscle for other things."

"But what about India? You think her death is unrelated?"

"I don't know," shrugged Bishop. "Maybe she saw something or heard something that she wasn't supposed to. Or...we're looking for motives where there aren't any."

"What do you mean?"

"Could be our suspect is suspended in the orgiastic ozone." Bishop shifted in his seat and twisted toward Dutch. "Look at what we got. A cutter with a prior. A rich trick with slick dick clientele. And some guy—"

"Watch the term, 'guy,'" Dutch cautioned. They still hadn't made a successful determination of sex in the investigation. And who knew what the hell Myke was anyway.

"Person. Perp. Freaky deaky donkey poker, all right?"

"Better," Dutch smiled.

"Look. All I'm saying is we're limiting ourselves by thinking man or woman. Murder 101. Intent, motive, opportunity. We need to focus on the psychological profile. Deviance—sexually or otherwise. Maybe what we're looking for here is someone who likes crossing the line just for the hell of—"

"What the fuck?" Dutch cut him off.

On green, without signaling, Gillette broke off Market Street and whipped hard right in front of the bus. Dutch jammed the gas pedal down to the floor at the same time the bus moved. Neither cop saw its left signal blinking. They assumed the driver had caught them in the out-mounted rearview mirror. But the SUV had been in the bus's blind spot. The driver's foot was on the gas. Hands steering the bus away from the curb. Committed to acceleration.

There was no time to react, let alone stop.

The towering bus bore down on the SUV. The massive grillwork filled the window on Bishop's side! Blinding globes of the bus's oversized headlights closed. An inevitable, fatal, broadside collision loomed.

A heartbeat away.

"Dutch!" Bishop gasped, clutching the dash.

Speed was the answer. The bus advanced, a yard from reducing the sports utility vehicle to scrap. Dutch crashed the accelerator down! The cylinders engaged, thrusting the SUV forward.

Too late.

They felt a large lurch, then a tug that threatened to fishtail the high profile vehicle. Dutch and Bishop stopped breathing. Colorless faces blanched by the light of the oncoming bus. Suddenly, like day turning to night at the flip of a switch, the blaze of the headlights vanished.

The SUV escaped. A large rubber-burn stained the back bumper, where the mammoth bus wheels had scraped across. Regaining their composure, Dutch and Bishop focused back to the road, where Gillette's hotrod had been.

Church Street was vacant. Gillette had vanished.

After half an hour of zigzagging a square mile of the immediate crossroads and alleys, they came up empty-handed.

"Guess our theories are going to remain just that," said Dutch, shaking his head. "Unless he made us. In which case, of course, we're fucked."

"Maybe not," said Bishop, optimistically. "Like you said, sickos are creatures of habit. They can't stop themselves from killing again. Even if they want to."

They returned to the Golden Gate station. Dutch parked beside Bishop's Camry. Black-and-whites rolled in with perps, others left with sirens blaring, lights flashing—a grim reminder they lived in a crime-ridden city.

Bishop opened the door, but remained in his seat.

"I didn't mean to be hard on Nicole, man. Just that the prom queen doesn't wake up one day cracking the whip in an S&M dungeon. That's not the way it works. I mean, this chick has been through it all. Tattoos, piercing, the club scene...but it wasn't enough. So she went underground where she met a guy. A svengali type. You know. The kinda guy that could show her the ropes. In this case, our boy, Gillette.

"He introduced her to the finer things—Mary Jane, coke, smack. And before she realizes it, she's in the big leagues and she's playin' way over her head. She can't handle it. Now he's made bad investments and she needs to protect hers, so it all of a sudden becomes a rock and a hard place type situation. And she doesn't know how to get out."

Bishop shrugged and continued, "Even if she didn't draw the knife, she's in on it and she's going to go down. I don't want you going with her. That's all. Half the guys we bust have trouble that way. They don't deliberately fuck-up. They just have trouble navigating the possibilities."

"Meaning?" Dutch asked cautiously.

"Don't wind up at the wrong place at the wrong time. You do that, and sure as shit you're going down with her."

"Thanks for the tip." Dutch's hackles were up.

Bishop rubbed the light-skinned palm of his hand over the five o'clock shadow. "You know, Dr. Tilton's probably right. These people can't even remember where they started from." Bishop turned to Dutch and faced his partner dead-on. "When did you start?"

Dutch stared back. Wondering how far Bishop wanted push it. His eyes were saucers without depth. "Start what?"

"Drawing the line."

Dutch laughed. "What do you mean?"

Bishop didn't even smile. "Everybody's got one, Dutch. A line inside drawn by their conscience. A line, just like their spine, that forms the backbone of their character and allows them to stand up straight."

"Hey, I got no problem standing up straight, if that's what you're asking. I'm all right with what I do."

"Are you?" Bishop threw it out there and let it hang. "Because if you start seeing Nicole, I don't think she's on the same side of that line. You'll have to cross it to get to her. And when you do, you may not even know it. So I'm asking you. Which side is Nicole on? Which side are you on?"

Dutch didn't like being pressed and now he'd been pushed up against a fence. He couldn't believe it. Now, even his partner was having doubts. Dutch didn't know if he was more angry or disappointed from a sense of betrayal. Nothing was working and everything seemed to hurt. There was nowhere to turn. He had everything to lose. A hole gashed in his side that refused to scar over. And wouldn't go away. He was on the verge of anger. True anger.

The kind that almost always leads to a physical confrontation.

Dutch's eyes thinned. He felt himself losing control. He glared at Bishop. About to blow up. Burn it off. Dutch's arms contracted. Tense as rope wrapped around a barrel. All the nagging frustration of the case and his marriage came to a head.

Dutch had hit his boiling point!

***

Bishop braced himself. Curled his hands into fists. If Dutch made a move, Bishop figured he could take him.

Beneath Bishop's calm exterior his mind raced. *Will Dutch really do it? Will he take a swing?* Bishop honestly didn't know. He'd never pressed Dutch this far, and now Dutch seemed ready to blow. Maybe he'd made a mistake. He had relied on a false sense of security, based on their friendship and their partner status, not to roll Dutch over the edge.

But did he really know Dutch that well?

"I'll see you tomorrow," Dutch said. "Thanks for the tip."

Bishop relaxed, seeing Dutch's eyes round out. Lose their edge. The air between them started to breathe again, like a lid removed from a boiling kettle, steam escaping. Dutch was back in his skin once more. Seen clearly, Bishop figured, Dutch had realized his partner was not being adversarial, but acting with the simple compassion of a friend who only wanted to help.

Bishop stepped out of the car, then leaned back in. "Listen. I've got to pick my kid up from school tomorrow night. We won't be able to get together."

"What about buses?" Dutch said. "Don't they have buses where your kid goes?"

"It's private school."

"How about a limo?" Dutch asked wryly.

"That's usually his mother," Bishop said tersely.

Dutch got the point and backed off. "That's all right. I've got to pick my stuff up from Elise anyway." Dutch shook his head. "Man. How did our lives get so fucked up?"

"Beats me," Bishop said. "We still on for the weekly game at the morgue?"

Dutch nodded. "Eight o'clock."

"Don't be late."

Dutch drove off. Bishop didn't move, thinking Dutch hadn't answered his question. *So I'm asking you. Which side is Nicole on? Which side are you on?* Bishop let it slide. Dutch was under enough stress. Maybe all he needed was a little more room. A little more time to figure things out. Then he'd make the decision to stop seeing Nicole on his own.

Bishop stood where he was. Waiting and watching for what came next.

He felt sick.

A Buick started up and tailed Dutch. Jett drove the unmarked, wide wheel-based sedan, passing close enough for Bishop to see his face. He could swear the FBI special agent smiled as he drove by.

Twelve.

When Elise first moved to the Bay area with Dutch, the clean lines of the Italianette architecture had immediately attracted her. Considering her tidiness, Dutch had joked, he wasn't surprised. Italianette homes comprised a good part of San Francisco's high building density because they ideally suited the space limitations the geography imposed. Distinctive features, borrowed from Roman mansions, enhanced their compact form.

The wooden structure of their home was finished to look like stone. A tall cornice, on decorative brackets, ran flat across the front facade, hiding the pitched roof. Elaborate arches capped the symmetrical windows. A pedimented porch added a subtle grandiose gesture to the front entry.

The first home Elise and he owned. They'd rented in Houston. On the middle-class edge of the wealthy Marina District, a pricey district with streets dropping in a sluice to the San Francisco Bay, it had been a bit of a stretch at first. The salary Dutch pulled down in the force had barely qualified them for the mortgage. The monthly payments left just enough aggravation over liquidity to keep the fighting down to about once a month. They dined in mostly, ordering so much Chinese, Dutch said he thought he was getting a squint. A joke with poor taste, at best, she thought.

Elise loved the house. And when she was happy, they were happy. And it made the whole struggle worthwhile. She enjoyed going down to the boutique stores and cafes for a weekend stroll. Even though they couldn't afford anything, she liked to window shop. Picking out dresses and fine bone china that would one day fill their dream home.

Then there was the view. A picture postcard seascape of yachts, sailboats, and cutters bobbing over the ocean. After Elise landed her big job downtown, she figured the fighting would end. But instead, it only got worse.

When Dutch first met her, she had been like a dutiful daughter. Easily molded. Easily led. Where her shyness and natural timidity caused her to falter, she relied on his strength for protection, his common sense to guide, and his bull-headed tenacity to prevail. For the longest time, he was her touchstone. If it weren't for Dutch, she may never have had the courage to leave her middle class insecurities behind. But borrowed courage, at least the kind Dutch gave, came with a price. She began to feel as if she were trapped under his watchful eye. As if there just weren't enough room in the house.

And then came the time demands.

In Houston, he had been carefree to the point of being unreliable. But in San Francisco, he had swung to the opposite end of the pendulum. He started to run his life like clockwork and she was expected to wind the watch. Breakfast at six. Dinner at seven. No less than two calls to the office in between. Then in bed by eight and asleep by ten.

His demands in bed were enormous. Insatiable. It was as if he walked around with a hard-on all day and then threw it into her for all he was worth when he got home. Nothing kinky. Just a powerful, primitive drive that she assumed was the product of a full day's frustration from putting up with the suits and skells, when all she wanted was some peace and quiet, some quality time alone with him.

But she knew better.

Even in their private moments, it was as if she was hardly there. He took his sex out on her with impersonal fervor, devoid of feeling, emotion, and intimacy. She never felt so alone as when they were actually having sex. Before that and after, he was there. Present. Alive. But during, he disappeared. She didn't know where. She feared some fantasy world where men go when they're tired of fucking the same woman. Once, she'd been really lit at a backyard barbecue for the precinct in Texas, and she'd overheard his partner say, "Forget all that, Dutchie. Chinese remedies, sex tapes, even cocaine on yer Johnson won't help. The only true aphrodisiac is new pussy."

That was before Elise had given up.

Their relationship had been a rocky road, but signs had been posted all along the way. Warnings. Only she kept running over them until they hit the skids. Another wreck down Lover's Lane. When they separated, Elise had loved the house so much, Dutch agreed to move out.

Elise looked out the window nervously. *Stupid, stupid, stupid.* Why had she allowed Dutch to invite himself over? She'd hoped the courtroom would be the last time she saw him. She'd walk away, making a clean break.

Emerald moss framed each brick, shining under the evening's sunset. A benediction from lingering rainfall. Taking a close look, she could see where cracks had sprung in the tight fitting paint. There seemed to be a relationship between mass and age and time and although Elise wasn't exactly sure what it was, she saw the results. The house suddenly felt smaller with the prospect of his arrival. Less durable. Azoic. She could barely enjoy the scent of La Belle Sultane roses—a bonfire of flattened, singular petals dusted in darkening tones of velvety crimson purple, with a prominent center of gold stamens. Elise had them potted on either side of the entryway to give guests the nostalgic impression they were entering a country villa.

Elise heard a car engine. She recognized Dutch's black SUV approach. Retreated quickly. Her throat rolled. Perspiration sprang to her forehead. She could see the ink smearing and running below that line on which she thought had been the bold, clean strokes of the signatures finalizing their divorce.

The car door slammed. *Angrily?* Then footsteps. Sure. Crisp. Her trepidation notched up. *Knock. Knock.* His hallmark. Two knuckle raps. Elise started forward slowly toward the door. A strangling sensation took her throat in a velvet mitten. Butterflies flew wild arcs in her stomach. Senses riding the edge of uncertainty.

Which Dutch would be there when she opened the door?

The charmer she'd married, or the monster she'd discovered.

***

Dutch was immediately captivated when Elise opened the door. In contrast to Nicole, who was cultivated, sophisticated and refined, everything about Elise was uncomplicated and natural. In her simplicity, Elise was, perhaps, the more appealing of the two.

She wore a yarn-dyed, plain-weave cotton fabric that could pass for gingham. Face devoid of make-up, with only a touch of mascara to bring out the toasted luster of her almond eyes. This was what Dutch knew. Just looking at her was like going home again, and he felt like a fool for ever having lost her.

There was a moment of awkward embarrassment before both spoke at the same time, with the same simple greeting.

"Hi."

Elise laughed and put her hand to her throat prettily. She looked extremely nervous. Dutch grinned, shuffled, and looked at his feet. An atavistic cowboy gesture that stayed with him from back home. When Dutch finally looked up, he searched her face for some sign she was glad to see him. But she was already reigning in. Elise held her arms stiffly by her sides, as if she might be taking a chance letting him this close.

"Come in," she said finally. Sliding back into the house and away from Dutch. Allowing him ample room to enter without the danger of physical contact.

He walked past her into the living room, where aureate rays of sunlight filtered through sheer curtains and bathed the neat, simple furnishings room in a golden glow. A laugh track erupted periodically on the TV. Dutch noticed his boxes behind the couch. Carefully taped, labeled, and stacked. Ready for pickup.

"No strings attached?" Dutch asked mordantly. Throat tightening. It's really over, he thought, still groping for the magic words that might reverse the annulment of their marriage.

"I gave you the wedding pictures," she said.   D u t c h just nodded. Silence. "Would you like something to drink?"

Then, she blinked. Was she regretting the offer? He couldn't tell. But he didn't want to take the chance. He nodded. "I'll have a beer." Then joked, "Old habits die hard."

Elise smiled. Dutch noticed that she did not laugh. He followed her into the kitchen. Shiny, copper-bottomed pans dangled in order of size above the stove. The countertop gleamed without so much as a water spot. The sink was empty, scrubbed, and bleached. Elise always washed and put away the dishes immediately. He stopped at the island and watched her movements.

Elise walked over to the refrigerator and opened it. Her full hips swaying as she walked. There was something slow and sultry about her even now. A purloined beauty that could only have come from back home.

"I want to apologize if I...hurt you," Dutch began, fumbling for the right words. He had to say something.

She looked over her shoulder. Her lustrous, shoulder-length hair cascading off her face. "Dutch. No. Don't start, all right?"

She removed two bottles of Miller and handed one to him.

"I'm sorry." He twisted the serrated cap off.

"Ow!" Elise cut her finger doing the same.

Dutch put down his beer and hurried over.

She bled heavily.

"Give me your hand." Dutch grasped her wrist. Opened the faucet over the kitchen sink, and put her forefinger under it.

Elise caught her breath. The water sent a stinging pain shooting up her hand. A diagonal shaft of crimson light sliced through the uncovered window. The sunset, now flaming red, cast a deep blush on Dutch, Elise, the kitchen, and the blood corkscrewing into the drain.

Dutch was riveted. Elise asked, "What's wrong?"

He broke out of it. "Where do you keep Band-Aids?"

"I don't have any."

"Paper towels?"

Elise shook her head. "I'm out. I used it all to pack your things."

The blood poured onto his hand. "I think you cut a vessel."

"Shit." She looked around helplessly. She rarely cursed and was surprised that she did. But when she looked at Dutch, she became even more unnerved.

He was smiling. A faint, inscrutable smile. "You know, Nicole and Gillette would consider this foreplay."

Elise looked uncertain. Without warning, Dutch closed his mouth over her bleeding finger. Elise went still. Not knowing what to do. As he turned his knuckles, her blood dribbled into the tiny creases. She laughed nervously. But this time it died abruptly when Dutch resisted her attempt to pull her finger out of his mouth.

He nodded to his knuckles. "Go on, taste it."

She didn't. She stood frozen, unmoving. He knew what was going through her mind. *What the hell am I doing?* Dutch eased her finger out of his mouth. Not entirely. Just far enough to let the cut bleed onto his lips. He knew her so well, so completely, he recognized the emotion shift in her eyes. *Fear,* his control stick, was back.

He boldly touched his bloody knuckles to her lips. "Go on."

Two short words.

Uttered with tender desire and a threat of violence.

If he played it right, Dutch thought, maybe he could use the moment to reunite what had long ago died. A sense of mystery and forbidden pleasure that had enticed her out of her shell. The air between them took on the texture of silk. A smooth, unruffled amalgam of anxiety and fear. Dutch watched her hesitantly taste a red rivulet. The cold, moist flick of her tongue sent his pulse racing. She tilted her chin, looking, not in his eyes, but at her bleeding finger.

"We shouldn't," she reacted, pulling back from his hand sliding between her legs.

"Dutch!" she said in a hoarse whisper, "I don't want to! I won't!" Her voice rose to a shrill pitch.

But he silenced her, crushing a kiss upon her lips, which were stained red.

***

Elise couldn't resist him. She hadn't been with another man. She opened her mouth to admit his tongue. Hers surged toward his. She tasted saliva laced in her own blood. He sucked her breath out. Her fingers dug into his scalp, tightening his face up to hers. She felt a shiver of pleasure start between her legs and roar across her body with the power of a wave crashing upon rocks.

Stop!

But her brain could not overcome her emotion. Her blouse was open and he was working the bra clasp with one hand. The electricity thrilling her nerves, she realized, was his other hand, which was in her panties. His fingers dipped inside her, touching her in a way only he knew how. She pulled them out. They were dripping wet.

She pulled away, shaking her head. "No, Dutch. Stop it.

I can't."

The sudden passion receded. She saw his eyes and caught her breath. Frightened by the utter lack caring in his gaze. Dutch didn't reply. He just pulled back, stood, and stared back at her. She saw his pupils attenuate to fine points of light.

Oh, dear god! The color of his eyes! It's shifting!

She'd been terrified the first time she saw it happen. Nuclear reactions, like stars being born. Only not kind, twinkling spheres; dark stars. Whirlpool voids of lifeless emotion. The transformation was somehow reptilian. It made her skin crawl with terror as memories rushed back. Fearful, threatening memories. Because she'd been here before, she knew what came next.

Fury.

She waited for him to roughly spread her legs and enter her. As much as she hated the violence, she thought, subconsciously she must enjoy submitting to his power and strength. Otherwise, why, within seconds, did she always find herself moving with him deep inside her, her ankles tightly locked around his hips, her fingernails tearing into his skin. Always, it was only as she fell away, sweating and panting and satiated, did she remember how their sex had started. It was wrong and humiliating, but she could never resist Dutch or stop him.

"Wait," he said, surprising her.

She observed his eyes move beyond her face, trail over her shoulder and focus with new possibility. His lips twitched in a smile.

She glanced behind her and gasped, seized by a new terror. "No!"

On the cutting board, within reach, lay her kitchen knife.

***

Bishop's heart and mind were not in the poker game tonight. Surrounded by a backlog of corpses, he sat at an autopsy table—which served as their card table—with Dr. Pease, Lee, and Magno. They had already made a visible dent into the variety of six-packs each had to bring to the game. Cigarette smoke hung in thick, stagnant curls. The loud air conditioners sounded helpless, trying to dissipate the combined odor of formaldehyde, tobacco, and alcohol, which would turn anyone's stomach but a cop or a coroner.

Pease dealt with the deftness of a card sharp. "What did the dumb blonde say when she found out she was pregnant?" Ignorant shrugs rippled. "Is it mine?"

Bishop, his most ardent fan, did not join in the guffaw.

Pease tried again. "What did the blonde say when she saw the banana peel?" He looked around. "Oh, no! I'm going to slip and fall again!"

Once again. Laughs all around. But not Bishop, who scowled, preoccupied, "What the fuck was I thinking when I agreed to snitch on my partner?"

"If he's guilty, fuck him," Magno said.

"If he's not?" Bishop asked.

"What does it matter?" Lee said. "You helped clear him. That's in his best interest, isn't it?"

"Right," Magno agreed. "You're looking out for him. That's the way I see it."

Bishop and Pease went back almost fifteen years. They'd been introduced to each other by Bishop's mentor and first partner on the force. Three years later, Lee, a generation younger, joined the friendship when he transferred from Los Angeles. They took on Magno, another generation down, two years ago. The difference in age and personality made the weekly get-together a welcome, break from the daily pressure-cooker of police life.

Six months ago, Bishop's partner had died in the line of duty, and Dutch arrived. As much as Bishop and the others tried to embrace him, the detective from Houston remained a fifth wheel literally and metaphorically. Bishop could not place his finger on a single reason, neither could the rest. D u t c h displayed two sides to every facet of his personality. Open and friendly on the one hand, secretive and guarded on the other. He took his job with a seriousness that they admired and found unsettling at the same time. His police work was top rate and they never doubted Dutch's single-minded determination to solve a case, yet questions nagged them about his integrity between shifts.

"I hope you're right." Bishop didn't sound convinced.

"Where is he?" asked Dr. Pease, looking up at the clock. 8:25 P.M. But then, Dutch kept his own time. They'd never known him to be punctual, on duty or off.

TrrTrr. TrrTrr.

Everyone reflexively reached for their cell phones, even if the ring tone wasn't theirs.

"Mine," said Bishop and grumbled, "Somebody should have smothered the inventor of this in his crib."

"What's the matter?" asked Dr. Pease. "Don't you like technology?

"Oh, I like technology," Bishop shoved his chair back, "I'm just not a techno junkie." He didn't answer the phone knowing he had four rings before his voice mail kicked in. He took the opportunity to release his frustration about the case by venting about something totally unrelated. "I don't like beepers, answering machines, car phones, cell phones, home phones, or any other damn way of getting hold of me when I don't want to talk. Reach out and fuck someone. That's what being connected is all about today."

The men laughed.

He flipped open the phone. Slammed it to his ear. Still angry. "This is Bishop." His irritation subsided at once as he listened in silence. "Je-sus."

He hung up. The others were already throwing down their cards and getting their coats. Some words spoke volumes. Bishop's reaction could mean only one thing.

"Bodies," Bishop said, affirming what they already knew. Then he added what they didn't, "Jett and Russell."

***

The two FBI agents had been shot through the head at point blank range in Jett's Buick. It was neatly parked between one of many parallel bumper-to-bumper cars lining the curb.

The quiet residential area was lit up like the Fourth of July. Residents crowded behind police tapes cordoning off the crime scene. Black-and-whites blocked the approaches, their lightbands sweeping across the closely-packed facades. An ambulance siren gathered, then pulled into view. Patrol cars backed up, allowing the ambulance inside the perimeter. Uniforms faced outward, away from the crime scene.

Dr. Pease straightened from an initial examination of the fatal wounds. A ribbon of moonlight replaced his shadow on the two bodies. "Nine millimeter. Up close and personal."

"Dutch uses a Browning nine millimeter," Schiff said.

Bishop knew it looked bad, but some part of him still had to back up his partner. "So does every gangsta on the West Coast."

"What the fuck are these two doing together anyway?" demanded Schiff. "Jett was tailing Dutch, and Russell was supposed to be following his ex-wife."

Bishop blanched as the realization hit him. "Elise lives around here."

"Do you have an address?" reacted Schiff.

"In my car." Bishop sprinted to his Camry.

Bishop and Schiff successfully slipped beyond the barricades unseen, skirting the onlookers. If the night was going to get worse, the last thing Schiff needed was a circus to publicize it. They cautiously ascended the brick pathway to Elise's front door.

The moon had risen high into the clear night sky. A strong gust picked up. Ruffling the leaves on the lone tree in the front yard, a thirty-year old Magnolia. The wind entered gaps, billowing their clothes, allowing a chill to take hold. Schiff and Bishop knew they were seeing what Dutch must have seen a few hours before. Only now, the house was obfuscated in nightmarish shadow. Branches and moonlight writing a chiaroscuro playlet to the tragedy within.

"I don't see any lights," Schiff said.

"She might be asleep."

"At nine-thirty?"

Bishop shined his flashlight on the white storm door. His heart sank.

There was blood around the knob.

"Don't touch anything," Schiff warned.

They unholstered their guns. Twin safety snaps popping in crisp, mechanical unison. Bishop checked the chambers. Six full. Then racked the cylinder back in and used the barrel of his Smith & Wesson .357 to press the bell.

DingDong! The door bell became the prelude to a long silence. No lights came on. They didn't hear any shuffle of answering feet. Schiff nodded. Bishop jabbed the bell again. *DingDong!* Again, only silence ensued after the echo of the chime died. Silence, stillness, darkness. Nothing.

"Hanky." Schiff held out his hand. Bishop dipped into his pant pocket and removed a clean, white woven cloth. Careful not to wipe off any prints, and making sure not to smudge the blood, Schiff grasped and turned the knob.

The storm door was unlocked and swung in. Schiff held it open, allowing Bishop to lean past and shine the light on the handle of the solid wood inner door.

More blood.

Bishop nudged it inward and skipped over the doormat in case there was evidence from a shoe sole. Schiff followed. Hugging the outer edges of the short passageway. Advancing, Bishop's heart did double time. Dutch's boxes remained behind the couch. Unmoved. Untouched.

Schiff raised his brows. "If he was here to get them, why didn't he?"

Bishop pondered the implications. Maybe Dutch hadn't been there at all? Then he froze. No. That couldn't be right. Or else Jett wouldn't have been in the car. He turned it over. Getting his mind around it. Maybe Dutch had been there. Maybe he was killed. Maybe he got too close. Jett and Russell could have seen Dutch go in, then the murderer had taken Dutch's Browning and gotten rid of the only possible witnesses. Bishop was only scratching the surface. Running possibilities around the one question he was avoiding.

Or, was Dutch a copycat?

Swiftly, silently, they moved in flawless synchronization. Bishop stepped in front. Schiff covered. Then the lieutenant went by and Bishop covered. They took no chances. Most cops lost their lives assuming the danger was past when they entered premises apparently deserted. The two men drew level in the living room.

Back to back.

No sign of foul play.

They pressed against the wall. Shoulder to shoulder. Between two doors. Schiff signaled and they rolled in opposite directions, appearing simultaneously in adjoining doorways. Guns outstretched. Trigger fingers a twitch away from firing.

Schiff and Bishop stared into the master and spare, respectively. At first glance, neither appeared to have been slept in. The master contained a queen-size mattress on an inexpensive, sleigh frame, sheets tucked in as fastidious as a fine hotel. The spare had a futon, maintained with the same tidy diligence.

With a nod, they each entered their bedroom and lost sight of one another.

Bishop ran a check around the louvered shutters of the closet, found them clean and opened them. Few clothes hung inside. Thick, woolen coats. Older dresses and neatly folded sweaters covered by a flimsy sheet of cellophane to keep off the dust. Bishop figured it was most likely overspill from the master bedroom, where Elise kept her day-to-day wear. He backed away and examined the window. It was undamaged and fastened from within. He scanned the floor, the walls, and the futon more closely. No blood.

"Bishop!" called Schiff, shattering the silence.

Bishop hurried into the master bedroom. Schiff beckoned from the doorway of the attached bathroom. Bishop strode across, fearing the worst.

Schiff nodded to the sink.

Bishop didn't have to peer closely to see tiny fibers dotting the white porcelain and dry, pink-black stains along the rim. Blood, diluted by water. Schiff then directed Bishop's attention to the bathtub. Long, dark tendrils like feather boas on the floor of the stall had gone slinking toward the drain, leaving a dry reticulated trail before they could empty.

Once again, the killer had taken his time.

"Shaved and showered just like India's place," Bishop murmured.

Emerging from the master bedroom, they approached the kitchen anxiously. They took a deep, resigned breath and went in together, turning their bodies to fit through the narrow doorway.

Both stopped dead in their tracks.

"Oh, man, this can't be happening," Bishop exhaled. From the moment he saw the blood, he had expected a murder, possibly even a gruesome one. He had steeled himself against it and accepted the growing dread that his partner may be a part of it. Even the previous murder couldn't have prepared him for what he saw on the solitary island in the center of the kitchen floor.

Elise lay on the island, naked. And dead.

***

Her arms hung over the edge just like her spread-eagled legs, knees bent at the edge of the countertop. Half-dry, half-wet drops of blood poised on the fleshy inner regions, uncertain whether to drip to the gathering puddle on the floor. Bishop couldn't help notice the blatant sexuality, even in death, of her pose. His eyes were arrested by the crude artistry etched all over her upper torso between her neck and waist.

If this were the same killer, he'd lost his touch.

Anger dominated the deep incisions on the lower half of each breast, simulating a stream of tears from the nipples. A bloody flower bloomed around the navel. Tiny, random nicks and cuts perforated the rest of the skin, including some brutal hacks to her upper torso.

Bleeding occurred in narrow lines, connecting one wound to the other, like a ball of red thread uncontrollably unspooled and impossibly entangled. Thin rivulets covered her entire body. Overflowed across the counter. Precipitated along her limp arms and legs. Sheeted down the escarpment of cabinets supporting the island. And purled into floor seams, exposing their fractal symmetry.

The men tiptoed to either side of the body.

Elise's eyes stared up at the ceiling, retinas dilated. Head resting on a radially diverging pillow of hair. Her throat was slit in the signature manner of the previous victims.

Bishop noticed something else.

No matter what other factors were involved, he couldn't remove his eyes from her face. The frozen expression. Identical to the one he remembered on the face of every woman under the knife at *Scars*.

A smile.

***

Having been on the other side of questioning, Dutch wasn't intimidated.

Indifferent cream walls, fading linoleum, and a naked

fluorescent tube cast a depressing gloom over the interrogation room. One narrow door opened out of this windowless space into an even gloomier corridor. The lack of comfort, character, and daylight was designed to suck out hope, break will power, and empower suspects with the bold tenor to sing.

Dutch sat alone in a straight-backed chair. Clean shaven. In front of him was a long table and more chairs, all but the two closest to him on either side were pushed in. To his left, sat Lt. Schiff. To his right, Bishop.

"I didn't do it." His eyes were red and downcast.

"Your prints are all over her house," Schiff adopted a conciliatory, paternal tone.

Dutch wasn't fooled. He knew the loot was trying make him feel comfortable and open up. "Because I dropped by to pickup my stuff."

Around 1 A.M. this morning, Dutch had been jolted awake by two uniforms he recognized knocking on his door. They said they had orders to cuff him. And did. Like a common criminal. Every minute after that, Dutch's ire mounted. So did an underlying anxiety as they drove him Downtown in the back seat of a cruiser.

Dutch had been on the force long enough to realize, if Schiff really had it in for him, the lieutenant would have shown up with an arrest warrant and made the charges stick. Even first degree murder. Grand Jury through to trial, it would be an easy case because sixty-nine percent of Americans believed cops were corrupt and used the power of the shield to kill.

"Then why didn't you?" Schiff asked.

"So I could come back another time." Dutch followed the rules of interrogation, making no gesture that a criminal psychologist could construe on a video replay as a signal of guilt. "We were coming to terms, you know. This was the first time in a long time that we actually had a conversation. No fighting. None of the old bullshit. We'd just kind of reached a new plateau."

"Where were you between nine and midnight?" Bishop asked.

"Home," Dutch snapped in disbelief of what was happening. *Elise is dead, and my own partner is questioning me as if he did it.* "Look, my wife—"

"Ex-wife," corrected Schiff, with emphasis.

Dutch let it pass with an irritated glance. "Was just cut to pieces. And I don't very much fucking appreciate—"

"Settle down, Dutch," interrupted Bishop. "You know the drill. We have to investigate every angle. As far as I know, we are still on the same side."

Dutch waited for Schiff to go *snap!* But the lieutenant controlled his temper and backed up Bishop, albeit skeptically, "So far." Schiff paused. "Anyone else with you at home?"

"Me," said Nicole, walking in.

***

Schiff had to turn completely around because she entered the room from behind him. His face widened with unconcealed astonishment. "Who the fuck let you in?"

A tall, serious-faced man, in a suit, carrying a briefcase, trailed in after her.

"William Salenger, attorney." He stuck out his hand. Schiff didn't take it. Salenger wasn't offended. "Was Mr. Holland read his Miranda rights before this Q & A?"

"This is an informal kiss and tell," Schiff answered.

"But your desk sergeant said he was cuffed when he came in."

Schiff's lips thinned. "Dutch can leave when he likes. But it's in his best interest to stay here and answer our questions. He knows that and now you do. So why don't you let us get on with our business."

"You never told me I could leave, lieutenant," said Dutch, shifting from defense to offense.

Schiff turned to Bishop. "I told him, didn't I?"

Bishop tilted his head. Ambiguously. Neither a confirmation nor denial.

"Maybe I am a little tired for this right now," smirked Dutch.

Snap! Schiff had reached his limit of being civil. He took his eyes off Dutch and took on Nicole with a sharpness that caught her off guard. "How long were you together?"

"You don't have to answer that," Salenger quickly cut in.

The couple of seconds her attorney bought her was enough time to compose herself. She walked behind Dutch and placed her hands on his shoulders. "I want to, Bill." She blinked over to Schiff, fully in control. "Until midnight."

Snap! The sharpness left Schiff's voice. Calm, acid-laced words dripped out of his lips. "So you tried to make up with your wife and then you were so happy you reached your 'plateau,' you decided to celebrate by playing hide the salami with the bondage queen?" *Snap!* Schiff jerked a thumb at Nicole and yelled, "Is that the bill of goods you're selling me, Dutch?"

Nicole's eyes flashed.

Schiff caught it. *Snap!* He shifted gears, adopting an avuncular tone. "Save the righteous act, sweetheart. Murder is a whole lot bigger than you are."

He'd seen her type a million times over. Women who'd married right, or lucked into the golden cage of well-being. They figured because they had dough and a fancy-pants lawyer, they moved up the food chain. But actions spoke louder than words. Schiff was an expert at judging actions. And from where he sat, she was nothing more than white trash sprinkled in perfume.

"He needed someone to talk to and I was there," Nicole said. "Nothing happened."

Schiff didn't even look at her, glaring at Dutch, who showed no guilt, remorse, or fear. Schiff's lips slanted cynically. "So both of you are in on it together, or you had nothing to do with it. That's nice, Dutch. Painted yourself a beautiful corner to walk into." Snap! His voice sharpened to a ragged edge and he pounded the table. "If this is bullshit, you better tell me right now!"

Schiff noticed Nicole increase the pressure on Dutch's shoulders. Her long nails dug into his skin, squeezing the words out of him, "It's true."

"Are you sure?!" Schiff yelled. "Because my bullshit meter is running way into the red! This is your last chance to come clean. And for your sake—"

"It's true," Dutch repeated evenly.

"What is?!" Schiff spat. "That it's bullshit, and both of you are in on it together? Or that you're innocent?"

"What do you think?"

"You tell me, Goddamnit!" Schiff's eyes bored into Dutch's face.

Dutch said nothing. His jaw moved once. From one side to the other. Trapping an angry reply. Schiff had hoped Dutch's temper would get the better of him, but Dutch stood up abruptly. "I'm through here. Next time, have a warrant when you come for me."

Nicole's hand slipped into his.

Schiff threw his chair back, drew himself to his full lanky six and half feet, looking truly ominous, and yelled, "Fuck you, Dutch! Fuck you, you ungrateful son of a bitch! You think you're home free? It's not that easy! Don't fucking forget who's in charge here! It's me! Not you! And I'm going to give you an ass-raping you won't fucking forget! Not by a long shot! You'll be shoved in a hole so dark you'll fucking forget what daylight looks like!" He shoved a long, bent finger in Dutch's direction. "Tomorrow, I'm going upstairs and the big wheels are going to turn! They grind slow, but they grind fine, Dutch. It's your badge, your gun, and your fucking life, you piece of miserable shit! Say hello to oblivion!"

Schiff ran out of breath. Dutch looked past him as if he

didn't exist.

At Bishop.

***

Bishop found it hard to catechize Dutch. But he had to. As strong as they might be, Bishop's morality did not allow him to put his own inclinations aside.

In this moment of eye contact, his innermost demons about Dutch roared back. The torment and baggage and issues that Dutch had brought with him. Lines blurred for that breed of cop. They slipped easily. 'Til they could no longer compartmentalize the good Mr. Hyde-like 'protect and serve' side of their job from the Dr. Jekyllian bad stuff that the shield provided.

Two guys, one person.

He wasn't alone, Bishop had realized, walking into the precinct earlier. The word was out. Dutch was being brought in and this latest insinuation didn't seem to surprise anyone. In fact, moments before Dutch's arrival, he got up to take a leak and found himself pissing in the urinal next to Gantry. The Desk Sergeant remarked that there as an edge about Dutch. An ambiguity. *Whatever,* Gantry said with his usual acerbic distance, this was better than any of that reality shit on TV.

Bishop released his doubts into his eyes.

Dutch's expression transformed.

Bishop never saw such hate and hostility before. Not this close. His blood ran cold.

***

Dutch didn't care what Schiff thought of him. He sought the trust, approval, and support of only one person in the room. Bishop. When he didn't get it, Dutch turned on his heel and headed for the door. Nicole clung thinly to his hand. Salenger hurried after them.

Outside Schiff's office, Dutch faltered. The squad room

never seemed so large. An eternity, stretching from one end to the other, all the way to the exit. Work ceased. Pencils froze in mid-air. The incessant tapping of computer keyboards stopped. Some looked at Dutch. Others chose not to. A rolling silence fell as the men and women watched him pass, then whispered in his wake.

Dutch and Nicole emerged into the booking area. The zoo subsided. Dutch looked at Gantry, who stared back dispassionately from behind his nightly perch. It took Dutch ten more strides to get to the exit. He was grateful for Nicole being at his side. He tightened his grip around her hand. She squeezed back reassuringly. He saw a gloating sparkle in her eyes. It sobered him up at once to the question, *why?*

Why did she lay herself out for me?

The wee hours left the roads empty for long stretches. Some traffic lights flashed red. A thin marine layer floated in off the ocean, periodically blotting out the stars, like a painter unsatisfied with his work. The chill in the wind was lost inside Nicole's luxury car. The windows were rolled up and the heater turned on low.

"Why don't you tell me what's on your mind?" Nicole said finally.

Dutch hadn't uttered a word. He didn't know whether to be grateful or suspicious. Should he thank her or roll her out on the mat? Question her motive or accept his freedom? He turned down Joshua Redman's tenor sax piping in on the Jaguar's radio.

"You lied back at the station. Why?"

"You're innocent," she said simply. "Aren't you?"

"Or," Dutch guessed, "you needed an alibi and realized this one cuts both ways."

Nicole's eyes crinkled. "If all I needed was an alibi, I could have used Gillette."

"A suspect doesn't hold a candle to a cop, if you're looking for something ironclad. Besides, he's got an acquittal of a similar prior. You telling me that's a coincidence?"

"Dutch," said Nicole with as much sincerity she could muster. "Gillette did not kill anybody. I did not kill anybody."

"Well, I didn't do it."

"Then what are we fighting about?" She gazed at him.

Dutch eased off. "I don't know. I'm sorry. It's me. I'm a cop. Even if I'm not on the force any more. Trust doesn't come easy."

She dropped him off at his apartment. He told her he wanted to be alone. She understood. Dutch was grateful. Nicole closed a hand over his. "The important thing is you're free."

***

Nicole came to Elise's funeral. She stood by Dutch, which made it awkward. Dutch had mixed feelings, seeing Nicole at the grave site. He hadn't asked her to come, but, like most things she wanted, she somehow managed a way and found out the date and time so she could be there.

The scarcity of mourners, gathered under black umbrellas, evoked a bleak image of a lonely life, lived anonymously and prematurely interrupted. Dr. Pease had leaked Elise's autopsy results when he released the body to Dutch. No semen, but extended intercourse. Sodomy. Uprooted follicles on the back of her head. Cutting before and during sex.

The details matched those from Lauren and India.

Dutch had driven behind the hearse bearing the priest, Elise's father and mother and Elise's body. He had tried to talk to them during the service, but all he received was a somber greeting followed by distrustful glances. Bishop might have come, if Dutch had called him, but they hadn't spoken since the interrogation.

Thick cloud cover obliterated chalky sunlight, casting a fitting, funeral pall. The lack of brightness diluted the green lushness of the lawn, which on a clear day, contrasted starkly with the sorrow that lay beneath the orderly rows of squared-off tombstones. An occasional droplet of rain pattered on the coffin and splashed off the polished surface.

The pastor read David's Twenty-third Psalm.

Rain started to come down. He realized he'd forgotten to bring an umbrella. He'd been wrung out and hadn't slept the night before. Nicole embraced him with such genuine sympathy, he couldn't doubt her intentions. She opened her umbrella and they stood together, under its protective canopy, sheltered from the pouring rain. When it was all over, Elise's parents left with a last resentful look in his direction.

Nicole stayed with Dutch. Two lonely silhouettes in the storm. She suggested coffee. He nodded. Dutch reminisced fondly about Elise. Nicole lent a sympathetic ear. When they got up to leave, Nicole invited him over to her house. Supportive as she had been, Dutch wasn't in the mood for company and declined the invitation.

"Maybe once this case is solved," he answered.

"Sure," she said, standing abruptly.

They walked in silence to the intersection. The pedestrian signal thankfully turned green. She gestured good-bye and crossed quickly against the light. Dutch veered along the sidewalk. Once on the other side of the street, Nicole looked over her shoulder. Dutch waved from the corner, feeling sorry he couldn't be more responsive. She had stood by him, displaying a voluntary caring and concern he hadn't expected.

But he couldn't risk it. He had to clear his name first.

Thirteen.

Had his gut failed him? If it had, that would be a first. Sitting in the dark, Bishop pondered about Dutch. His feet were propped up on the desk. Dutch's resume scrolled up the computer screen. Only the faint light of the old monitor illuminated the tell-tale creases of age that had begun to show on his face.

With no new leads, Schiff had assigned Bishop another homicide—four illegal immigrants slain on a fishing trawler found drifting under the Golden Gate Bridge. This was the first time in three days he'd reviewed the case, which had been stagnating into a miasma of inconclusive evidence. He hadn't spoken to Dutch since the interrogation. Each day that passed, without one calling the other, widened the rift between them and made it more difficult to cross.

Bishop extended his arms, threw his head back, and yawned. The empty squad room echoed his bored and tired moan. It was a holiday weekend. All plainclothes were on call. Uniforms were on duty. The Department doubled their street presence because road fatalities and drunk and disorderly behavior jumped like a jitterbug on long holidays.

A door slammed. Bishop glanced over. Schiff emerged from his office and asked, "Still here?"

Bishop grunted, "Did you know Dutch was some sort of prodigy all through school?"

"Yeah. Boy Wonder. So what?" Schiff kept walking. He wore some sort of cloth seaman's hat with a multi-colored fishing lure stitched to the side. He held a tackle box in his left hand and a cylindrical carry-all for his fishing pole in his right.

"Why would he kill India and not bother to remove the evidence he was with her? Why would he shoot two agents with a gun whose caliber matches his own? Then cut his wife, leaving a trail Mr. Magoo could follow with the lights out."

Schiff exhaled steam like an engine with a bad boiler. "You *still* think he's innocent?"

"Smells like a frame," Bishop persisted.

"That's just what he wants us to think." Schiff didn't break his stride. Bishop did not expect him to—this was the lieutenant's annual, three-day trout fishing getaway to Clear Lake. Nothing ever stopped him from taking this trip. It was a sort-of reunion of loots from all over the country. The Coast Range mountains were gorgeous in late spring. The lake shone like a mirror in an Ansel Adams photograph. It had been on his calendar for months. The one event he looked forward to every year. "That's why he's a fucking genius and nobody's nailed him. He's copy-catting and we're thinking up ways to prove he's not guilty! You prove that he is. That's what you do. I'm going fishing. Goodnight."

Schiff passed through the door without stopping. His footsteps receded. Bishop considered calling it a day. The telephone rang.

"This is Bishop." His manner changed abruptly. He rocked his chair back and stood up. "I'm on my way! Have Dispatch put it on the radio." He wanted Dutch to hear it on his police scanner. "Request all available units to respond." Bishop slammed down the phone and raced after Schiff. "Lieutenant!"

He found Schiff a step shy of the exit. "Almost."

Bishop pulled up, shrugging his coat on over the gun in his shoulder holster. "A patrolman saw Briganza! He called in the APB we've had out since the Cordoba Meat factory shootout."

***

Black-and-whites pulled into a dark alley a few blocks from Castro Street without any flashing lights or sirens. The SWAT van and Bishop's Camry arrived at the same time.

Schiff climbed out and took charge. Clapping his hands. "Listen up, everybody!" Crayton, the Team Leader from the first Briganza raid, his men, and an army of uniforms and plainclothes gathered around. "I didn't want our man tipped off. That's why I picked this alley two blocks away as the command post." He turned to Crayton, "Deploy snipers on the rooftops around the club, and do it quietly." Then to the uniforms and plainclothes, "Block off both ends of the street and every crossroad in-between. Don't draw your guns and make it look like a containment. Stay inconspicuous." And finally, to the whole group, "Dispatch has given us an exclusive frequency. Tune your radios to it." He looked around. "Questions?"

There were none.

"Let's move, nice and easy."

Bishop glanced over. Dutch was pushing his way through the disbursing cops.

"See you got the message," said Bishop. No smile. All business.

"Wasn't too difficult." Dutch kept it formal too.

"What the fuck are you doing here?" Schiff said, irritated. Turning on Bishop accusingly, "Did you call him!?"

"I picked up the call on my scanner," Dutch said. Then, before Schiff could speak, "Let me go in, lieutenant. You owe me one last chance—"

"No, Dutch. I really don't," Schiff snapped.

"Come on, boss. He's got a point." Bishop spoke up for his partner. "Briganza was our best lead. We find him in there, this could clear Dutch."

Seeing Dutch's eyes soften in gratitude for Bishop's support, Schiff shook his head. "You don't know how fucking lucky you are to have Bishop. But he's your partner. He should have your back. But I have to be crazy for even considering it.

Face it, Dutch, screwing up is a real habit with you. You're a dyed-in-the-wool fuck-up and I don't see that bleeding out any time soon."

The radio crackled, "Everyone's in position."

Schiff stared at Dutch for agonizing seconds, then exhaled the kind of ponderous sigh that accompanies the defeat of one's better judgment. "Are you carrying a gun?"

Dutch shook his head. "You took my piece and shield."

Schiff tossed his weapon and harness to Dutch. "You got your last chance." He turned, "Bishop, you're responsible for him. He doesn't leave your sight. He fucks up, it's your fuck-up. Got me?"

Bishop nodded.

"Thanks for the vote of confidence," Dutch sniped at Schiff.

"Hey. I was born at night. But not last night," Schiff growled. He was already beginning to feel the acid build in his stomach for the shitstorm ahead.

"Let's go," Bishop said.

The two detectives checked their weapons, holstered them, buttoned their coats, and strode onto the street.

As Schiff watched them go, he recalled that this was why he hated street duty. Continual chaos. One fuck-up after another leading all the way to the big, huge, colossal fuck-up that could cost a man his pension. That was the downside. He reached into his coat pocket and broke open a small plastic packet of Pepto Bismol tablets he'd secured from the station's first aid cabinet. He kept them for moments such as this. When his stomach needed it most.

Dutch and Bishop crossed into the crowd.

Then Schiff tried to figure the upside. He ground the pink tablets between his teeth and tasted the first soothing signs of relief. On the other hand, if they did get their man, if Briganza was the murderer, he wouldn't have to worry about negative publicity for a long, long time. That could lead to a promotion and put an end to circuses like this forever. Schiff began to build his castle in the air—then suddenly stopped.

The burgeoning smile on his face fell to a frown.

No, he thought, not today. Dutch, Bishop, and Briganza weren't good bets. And luck wasn't his strong suit.

***

Dutch and Bishop dodged the slow moving traffic. Passing police units lined the curb at either end of the targeted block. Blues climbed out and leaned against their numbered squad cars. Plainclothes officers hung around corners of the smaller roads and alleys. The detectives consciously did not look up because they knew SWAT crouched on the terraces, eyes pressed into the telescopic nightsights of high-powered rifles. A chopper flew by, probably with Crayton in it.

Dutch and Bishop turned the corner toward a nondescript building that, like all places of this type, would pass for office space. According to Magno, the resident expert, it was called *The Gauntlet: A Fetish Haven.* Like anyone needed to be told that, Dutch thought.

They jostled their way across the packed sidewalk and entered a surprisingly bland lobby. Immediately inside the door stood a reception desk. A bouncer stood in front of it. And a butch-brunette in a peek-a-boo, sporting nipple rings shaped liked horseshoes, chewed gum behind him. Dutch stared at the jangling horseshoes.

"They're for luck," she monotoned, delivering her response like a clerical worker who was used to being asked the same mind-numbing questions over and over. Like, does this train stop in Oakland? Or, how much for cock screws?

"Oh," Dutch replied.

As a result of the piercing, her nipples received constant stimulation, and like her attitude, maintained an erect, almost threatening posture.

"How are you?" Bishop said, trying to lighten things up.

She stared at him for five full seconds, then said, "*Exceptional.* How are *you?*"

Bishop's brow knitted. Words stumbling out like careless children. "Er...fine."

Dutch noticed she had an intense, castrating glare that could only come from a lifetime of discrimination and persecution. She looked like she'd heard and was tired of all the lipstick lesbian jokes. Was tired of hearing how every male-child thought lesbianism was cool. Was tired of how men wanted to watch women having sex so they could get into the mix and 'turn' the women hetero by showing them how it was *really* done.

"Originally, horseshoes weren't horseshoes at all," she said. "They were horse genitals. After a stallion was cut, they nailed his balls over the door of a barn for good luck. Hanging down like that in the shape of a 'U.' But it offended some men. Made them uncomfortable, I guess. Does it make *you* uncomfortable?"

Dutch stared back dumbly. Bishop drew a blank.

"Or insecure? You know how much bigger horses are."

Neither Dutch nor Bishop had an answer for that either.

She gave up when she saw she wasn't going to get a rise out of them. "So they hung up horseshoes instead." She shook her breasts, flipping the horseshoes up and down.

"Clip clop." She smiled coldly,

"That's very interesting," Dutch replied.

She took two sheets off a clipboard. "You have to sign a release."

Dutch didn't even read the closely typed sheet, throwing the pen across it in an illegible blur. Bishop carefully spelled his first and last name at the bottom. As he wrote, Dutch observed the greeter in his peripheral vision. She was regarding them with a jaundiced eye. She looked like she'd been working the door five nights a week, every week, forever. The way her eyes darted, Dutch sensed she suspected something wasn't right with the picture in front of her. White guy, black guy, both squares. Too old to be first timers, too jaded to be thrill-seekers, and too straight to be queer, which really meant only one thing.

Trouble.

"Would you like to buy gloves, condoms, or dental dams?" she smiled contemptuously. Maintaining the party line.

"Just looking," Dutch smiled back.

Her face cleared. "Voyeurs?"

"Yup." Dutch shrugged acting embarrassed. "It's our first time."

A smile stretched across her lips like she'd just received a present she didn't particularly like. "Entry's at the end of the hall. Watch your step."

Dutch and Bishop strode toward the door.

"Nice work covering," Bishop said.

"Don't think she likes breeders."

"Breeders?"

"Men who like women who like men."

"Look at you," Bishop raised his eyebrows, "an expert in the field now."

They pushed open the heavy, sound proof inner door, and were instantly assaulted by loud speed metal music. The setting was radically different from *Scars*. *The Gauntlet* catered to the hard core, one-step-beyond crowd that worshiped bands like Nine Inch Nails and Rage Against the Machine. Gone was the carefully nurtured showmanship of love and dysfunctional familial support. Tossed away in favor of hairy-chested, balls-to-the-wall Bangoria. Tuned into that alternative frequency that was specifically designed to take the participants to the edge of reality and give them a little push. Into Never Never Land. A state of sado-masochistic fervor never before experienced and never to be experienced again.

Bishop stopped dead in his tracks, jaw dropping.

Dutch didn't flinch. A Texas hick when he'd walked to *Scars* the first time. *Look at me now.* He felt completely at home.

***

There were so many different scenes—the term for S&M acts—happening at the same time. All appropriately twisted. Bishop didn't know which way to look. He directed Dutch's attention to the closest one, "Will ya look at this shit?"

A play piercing scene.

The young man carefully placed tiny hypodermic needles under the skin of his partner's face, a woman in leopard print catsuit lingerie. He recreated the neat semi-circular design of pins that protruded from her other cheek just below the eye. She emitted a short cry for each puncture. A small group of onlookers resonated with empathetic moans. Blood swelled to the surface around the needles without trickling down. The young man interlaced the two circles of needles and took a step back.

"Ready?" he asked.

The woman closed her eyes and clenched her fists. A hush fell over the gathering. The young man gave the laces a short tug. The two circles of needles leapt out of her skin! The woman wailed. The group howled like wild monkeys, bouncing and clapping and cheering all around her as the blood trickled down her cheeks, drying into crimson tears.

Bishop signaled Dutch to take the other half of the club and he started to circle his. *The Gauntlet* was an ever-changing freak show. Every time he shifted his eyes, he saw something else—topless people, bottomless people, people sporting a variety of piercings, and thanks to this investigation, he recognized people with 'hamburger cuts' and other 'documents.' On stage, in front, a feather-boa striptease played out. An audience, pockmarked with elaborate piercings and outrageous costumes, milled around, rapt. Brushing flesh.

Gyrating to the constant bump and grind of the bass-driven music. The echo reverberated in Bishop's chest. Shaking his body and surging through his veins, pumping his blood like a second heart.

Bishop moved on, shoulder-to-shoulder, through the pressed pack, and passed an executioner hoisting his girl to a dangling flesh hook. When the tip grabbed flesh, her cry rose above the *thumpthumpthump* of the blaring back beat.

The Gauntlet was a cornucopia for all but the faint of heart.

***

Dutch stepped aside for a woman leading a blindfolded man by a leash. Occasionally, she would strike him with a crop and he would emit a short bark, "Good boy." He panted and yipped after her. *Probably a big-shot CEO during office hours.*

Dutch circled around a bloodbath scene. Two good looking girls and two attractive guys slapped each other to bring their veins to the surface. Then they sank twenty-gauge needles into themselves. As blood spurted out, the couples sang, finger painted each other and covered themselves in palm prints. They were most definitely *in the zone.*

"Hey you!" a voice called out Dutch, who turned and found a man in silver-studded, leather, crotchless briefs. Old Jimmy One Eye facing north. He held a multi-stripped leather whip in his left hand. He asked Dutch, "Wanna take a crack?"

Dutch fought the revulsion rising in his throat. "No, thanks."

"Hey, man. I don't want to fuck you," the man explained, seeing the pained expression on Dutch's face. "It's for me and my girl." He used the whip to gesture to a striking blonde behind him. It was a peroxide job, because the top and bottom were as different as day and night. She wore a matching leather merry widow and had a come-hither look that Dutch found particularly unsettling. "We're celebrating our first anniversary as live-ins and we want you to spank us while we get it on."

Dutch declined the invitation again and moved away quickly.

Even if he weren't after Briganza, flogging the flaxen girl while her boyfriend pumped her wasn't, and never would be, Dutch's scene. The night he ran around with India, they saw a few like that, only less explicit. India told him the pain from the whip enabled lovers to measure how much one was willing to bear for the other's gratification. It established suffering thresholds, the yardstick for lasting romance.

He found Bishop gawking at a couple strapped to a turning Wurtenburg wheel. The man rode on top of the woman, having sex to the delighted cheers of spectators. Next to them, two lesbians engaged in a knife play scene. They cut each other with random slashes. Then rubbed their bleeding bodies, tongue kissed, and ground their sex together.

"And they say cops have the best drugs," remarked Dutch. Bishop could only nod. They headed over to the bar, where they had to shout to be heard above the music, screams, and other loud conversations. "Any luck?"

"Nope," Bishop confirmed.

A statuesque bartender, who looked more like a body builder than a swimsuit model, stepped up to their corner of the bar. "What'll it be?"

Bishop could barely hear her and shook his head. Dutch did the same.

"My name's Victoria," she said, "and my secret is there's a two drink minimum."

Dutch noticed she was indeed dressed only in lingerie. Her firm buttocks rippled on either side of a thong v-kini. Pendulous breasts thrust out generously. She strutted behind the bar like the queen of the St. Patrick's Day parade.

"What's in there?" Bishop asked the bartender and gestured toward a doorway curtained with strips of leather. Men and women walked in and out.

"Playrooms," Victoria replied with a knowing smile.

Bishop motioned to Dutch, craning his neck, and the two detectives moved toward the far-off door. When Dutch stood, his coat caught on the stool and flared open.

Exposing the gun nestled in his shoulder holster.

* * *

Victoria waited for the two men to recede. Then, she quickly picked up a house phone from under the bar and pushed a single extension. "We got a couple of cops. One white, one black. They are headed into the Playrooms."

* * *

Dutch preceded Bishop through the doorway. They entered a long, dark corridor. On either side of the scarlet linoleum, erotic graffiti covered both walls. With each step they took, the din of the main hall fell behind. All sound faded completely when they pushed through a second set of double doors and entered a video lounge.

XXX movies forced their way across massive high-definition screens. Extreme close-ups of entwined bodies flickering blue-white in the near darkness, bumping, pumping, and humping at 1080i. Twisted, tuned, and synchronized to a scintillating field rate of sixty thrust cycles per second. Tanuy speakers, mounted behind the screens, provided source direct sound for the urgent moaning in a state-of-the-art display of surround sound encoded without a trace of unwanted hiss from the accomplished actors, who were busily engorging and disgorging themselves for the grand finale—what Hollywood directors called the Money Shot.

"Guy...lives... works...with this shit? Can't be normal." Bishop looked overwhelmed by the filth of it all.

A man, half-naked, carrying his own trousers under his arm with his shirt unbuttoned and flying behind him, ran through the room trying not to look at the two detectives.

Dutch got the picture immediately. "We've been made."

They quickly stepped through a cellophane curtain into another narrow hallway. Stairs led down into a corridor with black, featureless walls. Fixtures were recessed into the low-flung ceiling that forced Bishop to keep his head bent as they descended.

Rushed, anticipatory noises filtered up the confined hallway as men and women discontinued their orgies, confirming that the patrons knew the cops had arrived. Soon, the hall was filled with partially clad bodies, barreling past the detectives, seeking the nearest exit.

Dutch led Bishop past a veritable drug emporium. Abandoned lines of coke on mirrored table tops, inhalers, hypodermic needles, syringes, half-rolled joints, and a spate of bongs, single hit toke bats, and sundry paraphernalia.

They put their hands into their coats, but didn't draw their guns. The free-for-all was beginning, like the leading edge of a stampede. Visible weapons would only make it worse. Some men and women shouted warnings to friends and fuck-buddies, breaking-up the remaining S&M soirees tucked neatly behind the private curtains secluding the beds of the hospital-like playrooms.

Bishop and Dutch each took a flank and began the hunt.

Dutch whipped back translucent plastic drapes and checked each individual cubicle as he moved down the line. Here was a middle-aged accountant, racked on a cruciform pedestal. Here was an Amazon, slapping a dwarfish Alopecian over and over. Here was an urolagnian being peed on by a woman. Here was a paraphiliac, alone, cutting and placing leeches on the body to suck the blood. They were the final phalanx of the degenerate army. So high on dope and pain, and getting off with such abandon, they didn't even notice Dutch invade their privacy and then leave. Shit, figured Dutch, these people, these incubi and succubi, were too far up the tortured pursuit of that elusive point of fusion between pleasure and pain to come back now.

Dutch flung aside the curtain of the last stall.

A naked man lay on a soiled mattress, his arms and legs tied to the four corner posts of the rickety metal-framed bed. His sobs were excruciating. His entire upper torso from neck to waist had been freshly tattooed with little regard to healing. Black ink and blood oozed from rope-size, crisscrossing, welts. And it looked as if he'd messed the bed, or been sodomized, or both.

"Jesus H. Christ," Dutch said, drawing his gun and stepping into the room. He felt nauseated simply looking at the man.

"Help me," the man pleaded.

Suddenly, Briganza charged from behind the curtains!

Snarling with hideous rage behind a full-leather face mask!

He lashed a whip with small, spiked balls hanging from the end! A cat o' nine tails! It sliced Dutch's hand before he could move. Dutch dropped his gun with a sharp cry. Then, what Dutch had mistaken for the man's sob became an uproarious guffaw. He'd baited Dutch for Briganza.

"Take that you fucking pig!" he shouted. The man's torn and bruised body bounced up and down on the bed, shaking the entire frame with shrill, hysterical laughter. Then, he let out a long, maddening howl as Briganza brought the nine knotted cords of the spiked balls lashing down for another strike.

***

Bishop spun and fired on Dutch's cry.

His .357 tore a single, molten hole through the frosted plastic curtain in the last room. He saw shadows behind it. Dancing and rolling. It looked like one of the men was down, but he couldn't tell who. Before he could investigate, the hallway was filled with bodies. The sound of the shot broke through the consciousness of even the most devout pleasure seekers.

These people liked pain, not dying. All of the remaining S&M scenes came to an abrupt finish. A bizarre and incredible flood of humanity filled the narrow hall. Scrambling in panic. Forcing Bishop against the opposite side. Cutting off his line of sight.

"Dutch!" he shouted above the trampling beat of bodies, thundering footsteps and screams. There was no direction to the fleeing masses. Just an overwhelming need to get the hell out of there. He tried to move forward, but it was no use. "Out of the way, damnit!"

Desperate to assist his partner, Bishop pushed his way through the unstoppable wave and tripped. When he hit the floor, he instinctively curled up in a ball for protection and held his gun close while the maul of feet kicked, jumped, leapt over, stepped on, rushed, raced, dashed, scrambled, fled, and careened for the door.

He heard Dutch yell out in pain.

And in trouble.

***

Dutch watched Bishop's bullet miss Briganza completely and take out the drug-crazed zombie on the bed instead. A single red dot right in the center of his forehead. A surprised, half-startled look on his face composed an expression, more curious than anything else. Now, even if he made it out alive, Dutch knew he and Bishop were going to have some explaining to do. Internal affairs had to be called in whenever a gun was fired. Those pencil pushers would have a field day with a situation in which a poor, drug-addled idiot tied to a bed had been shot through the forehead by a cop who couldn't even see him.

Fuck it. That nightmare is for later. Right now, Dutch's most pressing need was survival. Briganza return-whipped much faster than Dutch expected, and Dutch took another grazing shot to the face. The spiked spheres were light. About two ounces each, but nine of them together could crush a man's skull with a direct blow. Looking up at the squat, formidable frame of his attacker, Dutch had no doubt he was capable of delivering just that.

Dutch rolled across the floor, leaving thin, vermilion ribbons in his wake. He wasn't sure he could escape. He had heard Bishop yell out his name, but he sounded so far away. Now all he could hear was the knocking of feet, a sea of screams, and a strident ringing in his ears from where the medieval weapon had made contact with his head.

The cat-o'-nine-tails swung straight for his face again!

Dutch turned his cheek at the last moment and narrowly avoided another glancing blow. This time, the spikes skimmed so close, his skin felt the audible draft of air as the cylinders pushed past. The hair on Dutch's neck stood up. He panicked and reached for his gun. He thought he might even make it.

But even that short distance was too far.

And it took too long.

Briganza brought the metallic stock of the handle down hard into Dutch's spine!

Dutch went flat on the floor. Sharp, mind-numbing pain emanated from the eighth vertebrae of his back and marshaled across his body like a troop of angry soldiers. He moaned and then turned his head.

BoomBoomBoom.

The distinctive sound of Briganza's cowboy boots approaching. It wasn't a natural walking step. But light and clipped. Like a kicker lining up for the game winning field goal.

Dutch turned to face the attack. He saw metallic toes and spurs as Briganza lifted a boot well clear of the floor to deliver a terrifying punt to the side of Dutch's face. *This is it.* Lights out. Then, reflexively, without even a thought, Dutch's own leg shot out and into Briganza's anchor leg. Knocking him off-balance. Sending Briganza crashing down hard on the floor. Both men recovered with the same speed. Lightning quick. Piling their long limbs into an offensive crouch. Then launching toward each other in a powerful dive.

Their skulls smashed together.

Dutch and Briganza fell back, woozy. Briganza straightened instantly and bored in, swinging rough, gnarled fists in a ceaseless barrage. The first blow glanced Dutch's head, but the next three hit him squarely. He somehow stayed on his feet and stood his ground. Briganza threw an uppercut that cracked Dutch's chin and rang a bell in his head. Dazed, dizzy, and reeling, Dutch wambled unsteadily as he tried to step away.

His legs betrayed him. He couldn't move fast enough.

Briganza closed in for the kill. Fists poised like twin pistons.

Dutch looked down at his feet still refusing to move in spite of the hellacious pain coming his way. The ground began to turn. Spinning. He looked back up. Preparing to take the hit. He lisped through swelling lips, which now trickled with blood, "Come on then, motherfucker. I can take you."

A wicked right tore Dutch's head one way, then snapped it the other as Briganza followed up with a pulverizing left hook. Dutch raised his arms to ward off the blows, bobbed, and weaved, still stiff on his legs. Briganza changed to straight jabs instead, finding every hole, cutting right through Dutch's defenses and delivering crushing blows to his face and mid-section. *Bam!* A stiff left. *Bam!* Another. Then another, and another, and another.

Dutch's lights were blinking out now. He felt like he was caught in a fusillade of flashbulbs, unable to defend himself from the shadowy figure delivering the punches like white hot cannonfire. Dutch collapsed.

Wracked with pain. Eyes closing. On the verge of a blackout.

Then, through the dizzying madness, he saw the outline of a snakeskin boot. Something glistening at the top like a brilliant diamond. The reinforced metallic toe. Aimed right for his temple. Oh shit, Dutch thought, a second before it hit him. *Whack!* A concussion powered kick that could wake an elephant wrenched Dutch's entire head one hundred and eighty degrees.

Toward his fallen gun.

How he remained conscious, Dutch didn't know. That he possessed any reflexes at all astonished him. That he was still alive enough to know the moment of grace was at hand was completely incomprehensible. But somehow, even now, in his most trying moment, he was able to pull it all together and act.

Dutch reached out, swept the gun up, and fired as he turned.

One, two, three rounds discharged before he realized he was shooting into empty space. The bullets struck ceiling tiles and brought down a rain of cement and plaster.

Bishop burst through the door.

"Dutch! Are you okay?"

***

Bishop skidded to a halt. Dutch wasn't moving.

He's dead.

It was the first and only thought that tossed into Bishop's brain. He looked around quickly, desperately. *ShitShitShitShit!* His adrenaline was still running so high, the grief didn't quite hit him. The hallway outside had emptied.

Suddenly—a cough.

The instinct for self-preservation took over. Bishop's eyes snapped around! His gun ready to fire. Then he realized it was Dutch. *He's alive!* Dutch coughed again, a stream of blood-laced spittle leaking from the side of his mouth.

"You scared the fuck out of me," said Bishop, relieved.

"Yeah?"

Bishop reached down and helped lift his partner upright. "You good to go after this guy?" Dutch swayed and blinked twice. Bishop held two fingers in front of Dutch. "How many?"

"Twenty," Dutch said, then pushed Bishop's hand out of the way. "Don't worry about me. I'm good to go." He wiped the plaster off his face with his sleeve, checked his gun, then wobbled out the door toward the rear end of the club, where Briganza had fled.

Dutch and Bishop checked the remaining stalls. All empty. At the end of the hall, there was another long corridor. Filled with hanging curtains.

"I don't fucking believe this," Dutch exclaimed.

"Again," Bishop said, "one at a time."

Dutch stepped up the pace, angling his run down the left side of the hall. Bishop strode parallel, taking the right. For the next few seconds, curtain after curtain lifted and fell.

Then Bishop cried out, "I see him!"

Bishop ran smack through the curtained doorway and into a room, but here, on this side, there were no walls. Just frosted panels separating one playroom from the next. Briganza dodged through the maze, leaving a billowing swath of rustling plastic in his wake. Bishop followed. Losing and regaining sight of him several times. Bishop heard Dutch keeping pace in the outside hall. Unable to check the rooms without stepping in, Bishop kept an unsteady bead on the chase.

All sense of time and direction disappeared in the chaos of running feet, flapping plastic and zigzagging shouts. Bishop fired several times. Heard Dutch doing the same. Muzzles flared. Shots rang out. High-caliber bullets ripped through the flimsy maze without finding their target.

They both reached row's end.

Bishop cleared a curtain out of his way and stopped. He'd adjusted the direction of his run to arrive ahead of the wave of flying plastic. The curtains had stopped and he could hear the soft tread of careful feet on the running board.

Briganza was one curtain lift away.

Bishop leveled his gun. Waiting rigidly. *This is it.*

His finger squeezed tight around the trigger. Applying the few necessary pounds of pressure to draw the hammer back into a firing position. The pear-shaped curtain hangers scraped on the metal rod. The plastic doorway flung back!

Bishop felt the hammer engage.

Bullet about to pound out of the chamber.

"Hold your fire!" Dutch screamed, stepping into view.

Bishop jerked his finger. He did not know if he had squeezed the trigger or released it.

***

Seeing Bishop's surprise turn to fear, Dutch was sure Bishop had fired his weapon. The next split-second was the longest he had ever experienced. Waiting for the bullet to take him out at point blank range.

The hammer of Bishop's .357 fell.

Backward.

"Holy shit, man," Dutch breathed. "Holy fucking shit."

Another millimeter of depression from Bishop's finger, Dutch realized, and he'd be hurtling toward the white light right now. Dutch breathed again, slowly. Then they heard a rusty whine. Hinges! The detectives turned just in time to see Briganza duck through the Emergency Exit.

Bishop grabbed his radio. "He ran into the south side alley!"

***

From his command post, Schiff bellowed over the radio to the plainclothes at either end of the south side alley to move in. They started forward on a run. The alley was a delivery road. Empty to all appearances. *Thank god for small mercies.* Schiff ordered, "We're going in. Keep the eye in the sky lit up. I want daylight down in the alley."

"Ten-four," Crayton responded from the chopper.

Schiff watched it swoop down, outboard searchlight probing the street in an inverted funnel. Media helicopters and vans poured in. The crowds looked up, curious. They were used to seeing SFPD choppers making city sweeps all the time. Only not this close. As they checked each other out, Schiff knew they were all wondering if the potential threat was right in front of them. He was loving the attention, but he didn't want another disappointment like the post-lineup press conference. Briganza better be their man.

***

Briganza leaned against the cold, brick wall of the alley. Preventing a clear shot from the detectives in pursuit. Sweat rained down the front of his shirt. Breath pumping in short, agonizing bursts. He was about to make a mad dash for the end of the alley when he saw the four plainclothes posted at either side.

No way out.

Briganza's eyes darted through the holes of his face mask. On his left, there was a fire escape. Too high for a leap from the ground, but if he pushed over a trash can, he just might make it. Then again, he wasn't sure if the two cops inside, particularly the faster white one, might clear the door and take a shot at him before he climbed to safety.

There was just no time to think.

***

SWAT Team Leader Crayton steadied the black, stainless steel barrel of his .270 Winchester rifle. Targeted his night scope. He was using the rifle made infamous by the Attica prison revolt of '71, when nine hostages were killed along with thirty-one inmates by the state police officers ordered to contain the prison. Still a helluva gun, its potential was extremely lethal if inaccurately sighted. He amped up the gain until his field of vision glowed brighter than the noonday sun.

He could see the outline of a squirming human form pressed against the wall, breathing hard. Briganza. He couldn't be more than one hundred fifty yards away. Crayton sighted the subject's sternum, then lowered the cross-hairs almost three inches to account for the gain in trajectory over the line of sight. A decorated sniper as an Army Ranger, he set the barrel and eased his shoulder against the butt of the weapon. He lifted his index finger and took off the safety. Assuring certain death at the squeeze of the trigger.

The helicopter's spotlight picked out Briganza. The perp froze.

"I have him!" Crayton barked into his headset radio. Out of his peripheral vision, he saw the four plainclothes slow to a predatory walk, guns held high.

A loudspeaker blared, "You! At the door! This is the San Francisco Police Department! Put your hands up! Lay down on the ground! Lace your fingers behind your head!"

***

From the corner of his eye, Briganza could see that the Emergency Exit he'd used to leave was six inches from closing completely. He knew the spring-loaded lock prevented anyone from entering from the outside. On the other side of the door, the two detectives had to be just moments away from coming through.

Briganza backed up, raising his hands in surrender. He saw the plainclothes on the ground dip their muzzles. Briganza moved in a flash! Turned toward the Emergency Exit with the quickness of a bolting cat.

Whack! A bullet whizzed past his cheek and shattered a hole in the brick wall where his chest had been a split second before. It came from the chopper. All hell broke loose! Sniper fire rained down from the rooftops. The plainclothes in the alley pumped out wild shots. Bullets peppered the entire door and wall around it.

BamBamBamBamBamBam!

Reverberations rocked the narrow alley like a series of closely-packed thunderclaps. Briganza knew he'd beaten the bombardment by a second, no more. He was already inside, catching the door an inch before it closed. The sound cut off abruptly in muffled, distant pops.

His next running step brought him face to face with Dutch and Bishop.

***

Bishop, a stride ahead of Dutch, was caught flatfooted. He did not expect Briganza to return inside. *And alive.* He did not even see Briganza's arm swing. Just felt his teeth rattle. His eyes rolled up in their sockets. Pain crashed through his skull. As he went down with a grunt, he glimpsed Briganza swing that same arm at Dutch. There was a gun at the end of it. The barrel caught Dutch under the chin and he crumpled too.

Briganza fled.

"Police! Freeze!" Bishop stood up from an Indian squat. Fired!

Briganza dove through a curtain, rolled, pounded open a heavy iron door into another passage, and disappeared. Dutch scrambled to his feet beside Bishop. They started sprinting again. Passed through the plastic drapes. And skidded to a halt.

Steam reached for them like the warm embrace of a physical thing. They stepped forward cautiously, discovering showers and saunas. The roaring water, driven by air jets, kept the men and women oblivious to the police scene, still lingering. Peals of laughter and sex came from Jacuzzis and stalls, where couples, trios, and a ménage-à-everyone bathed in libertine venery.

"Look," whispered Dutch, pointing to a nearby gutter, where blood, the color of ground garnet, whirlpooled between the bars of the grate.

"He's hit," said Bishop.

They followed the droplets. If they belonged to Briganza, he was pushing deeper into the fog. The cops roughly shoved aside wet and naked bodies as they emerged through the swirling white mist. Seeing the detectives' guns, a blonde, who looked like confectioner's sugar, let out a knifing *screech!*

Pandemonium took hold.

The steam erupted into a chaos of shadowy limbs and slippery, well-built figures.

"What do we shoot at now?" Dutch asked.

"Fuck if I know," Bishop said, just as frustrated by the barrage of wet bodies, splashing water, and twirling towels.

Super-heated air burned a passage through his nostrils. The steamy conditions forced sweat out of every pore. His shirt was already drenched and his fingers were slippery on the trigger.

He raised a quieting finger and pointed toward a lonely shadow.

"Briganza?" whispered Dutch.

Neither man was sure. Bishop raised the radio to his lips and said in a low voice, "Can't see a thing in here, Lieutenant. Keep all exits covered."

"Roger," Schiff's voice crackled back.

Bishop took a moment to secure his radio, then turned around. He was alone. *Aw, fuck, not now.* "Dutch!"

No answer.

The mist broke for an instant in front of him and he saw Dutch darting behind a column of scalding white mist.

"Wait!" Bishop ran after him on the double. He shoved aside a couple trying to cross in front of him. They sprawled, slewing together across the tiles. He came upon the column of white. Blasted through it. Emerged into an empty passageway. Kept moving.

Half way down, he heard multiple gun shots!

His stride faltered and he almost slipped and fell. Around

the corner he pulled up short.

Dutch stood over a body. Briganza was dead at his feet.

***

At point blank range, the bullets had struck Briganza's chest with a force of three hundred and forty-one foot-pounds, lifting him clean off his feet into the wall. Blood splatter and streaks recreated his impact and slide to the floor.

"Goddamnit, Dutch!"

"It was white!"

The walls, the grout, the bath mats, everything, shared the same color. Depth perception posed a huge problem. Bishop could see that. But Schiff would pose an even bigger problem. A monumental problem beyond all comprehension. Bishop knew Schiff was going to hold him responsible, and sure as shit, one or both of them would be getting his walking papers. That was a price Bishop couldn't afford.

"Damn it, Dutch—"

"I couldn't see him clearly through the fucking steam!"

"He was—"

"I said I couldn't fucking see him—"

"—trapped against the wall!"

"—through the steam!"

"Fuck you, Dutch!"

"That's the fucking truth!"

"Bullshit!"

"Bullshit!"

Bishop stopped an inch from Dutch's face. Sweat raining down his forehead. "Fuck! Dutch! You fucked it up! Goddamnit! You needed that motherfucker! Don't you see that? His confession would have gotten you off! You stupid son of a bitch!"

Dutch shook his head angrily, "No way! No fucking way! This guy is my ticket out! We'll print the son of a bitch and it's over."

"No, Dutch. You're over. Get that? You're gone. You're fucking gone!"

Dutch moved in, eyeball-to-eyeball. Lids peeled wide. Thrust right up against Bishop's face. Bishop saw his partner's nostrils flare. Felt hot breath on his face. "What are you saying, man? That I deliberately whacked him?"

Dutch didn't blink. Neither did Bishop. "Maybe you didn't want him talking."

"What the fuck is that supposed to mean?! You think I'm guilty, too?"

"I didn't know, I don't know! Don't you fucking get it? It doesn't matter anymore! Guilty or not, you got no chance left in this department. He didn't even have a gun, man."

Dutch turned away and pummeled a fist so hard, the wall chipped from the force of his knuckles. Defeat bowed his shoulders and his head lowered. Tears welled up behind his eyes. Dutch's shoulders began to shake. "Oh, man, I fucked up...I really fucked up this time."

Bishop wanted to comfort him, but he was still so mad, if he even so much as touched Dutch, he was afraid he would beat the living shit out of him. Then, as if a switch had been flipped, Dutch stopped. He stared at Briganza.

Moved toward the body and breathed, "Holy shit."

"What?" Bishop tried to get a glimpse and edged around Dutch, who dropped to one knee. The steamy heat had separated a gap in Briganza's hairline.

He was wearing a wig.

Dutch pulled it off. The hair underneath was blond. The color of spoiled milk. He waved the steamy fog clear. He unbuttoned the black leather face mask. Peeled it off. The thin fissure of a scar ran horizontally under his right cheek.

"Holy fuck," Bishop said, getting a closer look, and dropping flat on his ass.

"Oh, man, that's rich," Dutch smiled.

Briganza was Myke the Dyke!

Fourteen.

Schiff stepped in first, hoping and praying he could finally close this case. It was the only acceptable consolation that would make up not going on his annual fishing trip. He flipped the switch behind the door. It turned on four free-standing lamps in a loft eight blocks from Castro Street. There were no ceiling lights. Measuring about twenty feet square, the room contained a twin mattress that rested directly on the hardwood floor. The same pine finish repeated on the exposed rafters of the roof, a four-way gable, which started at about seven feet along the edges and sloped to about thirteen feet in the center.

The loft belonged to Manuel Briganza, aka Myke the Dyke.

Dutch, Bishop, Magno, and Lee appeared on either side and fanned out, slipping on latex gloves. Schiff stood in the middle of the room like an august senator and watched his people work. Dutch opened the closet. Hanging inside were a variety of whips, belts, riding crops, and other S&M gear.

"Over here," signaled Magno. He rocked on the balls of his feet beside the narrow mattress. Schiff approached. Magno turned the mattress. Underneath were twenty neatly arranged bundles of fifty one hundred dollar bills.

"A hundred grand," Magno calculated.

"Where did he get that kind of money?" Schiff asked.

"From little planes in Aspen," Bishop leaned out and answered from another room.

Dutch and Magno joined Schiff, and they trooped into the kitchenette. A scale sat on the cutting board. Drawers were open. Revealing street sale baggies of cocaine.

"Must have skimmed drugs from his mob employers," speculated Dutch.

"Guys!" Lee shouted from the bathroom. The four men crowded in. Hanging across the mirror over the sink were two rows of bloody condoms.

"Souvenirs?" Bishop asked.

Lee shrugged.

"Or trophies," Dutch added grimly.

"We've got three victims," Bishop said. "There's more than three condoms."

"Sicko like this?" Schiff closed and opened his eyes. "Tip of the iceberg." He didn't speculate any further about the other possible victims indicated by the remaining prophylactics.

Lee held up a barber's razor and a butterfly knife. "Phenothalene tested positive for blood on both. Once we DNA match the victims, we'll know for sure."

"Look what he reads to unload," Dutch pointed to a stack of magazines in a rack beside the toilet bowl. *Fetish World, Cutting Edge, S&M Weekly, Bondage A Go-Go.*

"Hard core, hard core," observed Bishop.

"What ever happened to Better Homes and Gardens?" Schiff asked.

"Different garden variety," Dutch monotoned.

"Looks like we have our man," Schiff declared finally.

"I think so," Lee agreed.

Schiff was not the kind who apologized. And he was not about to start now. Though when he spoke he added a conciliatory tone to his voice. "I guess you're off the hook, Holland."

"Apology accepted," Dutch smiled back. "And appreciated."

"Welcome back to the team, partner." Bishop clapped Dutch on his shoulder.

"Thanks." Dutch turned to Schiff, "Sooner or later a

crazy was going to cut loose on America's other side. I'm just glad we got him."

***

Dutch drove his SUV up Nicole's driveway. The porch was empty. All four cars were in the garage. He got out and took a moment to enjoy the spectacular view of San Francisco from her lofty perch on the hill. The weather was gorgeous, losing the milky veil from the marine layer that had blemished the now aquamarine sky for the past few mornings. The trees bent to the gentle sea-breeze and emitted fragrant aromas.

Dutch practically leapt up the sweeping marble steps to Nicole's front door. Rapped his knuckles twice.

While he waited, he inhaled deeply. Drinking it in. The entire day, the entire world, from the rocky blue ocean to the furthest vault in heaven, seemed filled with possibility. New life. And fresh opportunity. He wanted to remember this moment. Live oaks, cypress, and eucalyptus rose out of the ground, gift-wrapped in the late-evening glow. Stretching up to the sky. The wonder of creation.

Bellisima! Bishop would have said.

Dutch's heart beat faster. Quickening the blood flowing in his veins. Even his skin felt energized, as if a current was coursing through him. He smiled. The first real smile, the first genuine mirth, he'd felt in a long, long time. He turned back toward the door when he heard approaching footsteps. The latch turned as she opened the door.

Nicole was expecting him. She looked ravishing in a short white dress. The wind entered the slit along the side and caused the gossamer fabric to billow. Allowing Dutch a glimpse of her pear-shaped breasts and bare hips.

"Congratulations on closing the case," she smiled.

"Thanks," Dutch grinned back. To hell with it, he thought, and swept her off her feet and kissed her deeply as he carried her inside the house.

"Won't you come in," she said, pulling back to look into his sea green eyes.

Dutch kicked the door shut.

"Would you like a drink?" she asked.

"This early?"

"Red wine," she winked.

Dutch remembered. It slowed coagulation.

"Sure," he set her down. Heart pounding.

"What's gotten into you today?" Nicole smoothed the ruffled creases in her dress. The times she'd seen him before, he'd always been so reticent. So withdrawn. Keeping to some part of himself that he refused to share with her or anyone else.

"Life," Dutch said. "I'm ready to live again."

She crossed to the wet bar. She'd already poured them each a glass of claret. She handed him one. "I'll toast to that."

As Dutch raised the red wine glass to make the toast, he realized that its shape was designed for seduction. Lifted toward the mouth, the thin rim required her lips to open in a kiss to take a drink. Nicole's eyes rose just barely above the heliotrope color of the alcohol.

She met his gaze evenly.

Inviting.

***

Bishop came into the station to complete the murder report and put the case to bed. It was Saturday. The squad room was deserted. While Highway Patrol and Traffic was out in full force, other divisions were off. Barely half of all the fluorescents flickered. He set down a steaming mug of French roast that he'd brought from home, he brought the preprogrammed form up on his computer. He missed typewriters. Missed rolling the form over the platen. Missed lining up the margins one and half inches in from either side of the page. There was something tangible about typing up a report. He pulled back his chair, pondering the contents of the

Supplemental Crime Report, Golden Gate Park Precinct, Case Number SF409-3376.

He would report that they had discovered Manuel Briganza had an alias, and that the alias was Myke the Dyke. He would note that Briganza was responsible for the wrongful death of at least three individuals, possibly more—though that could only be confirmed in another supplemental report following the lab's blood work. He would list all of the evidence collected, prefacing each with an item number and a terse, though adequate, description. He'd finish with a brief recapitulation of his thoughts on the case, and then scribble a few notes regarding the impending evidentiary confirmation from Lee in the sci-crime lab.

Same old, same old. Bishop plumped his big butt down.

Something was wrong.

Bishop lifted up out of his chair and stared curiously down at the seat. He was looking at a padded, brown envelope nestled on top of the cushion. No markings of any kind. Something in his memory clicked. He didn't touch the envelope. Opening his table drawer, he retrieved the envelope that Schiff had received, containing Dutch's confidential IAD file.

The two envelopes were identical.

Oh, come on, man. He took out a pair of latex gloves, slipped them, and lifted the envelope and turned it over. No postmarks on the other side. He quickly cleared a work area on his desk and dusted it from a kit he kept under his lower left drawer.

No fingerprints.

He undid the staples, blew hard, parting the opening and looked in. There was one item inside. He took it out.

A DVD.

***

Her hair flying, Nicole slammed hard against the wall!

Her lips, the centerpiece of her porcelain-perfect face, curled into a delicious smile.

"You call that foreplay?" she teased in her throaty voice. "Come and get it."

A moment later, Dutch's face descended. Devouring her lips like a ravenous beast. Colliding. Forcing her mouth open. He gripped her face in his hands. Refusing to let go. Nicole fiercely clawed into his scalp. Breaking skin, releasing blood. He felt her long, manicured nails. *So that's why she keeps them sharpened.* Dutch felt a tingle, not pain. He was so consumed by the blistering heat between them, he couldn't think, didn't care, about anything else.

Their tongues entwined. Darting in and out of each other's mouths. Wrestling for control. Like fierce animals engaged in a primal feeding frenzy, saliva rolled down their chins and dripped onto their panicked throats and heaving chests.

Dutch couldn't take it anymore. He shoved a hand through the slit on the side of her dress, cupped a breast, and pinched it between his fingers. Her nipple became hard and erect.

Nicole moaned sharply. Emitted a sharp gasp. And gyrated her hips against his, rubbing against the enormous, thrusting bulge charging against his slacks.

Dutch rammed his other hand up her thigh and grabbed a cheek, separating her legs, and allowing him better contact with the spreading silky wetness below. She lifted up on her toes, did a small leap, and wrapped both legs around his waist as he held her in his arms.

They continued to kiss and grind. Passion vibrating from one body to another. Dutch piled against her, pressing and mashing her body against the wall for all he was worth.

The sex scent in the room grew. They slammed back and forth, back and forth, until it reached such a degree, they could smell, feel and taste it in every unhesitating movement.

Dutch's legs and arms weakened.

He slowly let her down.

Her legs slipped from his lower back like a spider unfurling it's limbs from its prey. Her eyes were wet with desire. Glistening in the soft skylight descending on angels' breath from the window overhead. Dutch pulled back, chest lurching from the effort. Incendiary eyes burning uncontrollably. Charged with energy. Consumed with lust. He reached down to unbuckle his belt.

"Wait!" Nicole snapped.

She turned around and reached for her purse on the mantelpiece over the fireplace. Dutch stepped behind her and thrust his erection against her. Maintaining contact. Letting her know the immediacy and urgency of his desire. He slid both hands over her breasts, down her hard flat stomach, and then drove them down, down, down between her legs. Pressing hard against her sex and lifting her up onto her toes.

She arched her back with a sharp sigh and sagged against him, momentarily lost. Dizzy. And overwhelmed. She fumbled for the clasp of her purse as her legs parted helplessly, letting him wedge his fingers inside the folds of her swollen lips. Pressed herself against them. Rocking uncontrollably to the pleasure he was giving her.

Dutch responded with short thrusts and rolling fingers. She twisted her neck around. Their lips met again and locked. She dropped her purse and they wrestled with renewed fire.

He slid off the shoulder straps of her dress and drew his mouth over her breasts, sucking and biting them occasionally to send her over the brink. Nicole threw her head back. Her nipples felt like divine nerve endings that were connected to every sexual emotion she could handle. Dutch looked up. He could see her heartbeat rippling the skin over her jugular.

Nicole called out his name as if she were in love with the sound of it. He clutched her tighter, pulled her impossibly close, but couldn't hold on. She'd managed to somehow twist away and now stared at him with impish delight. He wanted to enter her. Over and over. He wanted her so badly, his body screamed with a hunger that could never be satisfied.

"Not now, Dutch." She slipped the straps of her dress back over her shoulders. He looked at her, puzzled. "Oh, don't worry, baby," she said as if talking to a child. "We'll get it on. It's just, well..." She drew her words out as if she were opening a very special gift and wanted to measure his every reaction. "I've got a surprise for you."

Nicole grabbed her purse, opened it, and dipped in. She didn't have to rifle through the contents. Her hand emerged at once.

With a barber's straight edge.

***

Stillness gripped Schiff's office. Bishop had called him in. Which Schiff didn't mind so much on this particular Saturday, because his wife was out of town. She had planned a weekend in the wine country with the girls, driving along the narrow two-lane highways of California's Central Coast, and saw no reason to cancel just because her husband's fishing trip fell through. Until Bishop had called, he'd been frittering away his time. *Snap!* Fulminating over his backyard barbecue, whose coals stubbornly refused to light.

Schiff stared at the DVD Bishop held in his hands, then pointed to the TV set in the corner. "Well, let's have a look."

Bishop inserted the DVD into the deck. The heads spun to life. He pushed 'PLAY' and stepped back. Snow appeared. Clarifying into an image.

India's apartment.

"Looks like a copy of the tape from the camera I found behind the mirror."

***

Nicole wracked open the razor and held it out. "You go

first."

Dutch hesitated.

"I trust you completely, baby." Nicole kissed him deeply and looked into his eyes. "It's all about trust, remember?" She kissed him again, stroking his cheek with a reassuring caress. Her effortless composure quieted his nerves. With a look, she commanded him to take the razor.

Dutch did. And turned it around, then over.

Getting used to the weight and the balance. While he got comfortable with it, Nicole walked over to a device, which looked more like a laptop computer than a high-fidelity audio component. Just like at *Scars,* a low, sensuous hum throbbed out over hidden speakers.

"Good fuck music," she said, showing him the case.

"The best," Dutch agreed.

She stepped in close and offered him the V of her hemline. "Slip the razor under my dress, through the side."

Dutch's fingers began to sweat. He could hear the tear of the gossamer fabric, separating, as he drew the blade upward toward her chest. Nicole raised her hand around his neck. To help steady her, he encircled his free hand around her waist.

"For this to feel like the safest place in the world," she said, "we have to let go of our fears."

Then, as if it had been planned to a beat in the music, she lunged against him, allowing the blade to slice into her chest and draw blood. Dutch jerked back, in reflex to the cutting. But her hand was already over his, keeping the blade pressed to her chest.

Dutch didn't know what came next.

"Just dance," she told him.

He moved with her. Swayed. Her hand guided his and he could feel the edge pierce her skin. Each cut drew a wince and a cry. A sigh and a moan. Stains of red appeared under her white dress. Tiny rubies flush against the fabric.

With each exclamation, Nicole's pain shifted toward

pleasure. Erotic moans. Soon, stars fired in front of her eyes. Anyone listening, without seeing what was happening, would have assumed she was having fantastic sex.

The music tempo increased.

The step of their apache dance quickened. The razor sharp edge piercing with greater frequency and intensity. Dutch held her closer. Tighter. Her lips emitted brief, ecstatic shrieks. By the time the song ended and they stopped dancing, the front of her dress was crisscrossed in scarlet. Nicole's face was suffused with livid exhilaration. Dutch turned the razor outward and cut her dress down the middle. It fell to the floor, revealing her naked body. Nicole followed his stare.

From neck to navel, she looked like a canvas of random red slashes.

Blood drying like paint.

"Now we're getting somewhere," she heaved between heavy, excruciating breaths.

She raised his hand with the razor. It was wet with blood. She touched the blade to her lips, kissed it. Then kissed Dutch.

She bent to his ear and whispered, "Foreplay's over."

***

On the videotape playing in Schiff's office, Dutch and India were naked on the couch. He ripped the packing off a condom with his teeth. India cupped his balls in one hand and rolled the condom down the length of his cock with the other. When Dutch was ready, India pushed the lamp on the side table to the floor.

The bulb shattered. Shards scattered across the carpet.

Bishop and Schiff flinched, anticipating India's pain when she rolled off the couch. She winced and emitted a short cry as she slipped onto the glass.

After a moment, she beckoned to Dutch. He lowered himself. Gingerly. But India grew impatient and pulled him down hard on top of her. She screamed in pain as his weight pressed her body deeper into the knifing edges. But she wouldn't let go. Sliding a hand between them, under his stomach, she grasped and guided him inside her. Dutch looked at India. Her face was ecstatic, her eyes shining and her cheeks blushing like bloodstone.

Carefully resting his arms on either side of her head, he buried his face in her hair and began to move. Barely perceptible at first.

A slow pulse.

Up, down. In, out.

She began to throw her hips against him. Demanding his deepest penetration. Arcing her back against the glass. Seeking the incomparable sensation of having him thrust hard, fast and long. Each time her back flattened against the floor, her voice rose shrilly.

Dutch didn't take long to respond. Her heavy breathing and ecstatic moans, flush against his ear, soon urged him into powerful, lunging thrusts. Like a furious wind before a storm. His movements matched and exceeded her intensity.

Her cries tore out of her throat louder and louder.

Blood came off her skin and onto his hands as he ran his fingers under her back for better support. Soon, Dutch was completely turned on. Pounding into her with unbridled fury. Enraptured by the forbidden thrill of India's response. Her pain and pleasure combined into a prolonged keening wail that ended only when she came. With rabid, animal-like violence.

Schiff and Bishop, feeling like voyeurs, turned away from the action on the screen to face one another, feeling a mixture of fascination and guilt at having pried so far into Dutch's private life.

"Now we know what he did on the night of the murder," Schiff said.

But there was more.

***

Nicole and Dutch made it upstairs. They were in Nicole's spacious master bedroom. Naked. Exhausted. Exhilarated. They lay together on Nicole's antique bed, a vintage Victorian frame supporting a plush Sterns and Foster mattress. The box springs placed them a full three feet off the floor.

The satin sheets were stained with blood.

Most of Nicole's cuts had dried. Exhibiting the same quick-healing capabilities that she had mentioned when she first met him at *Scars* two weeks ago. They resumed cuddling, their kisses full of sighs and sweetness. Their urgency had been exorcized by the unrelenting pace of their first session of lovemaking.

Now she was ready for more.

Nicole kissed her way down his body slowly. She reached between his legs. He was bigger and harder than the first time. She took him into her mouth. Dutch remembered how it felt then. It felt even better now. He gasped while the diamond stud on her tongue played rough and smooth, hot and cold, over his sex-wet cock. Jolts ran up his spine like bullets. Guttural moans undulated out of his throat to the ebb and flow of a growing sensation that shook his entire frame.

She took him to the brink and stopped.

"No!" he said. "Don't stop."

He didn't know why he was telling her anything. Nicole knew what she was doing.
Before the tingling build faded to the point where he would have to start again, she straddled him, bent her knees on either side of his chest, and trapped his arms under her legs.

Dutch's eyes widened in fear.

"My turn," she said, raising a hand over her head.

Dutch saw a glint of metal! Her hand slashed down! He convulsed and cried out!

Nicole drew the barber's straight edge diagonally across his chest. A clean incision. He felt a rush of terror. His heart beat faster. Blood filtered out on either side of the cut.

"Trust me now?" she asked.

***

Schiff and Bishop were stunned. Onscreen, there was blood everywhere. India and Dutch could both be mistaken for victims, if they hadn't seen what had come before.

"I need a break, baby," India told Dutch as she started to move away.

But quick as a snake, Dutch grabbed her. His sinewy, pale skin coiled and corded. Eyes glinting with a startling lack of mercy. He hissed, "Not yet."

***

Dutch and Nicole were screaming. He flailed from side to side. Nicole rocked with passion, slashing his chest every which way. She rode harder and cut faster with each movement. He pulled her down and pushed her up.

Loving every pain-driven minute of it.

Agony seared across his face. Flashed across his chest. And rippled out of his body like shafts of lightning from the multitude of sharp cuts delivered by Nicole. As his skin tore under the touch of the blade, he also felt an exquisite tremor radiating from where they joined. She bucked her hips mercilessly. And like a wild, sunfishing horse, he fastened his hands to her hips and held firm inside of her.   Nicole's wounds opened in the violent commotion. Droplets of her blood leaking down, mixing with his.

They worked toward a monstrous climax.

He watched her come first. An internal temblor that started at the base of her spine and shook every limb. Then he surged, wracking her with aftershocks, and responding with his own explosion, which roared out of him. He was not wearing a condom and felt their come mix, mingle, and spread warmly.

She collapsed. Her mouth resting against his ear.

Whispered, "Dutch..."

***

Bishop's heart bucked. Schiff couldn't take his eyes off the screen. Dutch pushed India powerfully on her hands and knees into a position of total submission, then thrust himself into her from behind. Bishop remembered Dr. Pease's conjecture. *The last act was anal sex.*

Bishop's eyes focused back on what was happening.

India's face was stretched in a *smile*. She was *enjoying* it. India's knees pressed and scraped the glass on the floor. She screamed in the agony and ecstasy as Dutch savagely pounded into her. They rocked back and forth, working to an explosive climax. India fell forward, face flushed. Tears of agony roared down.

But her eyes sparkled. With sheer joy. Barely able to get the words out, she panted, "That was awesome."

"We're not finished," Dutch snarled, still behind her.

He grabbed her hair and snapped India's head back. India emitted an excruciating cry! Bishop realized the ecstasy was all gone. Now, fear spread across India's face. Fear and a pain she didn't enjoy. Bishop swallowed.

Dutch, come on, man, no! Say it ain't so.

***

Dutch stared at Nicole, into those striking eyes the color of coruscating waves.

"Like it so far?" she asked, catching her breath. She tenderly ran her hands over the rapidly healing scars on his chest. She smoothed out the taut musculature with even strokes. Clearly defining the scar pattern and admiring it with a sense of accomplishment.

"Give me a minute and I'll go you one better." Dutch pulled her head down and kissed her. He took the razor and swung out of bed. Saw himself in the full length mirrored doors of her closet. Paused. Grinned and looked over his shoulder, "I like it."

She'd etched a constellation of three sharp-edged Xs across his chest.

"We're just getting started, baby," she smiled back, slipping under the sheets stained with blood, sweat, tears and come.

"So am I," Dutch replied and went into the bathroom.

***

Schiff got the jolt of his life. Even the habitually placid Bishop took a startled step forward.

India was being killed on camera.

She disappeared from sight until the murderer struggled to hoist her off the glass. Carried her to bed. And tossed her in uncaringly. India's head fell backward onto the pillow, her eyes open, her throat slit. Exactly like she had been found.

Schiff turned sharply toward Bishop, who carried the same wide-eyed disbelief as the lieutenant.

"Son of a bitch!" Schiff barked. "Where is he?"

Bishop's eyes leapt. "Nicole's."

Schiff yelled. "Get over there, now! I'll call and have backup sent immediately."

Bishop dashed out of Schiff's office.

***

Dutch stepped up to the sink and stared at himself in the mirror. His face registered little of the pain he ought to be feeling from the wounds on his upper torso. He twisted his chest right and then left. Examining the scars. Thinking she didn't do that bad of a job. *Silly, three Xs like that.*

Almost child like.

There was something about the pattern that intrigued him. He turned on the tap. Ran his finger under the water of the basin until it was hot to the touch. Modeled his chin from side to side. Wet the blade. And raised the razor.

He began to shave.

***

Nicole picked up Dutch's gun off the night stand and slipped it under the sheets. Then, she heard something and craned her neck, peered down the hall. The bathroom door was half-closed and she couldn't see inside. She thought it was a pipe at first. Or streaming water. *No. It's something else.*

Something cheerful and entirely different. An absurd sound echoing over the tiled expanse. It sounded like a nursery rhyme with a couple of bars missing. After a moment, she realized what it was.

Whistling.

Nicole frowned.

Dutch was whistling *'Somewhere over the rainbow.'*

That's when the cell on the nightstand vibrated.

She looked at the caller ID: *Unavailable.*

She reached over and turned it off.

***

Dutch nicked himself. A drop of blood rolled down his neck. He exclaimed under his breath, "Now what?"

Dutch looked at the razor, then to the bedroom door.

***

Bishop slapped a red light atop his Camry, put on his high beams and bulleted out of the police parking lot to the tourists-filled streets. It was the weekend. He was forced to ride sidewalks, even the median, because the commuters had no room to pull over and let him pass. They simply stopped and watched his car careen by as he dropped the hammer and damned all who got in his way.

At one intersection, he escaped the front of the tram with a foot to spare. His cell rang. It was Schiff. "No answer."

"Shit." Bishop checked his watch, sweating it out. He was going to be too late, and he knew it.

***

In Nicole's bathroom, the overhead light flashed off the blade washing under the tap and put a slash across Dutch's retina. For a moment, his eyes glinted.

"Dutch?" Nicole called out tentatively.

"Be there in a minute," he answered.

***

Bishop broke into an empty corridor of road. Traffic free. An unnatural sight in the congestion capital of the world. He floored the gas pedal.

The Camry spitfired past 90 M.P.H.

Schiff had called ahead and ordered Dispatch to get traffic cops to clear the intersections for Bishop.

All the way to Nicole's mansion.

***

Nicole watched Dutch emerge from the bathroom. Naked. Body rigid with anticipation. Water dripping. A stippled trail of rhinestones. She moved. Smooth as a silk snake. No bones, nothing solid. Seemingly devoid of resistance. She knew how he'd react. Heat rose behind Dutch's eyes. His hard-on returned. She curled up a smile that played like a flame on her lips. Dutch paused in front of the closet.

Nicole's exposed a leg, crooked it to the side, and exposed her shaven sex that blushed deeply with their recent activity. Dutch's eyes drew to it. As she hoped it would. She touched herself to ensure his complete attention.

Spellbound, he raised the razor. "Let's do it."

***

Bishop's Camry roared up the driveway. Coming to a

grinding halt just behind Dutch's SUV parked under the shade of the porte-cochere. He leaped out of the car and raced for the front door. He tried the knob, prepared to blow the lock open, but the door gave way.

Bishop hit the marble floor and his shoes slipped.

At first, he thought it was the polished surface, but when he looked down, skating for balance, he saw blood. The red trail led upstairs.

Bishop took the steps two at a time.

Toward the master bedroom.

***

Dutch twirled the razor, a grin blooming on his face. Then it froze. Nicole hesitated. Just enough. He saw movement in her eyes. And sensed someone behind him.

"Watch out!" she screamed.

Dutch whirled around!

Gillette!

Dutch didn't know who Nicole warned. He didn't have time to find out either.

Storming out from within the closet, Gillette held his barber's straight edge over his head. Poised to bring it down after his next stride. As Dutch raised his arms to defend himself, he saw Nicole in the mirror. She pulled his Browning out of the holster on the bedside table.

Gillette was about to release the razor when Bishop crashed through the door! Two guns cross-armed in front of him. Everyone went still. Bishop looked at Dutch, Nicole and Gillette. Then they began to shout. One voice over another.

"He was going to kill me!" Nicole screamed in the direction of Dutch and Gillette.

Dutch whirled, "Yeah. He was hiding in the fucking closet."

Gillette yelled, "Glad I was! He was going to kill her!"

"Bullshit!" Dutch blared. "Drop your razor, asshole!"

Bishop's guns wavered between the three of them.

"Take that fuckin' gun off me!" Dutch screamed.

Bishop did not. "Nobody fucking move!" he boomed. Shifting one gun between Nicole and Dutch, the other at Gillette. "You! Up against the wall!" Gillette stayed where he was. "Now!" Bishop shouted at him. "Do it now!"

"Oh, come on, man! He was going to kill her! I had to do something—" Gillette raised his voice, pleading.

"Back up! Back up!" Bishop insisted.

"What's going on?" Nicole stammered, Dutch's gun trembling in her hands, her face puzzled and drawn.

"Drop the gun, lady!"

Dutch swiveled back and forth. Gillette. Nicole. Bishop. With so much shit hitting the fan, it was impossible to keep it all straight. He was caught in the cross-fire with nowhere to turn. "Take the fucking gun off me, Bishop!"

Bishop took his eyes off Gillette. Moved them over to his partner.

And that's when Gillette made his move. Releasing his razor.

Dutch saw it. Spun. Too late.

Nicole swung her gun at the same time.

Bishop squeezed both triggers in reflex to the panic.

BANGBANGBANGBANGBANGBANGBANG!

Nicole and Bishop started firing simultaneously. Dutch had no idea whose bullets struck what. But he knew the situation had spun terribly out of control. The dominos started to fall.

A bullet split the side of Dutch's neck. Blood sprayed. Three red holes stitched across Gillette's chest. He pounded backward, striking and shattering the mirrored closet doors. He was dead before he hit the ground. Shards, sparkling with his dying reflections, rained down.

Bishop didn't make it out clean either

Nicole's gun pointed at Bishop's heart, but her hands

were shaking like a leaf.

"C'mon lady. You don't want to do that," Bishop said.

Dutch realized she was trembling because she was dying. Nicole skewed sideways and slumped in a heap against the pillows. Lifeless.

Then Dutch began to fade. He thought he was going to black out. Instead, he came to again. Bishop was shaking him. Dutch blinked. He could hear himself breathing. A roaring gust between his ears each time he inhaled and exhaled. *I'm alive. Shit, I'm still alive.* But just barely, Dutch knew, because the light dimmed again. His lips upturned slightly in a rag doll smile.

He didn't intend to smile.

He was trying to warn Bishop that Nicole's hand twitched.

She was alive.

Her eyes fluttered open. She curled her finger around the trigger of the Browning. The rest of her body went rigid. She half-turned on the bed toward them. She gripped the handle as steadily as she could and slowly raised the gun above the sheets.

"The Loot and I," Bishop was saying, "we saw the tape from the camera in India's house. We know..."

Dutch lost track of Bishop's voice. He was sinking fast. His eyelids closed. He dug his nails into Bishop's hand. Hoping that would alert his partner because he couldn't find his voice, let alone words. But Bishop didn't notice. He thought Dutch was just squeezing from the pain.

Dutch forced his eyes open. His pupils skittered to the corner of his eyes where he saw Nicole aiming at the back of Bishop's head.

Oh, shit.

Dutch mustered up every ounce of strength left in him, grabbed the barber's straight edge at his side, lifted to his elbows and whipped it forward.

"What the——" Bishop yelled, raising two arms in an 'x' to protect himself.

The razor tumbled end over end across the room.

The muzzle of Dutch's Browning flashed repeatedly. Dutch couldn't tell which came first. Her gunshot or his deadly strike. Nicole's body shot back against the headboard as bullets ricocheted in a wild frenzy. He lost sight of her as Bishop ducked, covering him. The rounds chipped the walls, ceiling, and floor. Plaster rained over them.

The deafening *booms* finally died.

A prickling silence returned.

Bishop rolled off him. Dutch's eyes opened. His aim had been true. He'd got her first. The gunfire, he guessed, was her finger reacting in a death spasm. Nicole was pinned against the mahogany of the Victorian headboard. Knife lodged in her throat. Blood spilling from her mouth. Down either side. Her eyes registered that funny look someone gets when they cannot comprehend what has happened to them.

Complete shock.

Nicole, so full of vitality, sex, and heat—all things physical—only moments before, was quite dead.

Dutch coughed. Spitting up blood from the wound in his throat. A splash of crimson spread down his shirt. Dutch looked at it. He murmured, "Blood ain't sexy, man, it's fucking painful."

"Tell me about it," Bishop replied.

Sirens gathered in the distance. Dutch remembered Bishop was hit too and not much else. A numbing pain extended in long icy runners, and finally robbed him of consciousness.

Fifteen.

Schiff stood in the critical care wing located on the second floor of St. Mary's Hospital. Bishop was lying under clean white sheets. Thick gauze pads over his upper right deltoid and on his back, just above his kidney. Schiff had driven down to the hospital as soon as he had heard about the 10-53. Schiff paced for three hours while doctors operated. Then another two hours while he waited for the anesthesia to wear off.

By the time Bishop resurfaced to the conscious world, it was past visiting hours and Schiff had to leave. Bishop called the station later that night and gave his report to the officer on duty, Eric Olsen, tying everything up nicely. But Schiff still wanted to put a few nagging questions to rest. Two of his detectives down, Schiff had to juggle the manpower crunch and couldn't get out of the office all day. By the time he made it in, it was 7:45 P.M., leaving Schiff only fifteen minutes to talk about what happened before visiting hours ended.

"You want to go over what happened?" Schiff asked. "If you're up to it."

Bishop tried to prop himself up on his elbows.

"Here, let me." Schiff adjusted the two pillows behind Bishop's head to make him more comfortable, then handed Bishop a glass of water from his bedside table.

Bishop looked fine, but his skin had blanched two shades from the significant loss of blood.

Nicole's bullet had missed his kidney by a few millimeters and gone clean through. A little more to the left and it would have hit his liver, in which case, Bishop wouldn't be here at all. A man can live with only one kidney, without any kidneys if he came in for dialysis three or four days a week, but if the liver was shot, that was cause for an immediate eviction from the Hotel Life. The doctors had insisted Bishop stay under observation.

"How's Dutch?" asked Bishop.

Schiff shook his head. "Doctor's won't call it either way."

Bishop slow blinked. "Goddamn that son of a bitch. I warned him about crossing the line."

"Come on, Bishop," Schiff rolled his finger impatiently. "Let's tie this one up, huh?" Schiff had a hard time effecting sympathy and playing the Florence Nightingale routine for too long now that he knew Bishop was going to be all right.

Bishop took a long, difficult drink, and handed it back to Schiff. His voice remained hoarse and sluggish from the medication. "Nicole knew Myke the Dyke was Briganza all along. He worked for her using both aliases. Cutting by night, running drugs through Cardoba Meats by day. Did you check them out?"

Schiff nodded. "Yeah. Cartel owned. I told them about the meat locker chase and how our perp hid in a carcass. They said that wasn't hollow by accident. He probably carved it out ahead of time for a cross-country smuggling operation. Go on."

"With the heat turning up, Nicole found the perfect out by putting on that little show in Myke's loft. He had all the credentials to take the rap for the murders."

"Slow down. Let's start with victim number one. Lauren."

"The way I figure it, she introduced Nicole to her mob clients and hooked her on the idea of using the club as a front for the coke. Once Nicole was doing well, Lauren got greedy and wanted a piece of the action—not realizing Nicole didn't like to share. Money, men, it was the same to her. She had to have it all. Bringing us to India."

"Victim two," Schiff said. "Nicole didn't approve when India went after Dutch...or didn't trust her not to tell him about their sideline business."

"That's where the motive shifts to the left a bit, from money to jealousy. Nicole, Gillette, and India were into threesomes, but I suspect the camera was a dirty little secret between India and Nicole, otherwise Gillette wouldn't have been out there videotaping himself cutting India's throat after Dutch left."

"Wait a minute," Schiff said, backing up. "They were partners, right?"

"Maybe Nicole was tired of him. She was the type that tired easily."

"Horse of the short race," Schiff said.

"Exactamènt," Bishop agreed. "Besides, with Dutch, she had a new boy toy to play with."

"But she didn't plan to keep Dutch around too long either," Schiff followed the logic. "That's why she tried to finger him. Sending his Houston file to us using her father's clout with the FBI."

"And to appease Gillette. You gotta remember, he'd killed twice for her, and she hadn't done anything to incriminate herself. So, it was only his ass on the line. The trust had bottomed out and he knew he could never implicate Nicole because of her father's connections. Besides, what jury would convict someone who looked like her on testimony of someone who looked and acted like him?"

"Good point," Schiff agreed. "And don't forget his similar prior out of Miami."

"This is where it all gets murky," Bishop's brow furrowed. "There was no need to kill Elise. Unless jealousy was a factor."

"That ain't enough for Gillette to kill for Nicole, not

once, but three times that night." Elise, Jett, and Russell.

"Not if Nicole threatened Gillette with the tape from India's murder. Or maybe, Gillette might have enjoyed killing. Pervert like that, anything's possible."

Schiff wasn't buying it. "No matter how many times I roll it around in my head, that sounds thin."

"Or, maybe she told Gillette that killing Elise would turn all the attention toward Dutch. After all, they were recently divorced and he had a history of physical abuse."

"But why would she show up and then spring Dutch? And what about Gillette? I know he isn't the brightest guy in the world. But you say he doesn't suspect a thing?"

"Why should he? She's just laid out a plan to frame Myke the Dyke instead."

"Of course, when she's telling Gillette this, she leaves out the part about sending us the DVD copy of the tape from India's apartment," Schiff filled in. "This is the part of your report where you say Nicole's working from a carefully laid out plan."

"Nicole wanted to wipe the slate clean for herself," said Bishop. "She was thinking way ahead of the game at that point and was ready to make her power play. She'd figured out how to get rid of them all and came up with a topper to get rid of Dutch—get him in the sack, then have Gillette kill him and claim self-defense. Think about it. Dutch had to go if she was to continue using her club as a front for the more lucrative coke business."

Schiff whistled, long and low. "Beats the hell out of Beavis and Butthead."

A soft knock sounded at the door.

"Can you prove any of this?" asked Schiff.

"Fuck, no."

The knock on the door repeated.

"Come in," Schiff growled, noticing he had three minutes left and thinking he was about to be prematurely ushered out by a CCU nurse. Instead, a sharply dressed kid, who couldn't be mistaken for anyone but Bishop's son, stepped in.

"Hey, Darryl," Schiff said.

"Lieutenant." Darryl looked past Schiff, "Hey, dad."

Bishop posted a wan smile. "Son."

"See you later," Schiff said to Bishop. "Get well soon." He patted Darryl on the back. "You're dad's vintage, kid. A class act. The best."

Then Schiff left the room.

***

There was that long silence when nobody quite knew how to start a conversation. Especially in a hospital. Bishop kicked it off.

"How's school?"

"Mid-terms coming up," Darryl replied off-handedly. Then asked, concerned, "How are you?"

Bishop looked at himself. "I'm a mess."

"You got that right," Darryl laughed and nodded to the tray of hospital food. Mashed yams, apple sauce, banana, mixed greens, and a pressed steak that looked liked it could bounce. "Nice spread."

"I'd kill for a chili dog," Bishop said.

Darryl grinned. "I thought so." He reached into his backpack and emerged with nothing less. "Chili dog with everything on it! Just the way you like it."

"You are your father's son, Darryl, don't let anybody tell you different."

Bishop immediately tore into it with a post-operative hunger. He hadn't eaten in almost twenty-four hours and he was dying for some comfort food.

"Been watching much TV?" Darryl asked.

"You kidding?" Bishop mumbled, his mouth full. Darryl handed him a wad of napkins from the take-out bag. Bishop wiped his lips. "Apart from two nurses who look like they got transferred from county, TV's all I got left."

"You want a TV Guide?"

"I want my gun."

Darryl threw his head back and laughed. "You're crazy dad."

"You got that right," Bishop said. The sun dipped through the window, just above the horizon, sending golden shafts through the blinds and making it difficult for Bishop to see his son. Bishop raised the flat of his hand to cut the light, and winced as a pain shot down his right arm. "Close the blinds, will you please? Can't see with that sun coming through."

Darryl crossed the room and spun the arm clockwise until the blinds fully closed. "When you gettin' out of here?"

"A week. Maybe less. Depends on how fast I heal. I woke up this morning, went to the john, and started pissing blood. Had to sit down fast, 'cause it nearly scared the shit out of me."

"Damn, dad," Darryl laughed uncomfortably.

"Anyway. Doc says I can go soon as it turns yellow."

Each tired of the small talk, neither knowing what to say. Silence descended. Then Bishop noticed Darryl had a look in his eyes. A question had formed, but he didn't know how, or couldn't bring himself, to ask it.

"What is it, son? What's on your mind?"

"How can you do it, dad? Everyday. Like that?"

Bishop knew exactly what he meant. The grind. The daily dose. Life on the streets. Each phone call to Bishop's desk brought a new tragedy to his attention. Each shift removed another layer from the city's onion until all that remained was the smell of something rotten.

"You can't let it get too close, son. You just can't let it get too close."

***

Schiff walked down the endless white corridors. He felt

a nervous shiver as his heels horse-clopped over the hard tile floor. Hospitals gave him the creeps. There was something too clean and orderly about them that held the predictability of death. Unlike the precinct. Even in its craziest moments, Schiff always felt secure at the station house. He gathered a sound, pillow-like comfort from the noise and the grime and the ceaseless chatter of keyboards, telexes and fax machines. The precinct was chaos he could count on.

Chaos, in his mind, was good. With chaos, Schiff knew what to expect. A drone here, a buzz there, a ring somewhere else...it all meant something. The precinct had a vitality and a life that filled him with invulnerability. But here, in the hospital, just like in the field, it was when things got quiet that worried him.

Because death was always there. And it didn't keep to the shadows.

In places like this, he thought, it was right out in the open.

Schiff turned left at the nurses' station and walked past a series of tall windows. There were mini-blinds on the inside finished in eggshell and blue. At the moment, they were parted half-way, revealing a dimmed room. The walls on either side of a single bed were stacked with special equipment that dwarfed the lone patient tucked under the starched white sheets.
Dutch looked shrunken. Pale. And weary. The spiking LED display bumped upward in a slow, consistent rhythm...but it was weak. Numbers in the upper right-hand corner of the CRT monitor read a steady 68. Every so often, the monitor would phase switch to the graph of another vital sign and display Dutch's blood pressure. Which was also reading low, because he had been in a coma now for just under twenty-eight hours.

The doctors had given Schiff the details. None of which sounded promising.

Dutch had lost a lot of blood.

And, since the wound was so close to his windpipe,

there was the possibility he may not be able to speak after he recovered. If he recovered. Everything relied on him regaining consciousness. And that was still only fifty-fifty.

Thunder rolled outside, foreshadowing rain. W h a t Schiff saw on the DVD was kinky. It would be rape if it was any other woman. But India enjoyed the rough play. They were fucking on broken glass, for God's sake. But Dutch wasn't on the clock. What he did on his own time was none of anyone's business. Schiff fished. Dutch fucked crazies. Different folks, different strokes. To each his own. That was the way to look at it.

Everything Bishop had said made sense.

Everything, except the murders of Elise, Jett, and Russel.

Their deaths just did not fit in.

He didn't buy Bishop's theory or his own explanations to himself. There was only one other possibility. And it wasn't a reach. Not in his mind, at least.

Still…there was no way to prove it. Not anymore.

But it came with history, means, motive, and opportunity.

Dutch was a copycat.

The End.